A POLITICAL THRILLER

THE PRESIDENT'S ASSASSIN

Alex Contorno

Black Rose Writing | Texas

This is a work of fiction. Names, characters, businesses, places, events, and incidents are either the products of the author's imagination or used in a fictitious manner. Any resemblance to actual persons, living or dead, or actual events is purely coincidental.

ISBN: 978-1-68513-585-0
PUBLISHED BY BLACK ROSE WRITING
www.blackrosewriting.com

Printed in the United States of America
Suggested Retail Price (SRP) $20.95

The President's Assassin is printed in Garamond Premier Pro

*As a planet-friendly publisher, Black Rose Writing does its best to eliminate unnecessary waste to reduce paper usage and energy costs, while never compromising the reading experience. As a result, the final word count vs. page count may not meet common expectations.

Praise for
The President's Assassin

"Perils ripped from the headlines, a taut political thriller that will keep you up at night, turning pages to see what happens next."
–George Weinstein, award-winning author of
Aftermath* and *Watch What You Say

Special thanks to my adopted families.

1

The Afghan boy came marching down the scorching hot desert road, carrying an old, cracked bucket and a dingy rag and making a direct line for where Dean Page sat in his truck. No one along the side streets and alleys was paying the kid any attention. He was a staple of the area, one of many children always begging for minor jobs in the little desert village of Zarghunay, Afghanistan. Dean had first spotted the kid three weeks ago. He'd watched how the kid walked the streets, how he asked car owners if he could wash their cars or even just clean their windshields.

More importantly, Dean noticed how no one paid any attention to the boy. He was just another beggar. Most people on the streets saw these poor children as nothing more than gnats, swarming and irritating. To those of higher stature, he was pretty much invisible.

He was exactly what Dean needed.

The kid took a quick look over his shoulder and hurried to Dean's truck. A ruined, burned-out car was parked directly behind him, roughly ten feet away from the dusty street leading out of the thin row of markets along the village entrance.

When the kid came to a stop beside Dean's truck, a bit of dirty water splashed up out of his bucket. Dean's window was already down because the AC didn't work, and it was over one hundred degrees outside. The boy leaned his head through the open window for a moment, but then seemed to decide it might seem too chummy to anyone who passed by. And discretion was part of their agreement.

"Did it," the boy said.

"You're sure?"

But Dean could see the pride in the kid's eyes—the triumphant look of a child knowing he'd done a good job.

"Yeah, sure."

"Tell me where, exactly."

"Dirty white van with bullet hole in back glass," the boy said in his broken English. "I put your metal box under the bumper."

Dean knew this would be easy enough to test. The metal box the kid was referring to was a state-of-the art recording device with a miniature yet powerful parabolic microphone installed.

"Good job," Dean said. He palmed the fifty-dollar bill and passed it through the window. The kid took it deftly, nearly dropping his bucket and rag in his excitement.

"You want windows cleaned?" the boy asked.

"No. No more work. You scram now."

The boy nodded. "I scram. And I tell no one."

Dean gave a nod and started the truck's engine. It grumbled to life, and the truck shuddered. He pulled out of his spot and headed down the dusty path that led outside of Zarghunay. He glanced in the rearview and saw the boy already making his way back into the village.

He drove for half an hour, taking a few turns further into the desert. He passed nameless little villages and markets; the truck kicking up clouds of dust the entire time. Dean had been down these winding desert roads over twenty times in the past two months. He'd used a variety of vehicles: vans, a old Humvee, a beat-up Jeep and several trucks. Each one of the three different US intelligence agencies had paid for and planted the vehicles.

Dean Page wasn't a spy. Not really. His official title was Intelligence Coordinator, but Dean knew what that equated to. It was nothing more than a fancy moniker for *spy*. And for the last two months, he'd been on assignment in and around the area of Zarghunay, looking into the movements and conversations of three different men, all of whom were affiliated with a terrorist group known as Nightwatch.

They were quite crafty. As a small network comprised of men with military backgrounds, Nightwatch members knew how to go unseen. But Dean was better than them, as was the small counter-intelligence group that had sent Dean out this way.

He was sure no one had spotted him during his time in the area. And he planned to keep it that way. If all went well, he'd be on a plane back to the US sometime tomorrow morning. Paying the kid to plant the device had been a necessary risk; it made much more sense for an ignored local who wandered through the markets to plant the device on the van of a Nightwatch guard as opposed to a Black American man no one in Zarghunay had ever seen before.

And now, with the device planted, the only thing left to do was wait. He pulled off of the road forty-two miles away from Zarghunay and into what looked to be a small auto repair shop in the middle of nowhere. A small hut attached to the back of it also served as a meager bar. When he parked the truck and got out, Dean took no time to look the place over. It was owned by a local, but that local was being paid handsomely for keeping quiet about the fact that high ranking US officials and military operatives often used it to stow supplies.

Dean got out of the truck and selected another vehicle—this one a busted up old Honda hatchback. The keys were beneath the floorboard runners and the engine cranked with a bit of rusty hesitation. He instantly pulled away from the repair shop and bar. He took a quick glance at the building before driving away and didn't spot a single person, despite the garage bay door being open and a truck being propped up to reveal its undercarriage.

From there, Dean drove another five miles toward absolutely nothing. He came to the edge of a ravine; the scenery revealing nothing more than golden and orange hues of dust and dirt all around.

Bagram Airfield was roughly one hundred and twenty miles to the east. Mazar-i-Sharif was about seventy miles west. But other than a few meager villages here and there, there was nothing else. All he saw in every direction was open desert. It was perfect.

He opened the Honda's glove box and reached under an old, slightly yellowed stack of maps and napkins. He stowed his smart pad there earlier in the day, not wanting to risk having the microphone and the operating system side by side, just in case he was discovered. It had only wasted about two hours of his time and besides…if everything worked as it should, there was nothing else he could do until the now-bugged Nightwatch van moved.

Dean switched on the pad and opened up the system that was synced to the device currently attached via magnetized strips to the underside of the van's bumper. The operating system, like the device itself, was so new that certain departments back in the states were still referring to it as "in development." But based on what Dean had seen of it, he was certain it was ready for full deployment.

A map of the desert popped up, showing an expanse of two hundred miles. A small flashing dot appeared to his north, toward Zarghunay. He tapped the dot and it instantly zoomed in on a satellite image of the village. Dean used his thumb and forefinger to pinch at the screen, zooming in until he could see the small shape of the dirty, white van in question.

Near the bottom of the screen, a toolbar gave him several options, one of which read: *Microphone detected. Audio On/Off.* He clicked the little slider to *On* and the results were immediate. Despite the distance, Dean heard crystal clear audio with no lag or disruption.

Because the van was still in place, all Dean could hear were sounds from the markets and streets. A murmur of conversation, the puttering of an old motorcycle passing by, someone coughing, a small child whining about something.

Even though the job was far from over, Dean already felt a stirring of success and accomplishment. The entire point of his mission was to find evidence that Nightwatch was planning an attack on American soil in the near future. The suspicions had come from the journals and notes of an American journalist who had spent some time in the area. He'd seen no real threat in the posturing statements from people closely tied to Nightwatch, but US Intelligence agencies had found it serious enough to send Dean out.

And now, nearly two months later, he'd identified at least five members of the group, as well as two of their vehicles and a primary lair. All he needed was for someone to have a conversation pointing back to some of their alleged plans.

And for now, all Dean could do was wait. He sat in the car, isolated and alone in the desert, sweating even though he was doing nothing more than sitting in a car with the windows rolled down. He sipped from a plastic bottle of water while watching the small dot on the smart pad screen, waiting for it to move and for the voices of Nightwatch members to speak.

2

The van finally moved an hour and fifteen minutes later. Dusk had settled in along the desert, changing the colors and the temperature. The software gave a small ding to show that the target was on the move. However, Dean had very little time to enjoy the moment because he noticed a rather large flaw in his plan.

The noise of the van's rattling engine and exhaust overwhelmed the parabolic microphone within the device attached to the van's bumper. The sound of the van drowned out the voices of at least two different men speaking in Arabic, although he could still hear them faintly.

Uttering a curse, Dean switched the audio toggle on the screen to off. Irritated now, he watched the dot move along the map. Within a few minutes, it had completely left Zarghunay and was heading in the same direction Dean had driven away. Dean knew where they were going. He'd watched them from afar through binoculars for the past two weeks, the white van and a few old trucks coming in and out of a little camp the Nightwatch kept out near an ancient cave system out in a thin canyon in the desert.

When they reached their destination in the van, the men inside would be less than twenty miles from where Dean was currently. It would also be night. Still frustrated, Dean tried the audio once more but heard only the groaning and grumbling of the van's engine.

So again, all Dean could do was wait. Because of the audio issues, he knew he couldn't take a chance. If he simply stayed where he was and waited for the van to stop moving, there was always the chance that the interference from the engine and exhaust may have compromised the device. And if that was the case, this was all for nothing. So for now, he had to rely on the locator and hope that if he trailed them and fell in behind them, the microphone might still do its job.

He did his best to time it perfectly, not starting his engine and driving off toward the dusty routes that led to the Nightwatch camp until dusk had given way to night. He drove without his headlights on, which was perfectly fine as he headed through the open desert.

The little Honda hatchback bounced and complained a bit, but that was understandable. It wasn't until he joined up with the minor roads that wound their way between several small villages that Dean got some strange looks from passing motorbikes and people making their way home between villages. One man he passed even made a blinking gesture with his hands, showing that he needed to turn his headlights on.

But Dean did no such thing. As he closed in on the location he was quite certain the Nightwatch van was headed, he had no intention of being spotted. Besides, less than two miles after passing the walker that had made the gesture at him, Dean veered off the road and onto a narrow path that could barely even be considered a road. He knew this little lane would take him to an even more hazardous, thin route. And beyond that, there was the downward trajectory of the path that led down into the canyon where Nightwatch hid out.

Tearing through the desert with the darkening night sky gobbling up the clouds of dust the Honda kicked up, Dean kept his eye on the moving dot on the screen; the software moved the map along in order to keep up with the van's progress, and Dean could see the thin line of the canyon tearing through about eight miles of desert floor, now less than two miles away from the van. Estimating that he was about ten miles behind the van, Dean kicked up his speed a bit more. The Honda rattled and rocked, and he knew he was pushing it to its limit.

A few moments later, the flashing dot showing the van veered left, taking a passage down into the canyon. Here, finally, Dean allowed himself to slow down. After all, the last thing he needed was for the men to hear his vehicle or see the ghostly dust wafting up into the night from his passage.

When the dot stopped moving altogether, Dean drove on for another three minutes before bringing the Honda to a stop. The engine seemed to sigh as he turned it off. Dean grabbed the smart pad and quickly estimated that he was no further than a mile and a half from where the van had stopped.

Now, the moment of truth. He grimaced as flicked the little toggle beneath the microphone option back to *On.*

His heart seemed to rest easy when he realized that the device still worked. The quality wasn't nearly as good as it had been when he'd been listening in on the sounds of the market and village, but he could easily decipher what the men were saying. Either the journey across the desert or the heat and jostling of the van had caused the device's power to deteriorate. He made a mental note of this, eager to pass it on to the team that had developed the device.

Dean, while listening in on the conversation taking place within a small cave and series of tents down inside a canyon a mile and a half away, had to refer to the notepad he'd been keeping by his side once again. He wasn't fluent in Arabic by any means, but he understood the gist of it. He'd been keeping notes of phrases and words he was unfamiliar with. The notebook aided him as he did his best to make sense of what the men were saying.

There were three men, and from the sound of it, one of them had been waiting in the small cave for quite some time.

"...waiting in this damned cave with no updates!"

"There are no updates. Things are still in a holding pattern."

"*Nothing* has changed?" the previously waiting man asked. He sounded confused, maybe even a bit discouraged.

"Everyone is still waiting," the third man said.

"Waiting for what?"

"The right time."

"There will never *be* a right time. We must strike soon before our financiers become scared."

The date has been finalized. You know this. It has been set in place for months. It makes no sense to alter our plans, because everything we need is on site."

"Not the drones."

"They'll be just a decoy. Make the Americans think they're the major threat. They won't know what hit them—with luck, we'll kill thousands."

Dean jotted down a summary of all that was being said inside the same notebook he'd been using to learn new Arabic words and phrases. As he listened, their voices grew static-laced and weaker. He wondered if it had something to do with being in a cave. Dean doubted the van was actually in the cave, but the voices being so dampened by the rock and desert certainly weren't helping matters.

"The longer it is all on site, the more chance there is of it being discovered," the waiting man argued.

"You know what?" one of the other men said. "If you're so keen to change things up, why don't you speak with the boss? Let him know you'd like to change things."

After a moment of silence, the man eventually answered with a bit more patience and understanding. "No. He knows best. I am just...I'm getting worried. The men at Bagram are smart. What if they find what we've planted? What if it all comes back to us?"

"It won't."

Bagram Air Base, Dean thought. *So the journalist wasn't completely correct. They aren't planning something on American soil. They're planning an attack on the local American military base we've reoccupied.*

In the long run, he believed that this could be a good thing because it was isolated and not on American soil. But the repercussions of such an attack would be very dangerous. It could lead to war or even a—

The sound of gunfire interrupted Dean's thoughts, immediately followed by the sound of the Honda's exterior being torn apart.

Dean cursed and ducked down in his seat. No longer worried about the smart pad or the conversation taking place a mile and a half away, he reached under his seat and grabbed the Sig Sauer he kept stowed there. As he grabbed it and reached up for the driver's side door handle, the back glass exploded.

Dean opened the door and fell out onto the hard desert floor. The shots had originated from behind the car, he knew. Furthermore, judging by the sound and speed of the shots, he knew that they were being fired from an AK-47 auto. It was unclear to him whether there were one or two weapons being fired. All he knew was that as he scrambled to the front of the Honda, the shots continued to come.

How? Had someone gotten the drop on him? Had he been followed the entire time he'd been tracking the van?

Dean lay flat on the ground, looking under the car and into the dark space behind it. He saw movement out there—something thin and fast. And then, when the shots stopped for a moment, he heard the revving of an engine. A dirt bike, apparently. But, again, like the AK-47 reports, he couldn't be certain if there were one or two of them.

Cautiously, Dean got to his knees and propped his arms up on the passenger side of the car's hood. As soon as he popped up, the shots came again. But even as Dean dropped back down for cover, he'd seen all he needed to see.

There were two of them, coming in fast, less than thirty yards away. They had their lights off and from what he could tell, each bike had one driver and one shooter. So, four of them.

He thought about getting back in the car and plowing them down, but that seemed dangerous. Yes, he'd be mobile, but he'd also be trapped. He would simply have to rely on his expert marksmanship and fifteen years of dealing with situations like these.

With his nerves on fire, Dean popped his head up again, at exactly the same spot. He then dropped as the shots came again and this time crawled around to the driver's side where he popped up behind the still-opened door.

He took quick aim and fired off three rounds off before the men on the bikes could return fire. Before Dean dropped back down for cover, he'd seen that at least two of his shots had landed. One took the shooter off the back of the closest bike and the other had taken the driver of that same bike directly in the side of the head.

He heard the engine die as the bike toppled, and it was quickly drowned out by more gunfire. One round tore into the ground less than three inches from Dean's foot. Others continued to tear into the car as the remaining bike drew closer.

As the remaining bike closed in on his left, Dean did his best to take stock of the situation. The way he saw it, if he didn't escape this situation in the next ten or fifteen seconds, he could be screwed. These men had either been intentionally following him or had lucked out in finding him on their way to meet with the three men down in the canyon. Given that, he assumed the men down in the cave knew what was going on, and soon he'd have even more men to contend with.

"Damn," Dean said. Grunting, he swung himself around the driver's side door as more bullets pelted the car. He dove inside for the smart pad, grabbed it, and then sprang up in an awkward position in the passenger seat. Glass exploded all around him, and he was sure he heard a bullet pass by the back of his head, so close he could feel the breeze of it.

Dean fired through the busted window as the bike had now drawn within just ten feet of the back of the Honda. His first shot took the driver in the chest. As the bike toppled while the driver fell, Dean's second shot went a little high, catching the shooter in the throat.

Dean acted quickly, realizing that even if the Honda *was* still drivable after the attack, he'd surely catch unwanted attention in a car that looked like it had been in a war zone. So, with the pad still in hand, he stepped back out and dashed over to the closest of the bikes. The driver was still moving, coughing and reaching for a gun on his hip. Dean placed a shot in the side of his head and then picked the bike up from the ground.

As he mounted, he heard static from the smart pad. Excited voices, laced with static, fading and getting softer. Dean looked at the smart pad and saw that at least one bullet had struck it. The screen had cracked, revealing the inner workings. Not that it mattered...he'd heard all he needed to hear. He now had proof that Nightwatch had devious plans in mind.

His job was over. Now it was just up to him to get out of here alive and pass the information on to Washington.

Stuffing the pad into the back of his pants where it pressed against his waist, Dean kicked the bike to life. He looked back toward the canyon just to make sure there were no other vehicles, that the three men from the cave had not yet made it up to join the fight.

But seeing only desert and darkness, Dean spun the bike around in a wild U-turn. With no lights and a treacherous speed that sent a spike of adrenaline through him, Dean tore through the desert night as if there were a demon on his heels.

3

Roger Commer, Deputy Section Chief for Intelligence Gathering for the CIA and Joint Chiefs of Staff did two miles on the treadmill and watched half an hour of national news before his wife came downstairs. Roger had always been an early riser, something instilled in him by his farmhand father and later reinforced by a rigorous, demanding job with the federal government. Roger couldn't remember the last time he'd slept later than five in the morning unless he was on vacation...and vacations didn't seem to come around much.

However, for the first time in about three weeks, there were no early morning meetings waiting for him. Not at the Pentagon, not at the White House, not in one of the stuffy congressional offices. So he could sit down with his wife at the kitchen table and enjoy breakfast without feeling rushed.

When Maggie sat across from him with a cup of coffee and the omelet Roger had made for her, a strange silence settled in with her. It was a silence neither of them had gotten used to—the odd quiet of having become recent empty-nesters. Their youngest son, Thomas, had left for college just under a month ago, leaving Roger and Maggie with the strange task of getting used to living in a house without children.

"Good morning," Maggie said, settling into her seat.

"And good morning to you, too."

"Looking forward to your slow day?"

"You know, I really am," Roger said. "I don't have to be anywhere in particular until nine thirty. It feels amazing."

The bit about the nine thirty meeting was true. Of course, he couldn't tell Maggie what the meeting was about. It was one of the few things that had caused more stress in their marriage over the years. There was so much that Roger heard and dealt with in the course of a day that he couldn't discuss at home. And whenever the pressures of work caused tension and anger within him, he had no one at home he could talk it out with. Trying to process classified information in a shaded and coded way with his wife was more maddening than not having any outlet at all.

"You think you'll be free Saturday?" Maggie asked.

"In the afternoon, sure. It depends on how things go on Friday with the Ukraine conference call. But I think things will go smoothly. What's up?"

"It's been a month…I think it would be nice to pay Thomas a visit. Well, I did until I saw the weather this morning."

He recalled that there was a tropical storm brewing in the Atlantic. Forecasters were predicting it would hit high up on the North Carolina coast and when it did, it would have evolved into a full-fledged hurricane.

Roger's first reaction was frustration. The last thing he wanted to do was to make the three-hour drive down to Williamsburg and fight their way around the William and Mary campus. But as he considered it, the idea of getting on the road—even if traffic would likely be congested on the weekend and a hurricane was looming—didn't seem so bad to Roger. Other than taking flights to important political sites around the world, he couldn't remember the last time he'd actually *driven* somewhere just for the hell of it. And besides, he wanted to see how Thomas was getting on at college.

Sometimes, it was very difficult to balance his job and his family. On stressful weeks when there were multiple fires to be put out and political tension on the brink around the globe, it was nothing unusual for Roger to work seventy-five hours a week. He knew this had taken its toll on his marriage and his children. Now, at fifty-five, he understood the harm it may have done. The good news was, his entire family—Maggie, Thomas, and their oldest son, Bret—had never seemed to resent him for it.

"Even with the weather, that sounds like fun," he finally said. "We can probably get out of here around eleven, even if I have clean-up from the conference call."

"We'll need to keep an eye on that hurricane, though."

"Sure," he said. But he figured if it was going to only hit the Carolina coast somewhere along the Outer Banks, they might only have to deal with a bit of rain in Williamsburg. "Perfect."

They settled back into their silence while eating breakfast. It was actually refreshing, in a way, to have been married for twenty-two years and to be completely comfortable and peaceful in the quiet of their home. Yet, as was usually the case with Roger's job, that quiet didn't last very long.

A soft chiming noise sounded out from the kitchen counter. It was a noise Roger had grown to fear. He'd set the tone of his secondary phone to be as different as possible from his primary phone. Roger used the primary cell for low-level work affairs, family, and friends.

Maggie frowned at the sound of it. She knew what it meant, too. Roger supposed she'd grown to despise it.

"Sorry," he muttered as he stood from the table and grabbed the phone. He carried it into the den, hating the fact that already, so early in the day, he was having to be secretive around his wife.

However, the chiming stopped as he reached the den. He looked at the home screen and saw that he'd received a call that had been ended before he'd answered, and then a text. They'd come from a man Roger knew relatively well and was coming to resent just as much as the sound of his secondary phone.

His name was Walter Everson, a member of the CIA with no actual title. He was more or less a spook, someone to deliver messages and information that needed to be exchanged without crossing official channels. Roger had only met the man three times in the ten years Everson had been active, but he's received many calls and texts with sensitive information.

Everson had apparently decided against the call at the last minute, opting to send a text instead. The text was brief and to the point, but it sent a flare of worry through Roger: **Private meeting being held at 10. Your presence is vital. Tell no one. Meet at the nest w/o the bird.**

It was the last part that made Roger feel concerned. *Meet at the nest without the bird.*

The Nest was a small and well-hidden conference room on one of the sub-floors of the Pentagon. The Bird was a title Everson and a few other CIA heads and Congressional higher-ups had given the President. If, in the course of their secretive messages among one another, the President and Secret Service wouldn't be attending, the messages would end with *w/o the bird.* But if President Seibert was going to be there (which wasn't often), the messages would end with *bird on site.*

So, Everson was requesting a meeting to be held in under two hours at one of the Pentagon's secret rooms...and with little explanation why.

This can't be good, Roger thought. He wondered if it had something to do with the upcoming conference call with all the Ukrainian leaders and officials. If that was the case, though, why keep it confined to the Nest?

There were too many unanswered questions to make assumptions. This was apparently clear on his face as he made his way back into the kitchen.

"Looks like your carefree morning just got taken from you," Maggie commented.

"Yeah, it did. I need to be at the Pentagon in an hour and a half."

"That's quick. Is everything okay?"

It was an odd question because throughout their marriage; it had held a double meaning. First, *is everything okay* with you? Second, *is everything okay* in terms of the safety of the nation?

"I think so," Roger said. "Too soon to tell. But I need to get going."

Maggie nodded and took another bite of her omelet. "Thanks for the breakfast."

"Of course." He walked over to her and kissed her on the corner of her mouth.

"Text me later," Maggie said. "Let me know if you'll be home for dinner."

"I will," Roger said. And he did plan to do that very thing. But as he ventured down the hall and grabbed his briefcase from his office, his mind was already back to the text that Walter Everson had sent.

It weighed heavily on him as he made his way out of the house and into his car. And as he pulled out into the practically non-existent morning flow of Occoquan, Virginia traffic, he did his best to shove aside the sudden feeling of doom that had wrapped itself around his heart.

4

Roger didn't feel the weight and pressure of the meeting until he stepped onto the elevator on the backside of the Pentagon's sub-floor. Everyone knew it was there, but only a select few could use it. It went down two more floors. Beneath that floor, on the lowest level of the building, was a catacomb-like chamber that would serve as the military's base of operations in the event of a direct nuclear attack on American soil.

Roger had never been to that lower floor and hoped he would never have to visit it. However, he'd been to the first sub-floor multiple times. For a while, during the early days of Russia's invasion of Ukraine, the Nest had more or less served as Roger's office while American intelligence and counter-intelligence agents worked overtime to ensure Putin wasn't able to bully his way across Ukraine.

He had avoided visiting the dimly lit conference room for several weeks, though, and every time he returned to it after being away, he found its grandiose nature striking yet again. It struck him yet again as he walked down the flat gray hallway and came to the door. It was already opened, a massive, black bulky thing.

As he'd expected, Walter Everson was already there waiting for him. He was sitting at the very end of the long, thin table. The recessed lighting shined down from above, reflecting from the polished table in a way that would make museum architects envious. For a place that wasn't used very often, no expense or security measure had been spared in its creation.

"Roger!" Walter said, getting to his feet and striding over right away. "It's good to see you."

"Likewise." This was true. Walter Everson was a good man, among the most honest Roger knew. And in their line of work, where they were surrounded by secrets and lies of monumental proportion, that was saying quite a lot. They'd never really worked closely together, but they'd crossed paths enough for Roger to know that Walter was a man of his word. As a former point man for the FBI and CIA and a secret, shadow agent for Homeland Security, Walter certainly had the right credentials.

Everson said, sitting back down, "We may as well get right to the point if that's okay with you."

Roger had expected nothing less, but he still felt a spike of worry work its way through him as he sat down across from Everson. "Of course."

"Are you familiar with a man named Dean Page?"

The name rang a bell. Roger recalled a hardened and tight, very dark-skinned Black man of about forty. "I know the name, but not much about him. CIA, right?"

"Somewhat. Although he is an intelligence agent, nobody at the CIA is going to admit it. He's more or less a spy. Currently, he is not listed on the agency's books or payroll. He's been on assignment in Afghanistan for the past five months."

"Looking for what, exactly?"

"Making sure Nightwatch is really keeping its promises and playing nice with the rest of the world."

"Nightwatch," Roger said, speaking the word with such annoyance that he practically spat it out. "Are they still causing problems?"

"They are. And according to Dean Page, they plan on causing quite a bit more problems in the coming weeks. Page caught them discussing plans to attack a military base in his area. He didn't get an exact location, but based on everything he's seen and heard while over there, he feels certain it's going to be Bagram."

"Okay...so why are you and I talking about this in the shadows rather than taking it directly to the Secretary of Defense?"

"Because our esteemed Secretary of Defense, Mr. Henry Frederickson, will not deliver news to the President if he knows it will upset him."

Roger winced. There was a rather simple equation to follow, though it was one he was ashamed to face. The current President, a staunch supporter of efforts to harvest more oil and natural resources in Afghanistan, was quite chummy with the head of Afghanistan's Ministry of Defense. In the three years he'd spent in office, President William Seibert had gone out of his way to *not* speak ill of the political or military climate in Afghanistan.

"How certain are we that Dean's intelligence is correct in this?"

"Dean doesn't half-ass anything. If he says this is what he heard, I believe him."

Roger could feel tension sinking into his shoulders, could feel the weight of the decision he was going to have to make in the coming seconds. "Is there any hard proof? Audio? Video?"

"No. There was audio, but I believe it became compromised when he escaped.

"Escaped?"

"Yes. While he was on the scene, he was attacked by people on dirt bikes with AKs—people we assume are members of Nightwatch."

"Do you know if he killed anyone?"

"He did. He knows there was at least one casualty. Probably two, though he can't be sure."

Roger thought it over, considering every path and avenue this could take. Did he really want to present this to the Joint Chiefs without hard, irrefutable proof? It would be easier if it would not collide with President Seibert's fondness for the Afghani Minister of Defense, Ebrahim Daraa.

"Let's sit on this for now."

Everson shook his head and sighed, clearly irritated. "Sit on it? You heard what I just said, right?"

"I did. And you know what I'm dealing with on my end, right? You know damn good and well that if I take this to Frederickson, he's going to want proof before putting it in the President's ear. And if it gets that far, do you know what Seibert is going to do? He's going to call Daraa and ask about it. And if your man Dean is right on his end, it's going to cause a lot of trouble and anger. You can see that, right?"

"Yes," Everson said, practically hissing the word.

"What I can do, though, is contact a connection I have who has close ties to Bagram." I'll let him know to be on full alert for a while...tighten up security measures and things like that."

Still visibly upset, Everson shrugged and stood up from the long table. "Yeah, I guess that'll have to do for now."

"What about Dean? Do you know where he is right now?"

"Trying to make his way back into the country. I spoke to him about two hours ago and he was working to line up a flight home with fake documents."

"I want to talk to him when he gets stateside."

"Yeah, I think that's a good idea."

"Thanks for understanding, Walter. Trust me...it bothers me, too. And I won't let it go unnoticed. Even if it comes down to just you and I monitoring it...."

"I appreciate that."

"I'll see the President later today. Maybe I'll mention that we have boots on the ground over there that are hearing rumblings about Nightwatch movement. That will at least get the idea moving around in his head. That way, if he *does* eventually have to face the fact that he's going to have to get rude with Minister Daraa or even President Shahin, the idea will have already been sitting in his head for a while."

Everson nodded his acknowledgement of the idea, but Roger could tell he'd hoped for more action. They left the Nest together, walking in silence. Roger assumed Everson was worried about Dean and that the information he'd just shared may go unheeded. Meanwhile, Roger thought about President Seibert and already feared that he might not listen to reason if Dean Page's information was eventually proven correct.

It sat heavily on him as he took the elevator back up to the top floors. Even when he was out of the building and back outside, he didn't know if he'd ever truly be free of the pressure.

5

The Cabinet Room smelled like coffee and faint aftershave when Roger stepped inside forty minutes after leaving the Nest. As he settled down at the conference table, he was very much aware that there was still a small part of him that, occasionally, felt like an awe-struck child when it came to his job. From the Pentagon, down Pennsylvania Avenue, and straight to the White House. That was his job. Walking through the historic halls, passing by secretaries and chiefs of staff, and settling down to the polished table in the Cabinet Room...it sometimes did all feel like a surreal dream sometimes.

That feeling quickly shattered when President Seibert came hurrying in. He had a sandwich in one hand and his cellphone in the other. A staffer followed close behind, typing something into an iPad.

"Well, boys and girls," Seibert said as he sat down at the table. "I hope the world isn't falling apart today because I only have about ten minutes before I have to get on Air Force One. If I don't show up in Vermont today for an appearance following those floods, the media is going to have my head."

There was a quiet murmur of laughter among the eight people currently sitting at the table. But Roger didn't laugh. His mind was still far too occupied with what Everson had told him. He was thinking about the men and women at Bagram who may or may not have a genuine threat headed their way.

When Seibert sat down next to Secretary of Defense Frederickson, it occurred to Roger that he could skip the middleman. To hell with running things by Frederickson before it reached the President's ear. The morning briefing would be an opportune time to lay out what he knew. The only question was whether it would be to his advantage to explain it all in front of the others in attendance.

The Press Secretary sat across from him, a hardened and no-nonsense woman named Claire Montgomery. The Speaker of the House sat across from her—sixty-year-old James Pelingra always seemed slightly paranoid and was currently eyeing everyone with suspicion, as if daring someone to upset the President.

"I have something," a voice from the back of the table said. This was Malcolm Henreid, a young Black Congressman from Delaware. He was soft-spoken, naïve, and Roger wasn't sure why he was even here today.

All eyes turned to Henreid, including the President. He was eating his sandwich quickly. At only fifty-one years of age, President William Seibert was still expressive and unpredictable. His blonde hair was going gray, but it suited him well. Somehow, it made his bright eyes and disarming politician's smile even more charming. As he wolfed down his sandwich and glared at Malcom Henreid with muted enthusiasm, it was apparent that he didn't want to be here - that rushing to the airstrip after dealing with small problems that could likely be handled on a State level was the last thing he needed.

"Well, Mr. President," Henreid said, "there is still a very present and vocal Green Party movement occurring in Delaware and Maryland. The numbers they're drawing to their events and demonstrations are about triple of what we expected."

"Okay...." Seibert said, waiting for the part that would explain why he should care.

"Well, you won Maryland by two percent of the vote. And you lost Delaware by less than that. If you want to have both states in your back pocket for re-election next year, I think we need to think of ways to stamp these movements out. To get in front of it before it's too late."

"Excellent idea," Seibert said. "You can lead the task force to get started on that. Give me a list of names from each state…maybe five at most. Email them to me, and I'll give you the green or red light."

"Yes, sir." Henreid was smiling, but it was a thin one. He'd clearly not been expecting that kind of response.

"Anyone else?" Seibert asked.

Roger watched as the staffer stood behind the President, waiting to type up the meeting notes. And in the silence that settled around them, Roger saw his chance. As he started speaking, he was aware of the firestorm this might stir up, but he also felt that it was necessary.

"I have something that you may find pressing, Mr. President," he said.

Seibert looked uncomfortable when he cast his eyes Roger's way. After all, the only time Roger spoke up at these meetings was to pass along bad news. "Yes?"

"One of our CIA assets believes Nightwatch is on the move again in Afghanistan."

The shock on Seibert's face was only there for a moment before he started trying to dismiss it.

"What channels are we getting this through?"

"From an asset who's been on the ground over there for the last several months. He barely escaped with his life last night after doing audio surveillance."

"Okay…so where is this audio?"

Before Roger answered, he knew everyone was looking at him—and they all looked very bothered by the conversation that was taking place. Everyone at the table was just as aware as Roger about how the President felt about his new alleged allies in Afghanistan.

"Missing," Roger said, "Gone. I won't have the full details for another day or so, but I believe the device used to get the audio went missing or was destroyed in the spy's escape."

"I see." Seibert looked gravely frustrated. He sighed and tossed the last few bites of his sandwich into a nearby wastebasket. "And what are your recommendations regarding the situation?"

Roger knew he needed to speak carefully here. If he recommended anything Seibert considered an overstepping of sorts, that could be the end of it. Roger knew what *should* happen; a platoon should gobble up Dean Page's intelligence and work to undermine whatever Nightwatch had planned.

But he knew Seibert would never go for that.

"I believe we should make a call to the generals at Bagram." We need to suggest that their security levels be heightened in the coming days. Maybe have a few more bodies running security controls."

Seibert nodded and tapped the table. "Good enough. Can you handle that, Mr. Commer?"

"Yes, Mr. President," Roger said. Surprised by the President's quick and easy agreement, he spoke up again. And by the time all the words were out of his mouth, he was pretty sure he'd made a mistake. "And what about Nightwatch?"

Was that a flicker of irritation darting across the President's face, or was Roger simply imagining it?

"What about them?"

"Shouldn't we get eyes on them as well?"

Seibert actually rolled his eyes. Roger had to hide his contempt at the expression. "Mr. Commer, you know as well as I do that Nightwatch is no longer a viable threat. That information comes from the CIA heads...the same people I assume this spy reports to."

"That's true, but we all know that terrorist organizations aren't exactly known for keeping their word when it comes to treaties and agreements."

For a moment, it seemed that no one else in the room was even breathing. There was an awkward tension in the air, hovering between Roger and the President. Roger was pretty sure everyone else at the table knew what was coming. Malcolm Henreid looked like he was prepared to slip under the table to hide, and Press Secretary Montgomery's eyes had gone wide as if she were expecting fists to be thrown.

"Mr. Commer," President Seibert finally said, "I have worked hard to establish a strong, trusting relationship with Minister Daraa and even President Shahin. Do you have any idea how much damage it would do to those relationships if I suggested Nightwatch was defying treaties signed between our two countries?"

Roger swallowed down the need to argue. It was pretty much what he'd expected, and he wished he's just kept quiet after Seibert had given him the okay to call Bagram. He made sure he had control of himself—particularly his tongue—before speaking again.

"Yes, Mr. President, I understand."

Seibert nodded and took one long, lingering look around the room. He smiled as he did it, as if hoping the charming smile that had helped win an election would clear the room of the collected negative energy.

"Anyone else have anything?"

But of course, after the exchange he and Roger had just shared, no one was going to say anything. A few people muttered "No, Mr. President," and that was it.

"Thanks for taking the time to stop by everyone," Seibert said, getting to his feet. And before he left the room, he looked directly at Roger one more time.

With that, the President left. Slowly, everyone else also started filtering out, but it took several minutes for Roger to get his bearings. He took a moment to sort out what had happened and then, with a seed of anger and worry in his stomach, he headed out hoping to find a solution to the Nightwatch problem before it could get any worse.

6

Following the disastrous morning briefing, Roger headed back across the Potomac River to hole up in his office. He worked out of a nondescript building just a mile and a half east of the Pentagon. The building itself wasn't a secret, but very few people knew the nature of the offices that were housed there.

It was a simple two-story structure that blended in nicely with the other featureless buildings around the block. Although the official CIA offices were not in the Pentagon, several unofficial branches of the agency operated from this one. The same was true of the Department of Homeland Security and, to some extent, the ATF as well.

As Roger guided his car to the underground parking garage, his mind was once again turning to the spy who had given Walter Everson the Nightwatch tip. Dean Page...a man with plenty of experience and expertise in a few different fields. But Roger was also very much aware of the fact that he didn't know the man personally. The way he saw it, Dean might be the only ally he and Everson would have if they were truly going to get something done about all of this.

He contemplated it all as he made his way through the dimly lit building. Every hall of the three-story architecture was exactly the same: marble floors, recessed lights in the white ceiling, and soft-beige walls. When he reached his office, he instantly went to his desk and signed into the CIA database. He typed in *Dean Page* and pulled up the man's records.

Roger could tell the man's record was incomplete, likely on purpose. He started out with the Marines at nineteen and was transferred to duties with the Military Police five years later. At thirty-five, he shifted his focus to more inward and government-based services and started a career with the CIA. He worked with the CIA in an official capacity for about six years and during the latter half of that period, he had been a point man for joint operations between the CIA and Homeland Security. The official record ended three and a half years ago. Roger knew that this was because he'd become what Everson had referred to as an off-the-books spy.

Roger didn't know the ins and outs of it exactly, but he knew that just about every agency in Washington had a secret pool of individuals they could pull from to carry out tasks that were controversial or too sensitive for public consumption. Spying on a terrorist organization that was said to have gone quiet after the President and the other country's authorities had signed peace treaties would definitely fall into that category.

Everson had told him that Dean Page had been in Afghanistan for the past five months. But where had he been before that? Who had he been working for?

There were lots of strange shifts and blank spaces in Dean Page's record. It wasn't completely unheard of in Roger's line of work. During his time in his current role, he'd worked with men who had no public record at all, not even in the resource files of Homeland Security or the NSA.

As Roger looked over Dean's information, he knew he had to meet the man. He had to hear the report for himself. Until then, there really wasn't much he could do. And as he waited, he was also going to have to come to terms with the obvious blind spots the President had erected regarding Nightwatch or any other potential threats emerging from Afghanistan.

Before he knew it was happening, Roger's mind was dragging up memories he had worked very hard to bury. In his mind's eye, he saw himself outside an apartment building in Kuwait, the roof crumbling, people screaming everywhere. A voice, barking in his ear to move his ass, to get to safety, to leave it alone. He remembered looking up and seeing the face of a little girl who was no older than ten, blood covering her face.

Roger closed his eyes and willed the image to go away. That had been nearly twenty-five years ago. Was this brief argument with the President going to be the reason all of those terrible memories resurfaced?

"Not if I can help it," he muttered to his empty office.

He closed Dean's file and looked at the database desktop. He tried to think of other routes to possibly find out some of Nightwatch's more recent rumblings. The difficulty was that no one had really done any surveillance on them since Seibert had taken office. It was one of the military operations he'd worked to shut down in order to start the peace talks.

It made him wonder what or who had sent Dean Page to Afghanistan. Curious, he picked up his cell phone, intending to call Walter Everson and asking him that very question. But before he could pull Everson's number up, there was a knock at his door.

He set his phone down and said, "Come on in."

He knew it would be his assistant, May Conklin. She was the only person who ever knocked on his door without having a meeting planned first. And she only knocked when it was of absolute importance.

The door opened and he saw he was right. May was a thirty-five-year-old mother of four who looked no older than twenty-five and as if she'd never had a single kid. That was because she hit the gym at least four times a week and averaged one marathon every four months. She was also hard-nosed and very organized, which made her the perfect assistant for Roger's line of work.

"Good morning, sir."

"Sir?" he asked. "What the hell, May?"

She rolled her eyes at him and tried again. "Fine. Good morning, *Roger.*"

"That's better. What can I do for you?" he asked with a smile.

She looked slightly troubled as she stepped into the office, her hands folded together, looking like a kid who had just broken something and was about to deliver the bad news to a parent.

"I wanted to tell you first rather than just buzzing you on the phone. But Vice President Warren just called for you. He didn't ask to *speak* with you. He just wanted to know if you were here."

"What for?"

"A meeting. Frederickson is on his way over right now. Apparently, he wants to discuss the announcement you made at this morning's briefing."

"And Warren is coming with him?" Roger asked, dumbfounded.

May only shrugged, a frown on her face.

"Ah, Jesus."

Still shrugging, May said, "Don't shoot the messenger."

"Fine," Roger said, sighing. "Is the conference room set up and ready?"

"It is." She started back for the door and then turned back to him. "Is everything okay?"

Roger stood up from his desk and, for a dizzying moment, he once again saw that building in Kuwait, the little girl's bleeding face.

"I'm not sure, May. Maybe ask me again when the meeting is over."

May gave an uncertain smile as she left the room. She closed the door behind her, leaving Roger to once again shake away the ghosts and memories of his past while the present continued to unravel around him.

7

When his high-profile visitor arrived, the first thing Roger noticed was that Secretary of Defense Frederickson didn't look nearly as authoritative or powerful without the luster of the White House surrounding him. He was out of his element and looked anxious.

As for Vice President Warren, he didn't show up after all. Roger actually preferred this. Warren was a man of renowned political experience and had friends on both sides of the aisle. Roger had never had much interaction with him outside of a few White House luncheons and mandatory meetings during President Seibert's tenure. But the man also had security shadowing his every move. And the *last* thing Roger wanted was for extra sets of ears that were linked to the President to be in his office after the way his day had gone so far.

"Is the Vice President going to call in?" Roger asked Frederickson.

"Yeah, that's the plan," Frederickson said as he placed his phone on the edge of the conference room table. Only Roger was fairly certain the phone was not Frederickson's. It looked like one of those cheap burner phones you could pick up just about anywhere.

"I think it goes without saying," Frederickson said, "that Vice President Warren does not want his involvement in this discussion to be public knowledge."

"Of course."

Then, as if on cue, the burner phone rang.

Roger knew he should be nervous. For these two men to request a private audience, something serious must be brewing. This morning's discussion at the White House briefing only made matters worse. But Roger felt slightly collected and calm. They were, after all, in his neck of the woods now. And that made him think they'd intentionally wanted to be away from the often-prying ears at the White House for whatever was about to be discussed.

Frederickson answered the call. "Mr. Vice President, I'm here with Roger Commer."

"In a secure location?" Warren asked, his voice soft yet somehow firm through the phone.

"Yes, sir," Roger said.

"Good. Thanks for your time, Mr. Commer."

"So what's going on, gentlemen?" Roger asked as Frederickson sat at the table, positioned to the right of the phone. Roger took the moment to close the door to the room to make sure Frederickson felt as secure as possible.

The Vice President began. As he spoke, Roger thought Frederickson looked very nervous. There was a slight sheen of sweat on the man's brow.

"I heard about the little bomb you dropped at the morning briefing," Warren said. "I won't lie to you…had I been there, I would have said nothing in disagreement with the President's stance. I will tell you here and now, however, that I have long thought the alignments he'd made with Daraa and Shahin were dangerous."

"Then why would you have not spoken up if you were there?" Roger challenged.

"Honestly?"

"Of course."

Warren sighed through the phone. It communicated so much: worry, fear, the weight of a million decisions. "Polls show that most Americans also disagree with his stances on Afghanistan. They think it's only because of vested oil interests and potential weapons financing. But I fully plan to run for election in a few years, whether or not the President gets re-elected. So for now, I'm going to agree with the President if I have to. It's not very genuine of me, I admit…but it's the honest answer."

Roger looked at Frederickson and said, "And you feel the same? Do you oppose the President's stance over there?"

"Yes. Vehemently. As do many in Congress."

"And half of the Joint Chiefs of Staff," Warren added.

"Okay. So why talk to me? If I wanted anything done, I'd have to go through channels that lead to both of you."

"Because we have an idea," Warren said. "Two ideas, actually. And they both involve you."

"Will I like either of them?"

Frederickson chuckled softly. "Not likely. The first option is to place you in charge of a secret team that would work with your buddy Walter Everson and this spy of his...Dean Page, right?"

"That's right."

"We'd want you to work closely with Page to see if there is any intel at all that provides irrefutable proof of the actual reasons behind these sudden peace treaties."

"That's right," Warren said. "I'd like to know why the President got so upset this morning when you suggested Nightwatch might be moving again. When you mentioned it, I was sure it would become a bigger conversation. But to just brush it off like that...that seems dangerous and naïve to me."

"Okay," Roger said. "So, the first option is working on intel with Page and Everson. What's the second option?"

"To keep pestering the President with this," Warren said. "I know how the man works. He'll already have brushed this under the rug. But if you keep talking about it in meetings, more people will hear about it. Eventually, if the right people hear it...*talkative* people, let's just say—I'd imagine it would get into the press. And if that happens...well, the President won't be able to keep it under the rug."

Roger nodded. It was a good idea for sure, but it wouldn't be easy. If he pushed too hard, he might even lose his job.

"I like it," he said, "but it sounds like you want me to be the whipping boy on this. To sort of be the target of the President's irritation and anger."

"It makes more sense that way," Warren said. "If it's someone like me or someone on the Joint Chiefs, he'll be expecting it. It'll be like a landmine he just steps around every day. But from someone like you, someone he doesn't see every day or who has any responsibility to report to him unless it's absolutely crucial, he may rest easy, thinking that the matter is dead and buried. If we go to him with it, it's like a house on fire. But coming from you, you're just the pesky bee at a picnic."

"In other words," Frederickson said, "if you pester him with it occasionally, you're nothing more than a pesky buzzing bee he can shoo away. But if it's somehow higher up—"

"If it's someone higher up," Roger interrupted, "it's more like the wasp nest on the porch you can't ignore anymore."

"That's right," Warren said. "And it has to be coming from the pesky bee. He needs to be reminded of it, but it can't be in his face. Does that make sense?"

Yeah, it makes sense, Roger thought. *That's politics, I suppose. One big wasp nest and many pesky, buzzing bees.*

"You said Page gets in soon, right?" Frederickson said.

"I did. I'll reach back out to Everson to see if he has a clear timetable yet."

"Also," Warren said, "it may help if you reach out to the President's office tomorrow. Try setting up a meeting and speak to him about it in private."

"Why would I do that?" Roger asked. "Seems like willingly stepping into the lion's den."

"Because I'm hoping this morning's frustration out of him was a performance for the others in attendance—myself included. If he's alone with just you, we may get more truth out of him. We may get in front of this thing with little trouble. It's a longshot, but worth a try."

"I can do that," he said. Then, looking to Frederickson, he said: "Before I get in touch with the folks in Bagram, can you get me the specs on what their security looks like?"

The Secretary of Defense thought this over for a moment before finally nodding. "It will have to come from unofficial channels, so it may be a few hours, but yes. I can do that."

Roger sighed and got to his feet, suddenly feeling the weight of everything he needed to get started on. "Is that all?"

"It is," the Vice President said through the phone. "And Commer, I shouldn't have to say such a thing, but you know this meeting never happened, right?"

Roger smiled thinly as he walked over to the conference room door and opened it back up for Frederickson. "What meeting?"

8

Dean woke up to the vibrating of his watch. He sat up slowly, his body still fatigued with the wash of adrenaline from just seven hours ago. He'd spent that time making his way through the cool desert night, eventually ditching his commandeered dirt bike twenty miles from the site of the confrontation. He was sure they'd be looking for him now...and because they had no real understanding of who he was, it wouldn't be easy to figure it out. After all, there weren't many people milling about the desert roads so late at night.

He'd then walked for another few miles before catching a ride from a goat farmer headed toward Zarghunay. It had taken some bribing, but after offering the farmer the equivalent of ten American dollars, he'd been quite agreeable.

Dean asked to be let out roughly two miles away from the combination auto garage and bar that he'd been using as something of a safe house—the same place he'd been parking and exchanging his vehicles for the last few months. It also served as a makeshift motel during days when he felt the need to lie low.

When he finally arrived, it was nearly five o'clock in the morning. The little business was quiet and desolate. Dean was sure that if wasn't for the constant flow of cash from American sources, the business would have closed years ago.

Apparently, none of the locals found it odd, though. From what Dean had seen from his bit of time here, the place was frequented more as a bar than an auto garage. In fact, he was pretty sure the same motorbike and Jeep that had been in the garage two months ago were still there.

When he opened the front door, he saw the owner was still asleep. He was an older man, and Dean had never learned his real name. He claimed his name was Ernesto, but Dean had never met an Afghani with such a name.

After retrieving a blanket from a small closet in the little wooden alcove that separated the bar from the garage, he visited the back room, not much larger than a coat closet, and bedded down.

That was why he woke up with a terrible ache in his neck. As he sat up in the little room, he could hear Ernesto tinkering around somewhere in the bar. Dean left the room, taking the blanket with him and returning it to the closet.

He found Ernesto at the bar, washing out a glass. He was smoking a cigarette and humming a tune under his breath. Smiling, he turned to Dean with the cigarette bobbing slightly between his lips.

"You come in late?" Ernesto asked in broken English. He was pushing sixty, but looked closer to seventy. His hair was gray but always slicked back to reveal a widow's peak that was rapidly taking over his head.

"Very late."

"You look tired."

"Not much sleep," Dean said. "Ernesto, I'll be leaving today. Back to the States. Would you allow me to please use your shower?"

"Aye. Help yourself."

Dean nodded his thanks and went back to the little closet he'd taken the blanket from. Dean's travel bag was tucked away in the back, behind an old barrel of oil. He'd used Ernesto's shower before and the older man seemed to find the idea funny. He never asked questions, though. All Ernesto knew about Dean was that he was here on secret business for the US government. And Dean wasn't the only American that came through Ernesto's business. There were usually anywhere between five or six a year, and Ernesto treated them all with great respect. Probably because of the chunk of money that came to him twice a year from a secretive and non-traceable US bank account.

Dean walked through the cramped apartment behind the bar. Ernesto stayed here most of the time, though he often also stayed at a nearby village now and then. Dean was pretty sure there was a special lady in Ernesto's life who lived there.

The shower was not satisfying. The water was quite cold, helping Dean to wake up. Following his shower, he shaved in front of Ernesto's cracked mirror, and then got dressed. He wore only a white tee shirt, well-worn jeans, and a pair of sunglasses. Due to his belief that baseball caps were a true symbol of an American abroad, he never wore a hat. He already stuck out enough as it was. Why draw more attention to himself?

He walked back out to the bar and saw that Ernesto was already sitting at one of the three tables, scrolling along on his beat-up cellphone. It was only eight in the morning, but he'd poured himself a tall glass of rum.

"Thanks," Dean said. As he passed by, he slapped the equivalent of fifty American dollars on the table. "I need you to do a favor for me."

"Yes?"

"I'm about to drive out toward Zarghunay. When I get about five miles outside of town, I'm going to park my car behind an old, abandoned house. It's the one that appears to have been burned along the backside a long time ago. Can you make sure it gets back here somehow within the next week?"

"Aye."

Dean then extended his hand. "Thanks for all you do, friend."

"Aye, be careful, yes?" Ernesto said, shaking Dean's offered hand.

"Always."

With that, Dean walked out of the bar and back out into the desert. He was tired, and his neck hurt, but he knew this was going to be a very long day. Flying back to the States always took it out of him...not just the jet lag but knowing he'd have a day or two of debriefs when he got back.

He climbed into his remaining vehicle and pointed it toward Zarghunay. The sun was already beating down on the desert, as if giving Dean an an inkling of what the rest of his day was going to look like.

9

It took Dean six and a half hours to get to Kabul International Airport. It had taken his initial drive toward Zarghunay, and then three different cabs—one of which wasn't so much a cab as it was a random, sketchy bus that didn't seem to be affiliated with any official form of public transport.

The last cab took him directly to the parking garage on the western edge of the airport. As Dean got out and paid his fare, he looked up just in time to see a Delta plane landing on the runway behind the large building.

He hoped that the time he'd waited to leave, as well as the distance and taking four different modes of transportation, would have shaken any Nightwatch members or hired hands off his tail. He checked his watch and saw that it was nearing 2:30. His flight left in an hour, and he still had one quick task to wrap up.

He walked into the parking garage and made his way to the stairwell. The garage was three stories tall, and he only needed to visit the second level, so he had plenty of time. Once there, he slowly made his way through the rows of cars along the second level; there weren't very many, enough to take up a little less than half of the space.

He spotted the old Honda, a car with much wear and tear, the paint faded from the desert sun over countless years. An old decal along the back showed faded Afghani writing, a political slogan of some kind. It was a perfect match for what he'd always called the "pivot car." This car was rented by another American spy, probably from another agency, and parked here for any other spies or intelligence officers who might need to discreetly contact their American links before leaving the country. In about a month's time, that spy would return the car and then rent out another one a few days later, always keeping such a car in the garage, hiding in plain sight.

Dean approached the car quickly. He needed to make a quick call to Walter Everson. He'd called Everson last night from his throwaway phone to let him know he had the information but had lost the physical audio in his escape. Everson had implored him to contact him when he was about to get on a plane to come home, and to do so privately—hence the pivot car.

As he reached the car, Dean caught a flicker of movement in the glass along the passenger side door. He pretended not to see it, to carry on without stopping. But what he had seen were two men coming up the ramp corridor from the first-floor level.

Dean finally stopped and paid the men no attention...not yet anyway. He put on a bit of a performance, patting his pants pocket as if looking for his keys. He then sighed, hunching his shoulders in fake defeat. As he did, he checked the window again. The men were closer. One was gripping a pistol to his side. But Dean didn't let that bother him. If they were going to kill him, they would have already done it. He assumed they were Nightwatch and by now, given what had happened in the desert last night, they probably knew they'd been bugged. And if that were the case, they would assume there was a physical copy of a recording somewhere.

Ha...the joke's on you, Dean thought.

Still, he knew he would not be getting on a plane in the next hour as easily as he'd hoped. He finally turned to the men, acting surprised but not frightened, and set his features with an irritated look.

"I lost my damned keys," he muttered.

The man holding the pistol stepped forward. He was skinny with dark black hair and eyes, his skin the same dark tan as most of the other Nightwatch members. He sneered and said, "'ilaa sawt allughat al'iinjilizia?"

Dean wasn't great with the local dialect. He was pretty sure he was asking who he was. Or maybe specifically for his name. He wasn't sure.

"Gun?" he said, pointing to it. "Why?" He then raised his hands as if he were just a normal man, getting slowly scared of the sight of a gun held by strangers.

As he thought, the armed man held up his gun. The second man stood just a few paces behind, crawling to the left to flank Dean and trap him between the car, the two men, and the concrete barrier that served as the garage wall. This man was larger and, from what Dean could tell, had no gun.

The armed man took one more step forward, and Dean continued to stretch his acting skills. He was simply waiting for the right moment. If the idiot would just take one more step closer....

"I...I don't know what you want, I swear," Dean said, making his voice tremble. "I don't know who you are, and I don't have money, and—"

The man took another step forward, the gun still held out, pointed directly at Dean's chest.

"—and I know what you want, but it's gone," he said, smirking now. "And you couldn't have it, anyway."

Swift as lightning, his right hand acted as a battering ram, knocking the pistol away from him, while his left hand reached out and grabbed the armed man's shoulder. He wheeled the man around so that his back was to Dean, pulled his right arm up high over his head, brought it back, and twisted. He did this all in less than two seconds. The armed man's wrist snapped cleanly. He screamed and dropped the gun.

As Dean predicted, the other man hunched down to pick the weapon up. When he did, Dean delivered a hard, swift kick to the man's jaw. He was lifted and went sprawling back. Dean could tell by the way he hit the pavement that the kick had knocked him out cold.

Still holding the other man by his newly snapped wrist, Dean spun him back around so that they were face to face. Dean bent the broken wrist back even farther and when the man hunched over to escape, Dean released him but, brought his knee up twice in rapid succession.

The first strike shattered the man's nose and knocked at least one tooth out. The second landed right between the man's eyes. Dean was pretty sure the blow hadn't been fatal, but when the man fell back to the pavement, he was limp and completely motionless. Dean had killed people before, but he liked to avoid it whenever he could.

"Damn," he sighed.

He looked all around him and saw that he was fortunate that no one had been up on the second level to see him. Not wanting to draw any attention to the pivot car, he moved the bodies over to the stairwell. One by one, he slid them inside and left them there. The larger man had groaned, so Dean made sure he'd remain knocked out for a while with a stiff right hook to the face.

Shaking the jolt from the punch out of his hand, Dean walked back to the pivot car. He dropped to the pavement and retrieved the key from the top of the axle along the rear wheels. Next, he unlocked the door and opened the glove compartment. He fished around behind some maps and an old pocketknife before finding a few old napkins. He used them to pick up the handgun the armed man had been carrying and pitched it over the side of the concrete barrier.

He kept his eyes on the stairwell door as he got back into the car. He reached under the passenger seat and removed the small safe. It was a tiny thing, no larger than a paperback book. There was a digital combination plate on the side. He punched in the eight-digit code he'd memorized several months ago and popped the safe open. Inside, there were three cellphones. He picked one at random and auto-dialed one of the three numbers that were programmed into it.

Everson answered on the second ring. "Yeah?" is all he said, careful not to give important information to clever enemies that may have gotten their hands on the phones somehow.

"It's me, Everson," Dean said, his eyes still on the stairwell door. Massaging his right hand a bit, he said: "I'll be in the air in fifty minutes."

"Good. I need to know the moment you land."

"Yeah, I figured."

"One thing to keep in the back of your mind: in the next few days, I may need you to speak with the President."

"Oh. Okay."

Everson gave him a moment to let that sink in. After a few tense seconds, Everson asked: "Any problems getting out of the country?"

Smiling toward the stairwell, Dean said, "You know...same old, same old. But nothing I couldn't handle. I'll talk to you soon."

With that, Dean hung up and placed the phone back in the safe. He locked up the pivot car, returned the key to the axle, and headed toward the exit. He gave a little mock wave to his two would-be attackers as he made his way down the stairs.

Outside, with the garage behind him, Dean quickened his pace a bit. He had a plane to catch.

10

Roger realized that this day would be one of those where it was pointless to consult any clocks. Somehow, the half an hour he allowed himself for lunch had come and gone. He was drinking enough coffee to keep his hunger at bay. By the time he realized he was getting hungry, it was already after 3:00 in the afternoon.

He was still in his office, working his way down a list of priorities and strategies he thought would help to stay in front of the potential Nightwatch threat. They had already taken care of Bagram. In the meantime, he was looking at the schedules of all US Navy and Air Force training schedules, looking for any potential ways covert enemies might use them to sneak into the country.

He was also downloading the most up-to-date satellite imagery from the East and West Coasts. He knew most people would consider this the acts of a very paranoid man. The threat Dean Page had reported seemed to be isolated to potential incidents at Bagram Air Force Base. But Roger had spent a good deal of his time studying the policies and approaches of their enemies overseas. He knew that sometimes events like that could lead to larger events...sort of like a terrorist's Trojan Horse. Get everyone's attention on Bagram and then hit the country hard on their own soil.

They'd busted up four attempts with that exact blueprint over the past twenty years. And with a threat as unpredictable as Nightwatch, Roger wasn't about to take any chances.

With a heavy sigh and now-growling stomach, Roger tore his eyes away from the hyper-colored blobs and blurs on the satellite maps. The East Coast maps showed nothing out of the ordinary. Of course, that was an over-the-weeds study—sort of like a man looking for a diamond ring in a farmer's field by hovering over one hundred acres of wheat.

A new thought occurred to him as he reached out and buzzed May. Ever diligent, she responded right away. "Yes, sir—I mean Roger. You need lunch, right? You haven't eaten, have you?"

"No, Mom," he teased. "Do you mind calling in my usual?"

"On it."

His usual was a pastrami and mozzarella on rye. It made his office reek, but it was easily his favorite sandwich. Best of all, it was from a hole-in-the-wall sub shop just three blocks away and they delivered without any of that ridiculous Uber Eats nonsense.

Knowing that food was now on the way, Roger directed his attention to the idea he'd been forming. He'd been so perplexed over the report from Dean Page and Walter Everson because the idea of a blatant attack on an American airbase, no matter where it was located, seemed grandiose for an organization like Nightwatch. Because of that, he wondered if maybe Everson had maybe muddled up Page's report. He just couldn't know for sure until he spoke with Dean himself.

In the meantime, he had to work on his own speculations. And right now, that included wondering what the situation around the Parwan Province looked like. The nearest town of any merit to Bagram Air Force Base was Charikar. If anyone was going to carry out an attack on Bagram, certainly Charikar would be a point of interest for the attacker.

Roger reached for his phone. There were a few people he could call to ask about the current climate in Parwan Province. Everson was actually among them. But he also knew that, given Seibert's newfound treaties and agreements with Afghani officials, making such calls might be seen as going behind the President's back.

It was a damn shame Dean was coming back. He would have been the perfect candidate to send into Charikar. But, of course, Roger understood his need to leave the country. If someone discovered him and he got involved in some sort of shootout, then he would definitely become a target.

So, for now, all the information that would do any good was likely wrapped up in the Bagram documents he was waiting on. Deep down, he was already wondering if Seibert had people working against him...maybe a small team keeping eyes on all information about Bagram coming in and out of the Pentagon.

He stared at the ceiling for a moment before turning his attention to the West Coast satellite maps. But really, he was just checking boxes. His mind was already elsewhere, trying to figure out if there might be other ways to find out exactly what was on the ground in Bagram without drawing attention to himself. Everson might know, but that was a long shot.

As he looked at the screen, his eyes zoning out as he lost track of time again, there was a knock at his door.

"Come on in," he said.

It was May, and she was carrying his sandwich, as well as a bottle of the root beer he kept in the fridge out in the shared break room and cafeteria.

"This is amazing. Thanks, May," he said as he took it.

"Smells awful."

"Then get out," he joked.

She laughed and left. Roger picked up his sandwich and was about to take a bite out of it when his cell phone rang. A call that didn't come through the main line to be received and filtered by May usually meant it was something fairly secretive, or a call from Maggie at home.

He picked it up and saw that the number on the caller display was Frederickson. With a sigh, Roger put the sandwich down and took the call.

"Hello?"

Frederickson said. "Hey, remember I told you that you'd probably need to speak with the President in private?"

"I do, yes."

"Well, he's on hold right now. On the line."

"What?"

"I mentioned it to him about an hour ago, and he thought it was a good idea. He wants to make sure you're on the same page with all of this. He's on

Air Force One right now with a bit of spare time and wants to speak with you."

"Jesus, Frederickson...."

"This may be good, though. He's voluntarily speaking with you on this. Just...try to be calm. You may make this entire ordeal a lot easier."

"I will. But you've ruined my sandwich, so I promise nothing."

"I what?" Frederickson asked.

"Nothing. Never mind. Okay, put the President through."

There was a click as Frederickson switched over to President Seibert and then, ten seconds later, the voice of the President was in Roger's ear.

11

Roger placed the call on speakerphone, allowing him to pace little circles around his desk while he spoke. It was a habit he often resorted to during particularly tense calls. And there had been more than a few of them in his office over the years.

"First and foremost, Mr. Commer, I'd like to apologize for how things went this morning. News like that...what you were putting out there...it took me by surprise. And I'm sure you know it's not the sort of thing to jump the gun over. Especially not in a setting with so many ears."

Well played, Roger thought. *An apology that is twisted at the end to point out how he thought what I did was stupid and ill-advised.* It was yet another reminder of how this man had won the election. He was adept at swaying a conversation to meet his needs.

"I hope you know, Mr. President, that I would never lay out simple rumors and hearsay. I brought the situation to your attention this morning because I believe this is a credible threat. I trust the man that delivered the news and, as such, the man he is communicating with out in the field."

After a very brief silence, the President said, "Secretary Frederickson, what are your honest thoughts on this?"

There was more silence on the line. Roger could just imagine Frederickson's eyes going wide and alarmed as he tried to think of the right thing to say. "Well, sir," he finally said. "I don't know Everson nearly as well as Mr. Commer, but my gut says we should at least look into this," Frederickson finally said.

"Mr. Commer, you've reached out to the commanders at Bagram, correct?"

"I have, sir. I'm expecting the documents and plans from them any moment now."

"And if there is indeed some sort of planned attack on the base, would you be able to identify any weaknesses or inefficiencies in how they have things set up over there?"

"I believe so."

"And you'd obviously be looking for any red flags that may point to any inside interference that may undermine their security, I assume?"

"Yes, sir. But I know they keep things buttoned up quite tight over there."

"Ah, as do I. And maybe now you can see why I am thinking this is nothing but scary stories being spread around by...well, by folks across the aisle, trying to drum up some fear-mongering in a part of the world I've worked very hard to forge friendships with."

"With all due respect, wouldn't those very public friendships and partnerships be the perfect cover for a group like Nightwatch to stir up things again? They'd see it as either the naivete of their own government or a sort of immunity."

"Immunity? How so?"

"For the very reason we're discussing," Roger said. "Because they know there would be great concern and a cause of hesitancy on your part."

Roger knew he'd perhaps crossed a line with that final comment, but was almost beyond caring.

"Mr. Commer, I don't expect you to know the pressures and absolute chaos of trying to establish treaties and peace with a country that has historically been our enemy. I've worked quite hard to make sure the threats in that area of the world have been abolished...that we can consider ourselves allies."

The President's way of speaking to him like a child overshadowed the irritation in his voice, which Roger could hear. *I don't expect you to know....*

"With all due respect, Mr. Pres—"

"You say 'with all due respect' but your constant questioning of my policies and assurances that there is nothing to worry about here isn't *showing* respect. Now, if you have anything further to discuss after seeing those documents out of Bagram, you let me know."

Roger opened his mouth to respond, but the President had already dropped off the line. Roger's office went quiet for a moment, finally interrupted by Frederickson.

"You still there, Roger?"

"Yeah, I'm here," Roger said through clenched teeth. He couldn't ever remember being so angry with something the President had said. He knew Seibert wasn't a stupid man; he was exceptionally bright, in fact. But in this case, Roger felt certain the President was being blinded by his own delusions of grandeur concerning his foreign policy. And that could be disastrous.

"Any ideas?"

He had no *new* ideas, so he mentioned an old one. "I think I need to take your advice from our earlier call. I need to put a team together without the President knowing about it."

"It would have to be a small one. The more people that are involved, the bigger the chance it gets back to the President."

"I know. For now, I think I just have to wait—on the Bagram documents, on Everson and Dean Page."

"Yeah, that seems sensible. I mean…we don't know what sort of clock we're looking at on this thing if it *is* legitimate."

"True."

"Let me know when you've connected with Everson or Page."

"Will do."

They ended the call, and Roger took a few more laps around his desk, just to cool off. When he finally settled back into his chair, he saw that he had one bit of good news.

During their call, the information from Bagram had come in.

12

There were three documents. One was a rather simple blueprint of the base. Another was a fifteen-page document labeling best-practices for security and the chain of command all security events were ordered to follow. The third document was longer and more than Roger had been expecting.

This document detailed all construction jobs that had taken place on the base over the past two years. It was complete with a list of all materials shipped in, used, and any excess that had been shipped back out. It then detailed any security measures and protocols that had to be changed to accommodate these construction jobs. It was over two hundred pages long, complete with an index detailing the perimeter of every construction site.

A secondary index detailed recent attacks on the base, which happened more than the American media let on. The base was so heavily fortified, though, that nearly none of these attacks were effective. The most recent occurred three years ago, when five rockets were fired at the base. Four of the five had been knocked out of the air by personnel on the base. The fifth had struck just outside the base, resulting in one of the construction jobs listed in the lengthy document.

Roger recalled this incident, but not the specifics. He went on Google and typed in the pertinent information. The attack had caused one casualty—an Afghan civilian—and a terrorist organization that was currently defunct claimed responsibility for it. It was, however, a terrorist organization that had very close ties to Nightwatch. And it was there, in two different articles he read about the attack, that he'd found perhaps the most important nugget. He carefully read the line, unsure if it was a lead for him...but certain that he should at least check it out. It came as an edit to the original article.

NOTE AND UPDATE: Two days following this attack, authorities apprehended Devante Abdul of Baltimore, Maryland for attempting to plant a chemical bomb behind the loading dock of a Baltimore, MD post office. He claimed the act was to make up for the failings of terrorist bodies overseas, most notably the infamous Nightwatch, of whom he claims membership.

Roger shut down his browser and pulled up the CIA/FBI database. He typed in the name Devante Abdul and was looking at his criminal profile within just ten seconds.

Abdul was of mixed-race descent, with a father from Sierra Leone and a mother from Kunar, Afghanistan. He'd been arrested for the first time at nineteen for throwing Molotov cocktails at a military parade. He had been released from prison after serving three years and his name had come up on multiple cases where the CIA and Homeland Security had been tracking down the export of bomb-making materials. He'd never been formally charged on anything, though. Not until he'd been caught with the homemade chemical bomb behind the Maryland post office.

That was five years ago, and he'd been in prison ever since. According to the file, he was being held in DC, locked away in a building maintained by the Federal Bureau of Prisons. That he'd been sent to this rather mild prison system surprised Roger at first, but then he realized it actually made sense. If you had a local prisoner with alleged ties to terrorist organizations, you wanted to keep them close. It had been a strategy implemented by the US ever since Vietnam, keeping suspected traitors and terrorists in institutions where they could be easily questioned at a moment's notice.

It felt like a long shot, but if he was getting no help from the White House, he had to take every lead he found. The prison was only half an hour away, so it certainly couldn't hurt to question him. He sent the file to his phone and then, before pushing himself away from his desk, figured it might be a smart idea to call Everson. To sit at his desk and go through records, construction logs, and criminal databases was one thing; but once he started actively questioning people about a matter the President was considering dead in the water, it became much more dangerous.

Everson answered on the second ring. Even before Roger said a word, Everson was talking. "I'm sorry. I still don't know when Dean is getting back."

"Is there any need to be worried about him?" Roger asked.

"I don't think so. I know that as of about two hours ago, he placed a call to his supervisor and said he'd be getting on a plane soon. So even if he gets in the air within the hour, we're talking about him getting home in the early morning hours. So you'll have some time to wait."

"I need his number."

"Roger, I don't know. I mean, the whole appeal of having someone like this working on our side is the whole anonymity thing."

"Look, the Bagram stuff isn't helping like I thought it would...though it *was* thorough as hell. And I've had the President's ear twice, and he's refusing to listen. I need all the help I can get."

"It won't matter anyway. He's likely in the air by now. Trust me on this, Roger. I'll let you know the moment I hear from him."

"Fine. Anyway, I was calling to let you know I'm going to speak to a guy being held by the Federal Bureau of Prisons: Devante Abdul. You know him?"

"Sounds familiar, yeah. A small-time terrorist wanna-be. A Timothy McVeigh type, right?"

"I don't know. I'm about to go find out. He once claimed to be an actual member of Nightwatch. I don't think anyone took him seriously, though. Still...it's worth a shot."

"Yeah, I agree. Listen, let me know if you need an assist through any of this, okay? I can't guarantee my availability, but I can try my best."

"Thanks. But I think I'm fine for now."

"Be careful out there."

Roger ended the call and headed for the door. He thought about calling ahead to the prison, but decided against it. His mind went back to the possibility that maybe President Seibert had eyes on him. A call to the prison would be just one more piece that the President could use as proof against him...if it ever came to that.

Feeling true worry settling in for the first time, Roger made his way down to the parking garage and was already thinking of what types of question he could ask Abdul without showing too much of his hand.

13

Roger followed the tall, uniformed officer down the hallway, their footsteps like little bomb blasts in the otherwise quiet passage. Afternoon sunlight spilled in through the windows to the right, making the place look deceptively cheerful.

Because Roger had not called ahead, the woman he'd spoken to at the front gate had to call someone in management and request an urgent meeting with Devante Abdul. However, upon giving his credentials and over-stating that he was here as part of a high-ranking investigation with the CIA—it wasn't *all* a lie but not anywhere near the truth, either—the prison made some quick moves and was able to make Abdul available within ten minutes.

Roger was introduced to a guard who led him down the sunny hallway. They came to the end of the corridor, where the guard used a keycard to buzz them through a large metal door. When he opened it and ushered Roger through, they were in a darker passageway. On each side were several doors, all painted a shade of dull gray. The guard led Roger to the first door on the left and, once again, buzzed it open.

Roger peered in and saw a small, muscular man sitting at a square table. He had dark caramel skin and close-cropped hair. Davante Abul's face was familiar, as Roger had been looking at it on the database less than half an hour ago.

The guard stepped to the side and said, "If you need anything, sir, I'll be on this side of the door. Just give a holler."

"Thanks," Roger said. "But I think I'll be fine."

He stepped into the room and closed the door behind him. It was little more than a basic interrogation room, like the ones in countless police precincts all over the country—maybe larger and cleaner. When he took the seat across the table from Abdul, the man just looked back for a moment as they sized each other up.

Roger saw defiance in Abdul's stare, as well as a hardened, stubborn nature. That a higher-up from the CIA—as far as Abdul knew, anyway—was here to question him didn't bother him in the slightest.

"Did they tell you who I am, Mr. Abdul?"

"Some CIA spook, right?" His voice was low and lacked any sort of emotion. He may as well have been speaking about the weather with a friend.

"That's close enough, I suppose. We don't really have the convenience of time for me to explain it all to you. I'm here to ask you some questions about your involvement with Nightwatch."

There was a flicker of surprise in the man's eyes, but he shut it down quickly, keeping his composure. Roger assumed anyone from the government who spoke to him—if ever, at all—had been interested in the creation of his chemical bomb, not his Nightwatch ties. Especially not since everyone at the higher levels assumed they were no longer a threat.

"Well, you're wasting your breath," Abdul said. "I'm not a snitch."

"I don't need you to be. I don't need names, locations, anything like that. But the bomb you made and tried to blow up a post office with...was that at the request of Nightwatch, or were you just you trying to earn their good graces?"

"Why does it matter one way or the other?" Abdul was nearly reclining in the straight-backed chair, an arm cocked up over the back corner. He was actually smirking at Roger, as if daring him to lose his temper.

"It matters because if it was just you trying to look like a bad-ass for a group of terrorists, then I *am* wasting my time. I need to know information about the plan and strategy. I need to know if there's a chain of command that's followed."

Abdul sneered at the slight mockery, and his posture went a bit more rigid. "What are you wanting to know all of this for, anyway? Nightwatch isn't even at work anymore."

"Yeah, that seems to be the consensus these days. But I think otherwise. And I don't exactly have everyone in agreement on that, so I'm having to go to unconventional sources like you for information."

"Then you're shit out of luck, man."

Roger felt himself getting angry. Though he considered himself a moral man, he wasn't above lying to men like Abdul to get what he needed. He'd done more it over the years and was good at it. In his current position, though, he rarely got the chance anymore. Hell, it had been years since he'd actually interrogated someone like Abdul face-to-face.

"I've read over your file" Roger said. "I know you've done five years of a twenty-year sentence. And because your crime was considered an act of terror, you and I both know the whole 'getting off early for good behavior' thing isn't even an option. You know that, right?"

"Let me guess," Abdul spat. "You're going to shorten my sentence if I play ball?"

"Maybe. Again, you tried to blow up a post office. There's very little leeway there. I know I can shorten the sentence, but it wouldn't be anything huge. Far too many people have to sign off on it."

He could tell right away that the *no doubt* part of it got Abdul's attention. Roger knew how men like this thought. Abdul thought that for a guy in Roger's position to admit there wasn't much he could do, he might have a chance here. When someone wasn't offering the moon and kissing ass, they meant what they said.

Too bad for Abdul, Roger was lying. He had no power to shorten the man's sentence and would have no interest in doing so even if he could.

"How much time are we talking?" Abdul asked, probably with more interest than he wanted to show.

"Again...it's not much. At the most, I'd say three. Maybe four. But in all actuality, we're looking at maybe two. It really depends on who the President is at the time and their stance on domestic terrorism regulations and laws. It won't come down to any bills or laws that are passed. It would be because of some...well, let's say *accidental* fudging of the numbers on your record."

"You shitting me?"

"No. If I wanted to lie to you, I'd come at you with better than two years."

Abdul was sitting all the way forward now. No longer sneering and stubborn, he looked nervous—which made Roger certain he was about to reveal something.

"It was more than me showing off...the bomb," he said. "I was in contact with this guy who was connected with Nightwatch. He said he'd call on me if he ever needed an assist up near the Capitol. So that's what he did. He called on me, said one of the lead guys with Nightwatch wanted to bomb a post office."

"What was this guy's name?"

"The man with Nightwatch was something stupid, some codename like Wolfen or something. But the contact...yeah, I don't want to give you his name."

"Why? Is he local?"

"Sort of."

"Where? Here in DC?"

Abdul hesitated for only a moment. He sighed a bit as he answered, but he seemed relaxed. Roger knew the look on the man's face well; Abdul thought that if he'd already started peeling at the band-aid, he may as well yank it off.

"I'm not giving you a name," he finally said. "But I'll give you a location."

"Okay," Roger said. He was afraid it would be a dead lead, though. What if Abdul was only giving up the location because it was somewhere on the other side of the country?

"There's a small hub of operations in southern Virginia. A real backwoods vibe. Trailer parks and sheds, that sort of thing."

"This is a Nightwatch hub?"

"Yeah. And a few others, too. Al Qaeda used to have some folks there, planning and scheming."

"Are you lying to me?"

"No," Abdul said. "But how's it feels to have to wonder?"

Ignoring the jab, Roger said, "And you've been to this place?"

"Yeah, a few times. It's been years, though…at least five or six."

"You think they might still be there?"

Abdul chuckled and shrugged, once again reclining in his chair now that he sensed he had control of the conversation. "I don't see why not. Man, they've been there for at least twenty years. Maybe more. Out in the middle of nowhere, hidden behind this small Amish farm."

"Okay, let's say you're telling me the truth. Why would you just give them up like this?"

"Because when I said I did what I had done for them, there was no appreciation. They went on with business as usual. And from what I hear, the moment Seibert had his little campfire kumbaya with the Afghani officials, they acted like good little boys and broke apart."

Roger almost asked if he knew this for sure. But he knew the only access Abdul had to the outside was in newspapers and whatever limited internet access he had. And as far as the media knew, Nightwatch had indeed gone underground in the last few years because of a changed political climate.

"Where in Virginia?"

"A little town called Pamplin. Hell, it's not even *in* the town, but down some back roads."

"Can you tell me how to find it once I get into Pamplin?" Roger asked as he took out his phone.

"Yeah," Abdul replied. He suddenly seemed very excited, as if he might be feeding off of Roger's hurried attitude. Abdul told him where to go and how to get there—and all the while, Roger knew he had to be careful. Abdul had ties to terrorists, after all. This could all be one gigantic trap.

But without the aid of the White House and having to do this entire job in the shadows, he really didn't have any other choice.

14

The only reason Roger gave this Pamplin, Virginia lead any credence was because history supported it. Ever since the late 1970s, there had been countless unofficial terrorist encampments and training grounds scattered throughout America. They were usually in smaller towns, either in rural areas through the southern part of the country, or in barren ghost towns out west. He could think of four or five busts just in the past three years in such locations. Sometimes these groups weren't actually affiliated with legitimate terrorist outfits, but it happened enough to take the threat seriously.

As he drove out of the prison parking lot, Roger tried to sort out the rest of his day. Based on the directions he'd pulled up on his phone, the drive to Pamplin would take nearly three and a half hours. That meant he wouldn't even get there until five in the afternoon. And even if he got down there and found absolutely nothing, that meant he wouldn't get home until well after nine.

Thinking as quickly and as rationally as he could, he pulled up his office number on his phone and set the call to Bluetooth. May answered on the first ring.

"Hey, boss."

"May, I need you to do something for me. I need you to go onto the database and run a search for a town called Pamplin, Virginia. Call me back to let me know the results."

"Got it."

He ended the call, feeling uneasy about sending May to the database. She'd done a few things like this for him in the past because she had certain levels of clearance that allowed her to see the first few rungs of the database. A secondary password would protect anything that she didn't have. He hoped that she'd find at least a nugget or two that would back up Abdul's claims. He could then spend the three and a half hour-drive confidently knowing he wasn't chasing an aggravated prisoner's lies. It would also save him the drive back through DC, and he could just get on the Interstate and head south if—

His thoughts were interrupted by an explosion of glass. In the blink of an eye, his driver's side window imploded. His first thought was a rock, then maybe that an errant driver had hit him, but it all became clear quickly.

He screamed out a curse, swerved and nearly hit a beer delivery truck, and finally righted the car back into his own lane. In the process of all of that, with glass in his lap and little flecks of it having cut his face, Roger knew what had happened.

Someone had taken a shot at him. And they'd done so with a high caliber weapon. His driver's side window was not just cracked; it was completely shattered.

As this realization set in, he lowered his head, hunched his shoulders, and sped on. Suddenly driving for his life, it was hard to keep track of exactly where he was. He was headed west, on a two-lane. To his right, there was a concrete barrier preventing cars on that side of the road from falling off onto the underpass below. To the left, there was a business park and a few retailers—a small chain of shops ranging from a Thai diner to an office supply store. And because the round had come from his driver's side window, that was the source of the shooting.

As he stared ahead, his face stinging with multiple knicks from the glass, he sped past several cars. When he came up behind a city waste truck, he cut hard to the left, blazing down the breakdown lane with rumble strips complaining beneath his tires. He waited for another blast even though he felt certain one wouldn't come. For the shot to have taken out his driver's side glass, the shooter was stationary on that side of the road. They'd been waiting for him. Which also meant they knew where he would be.

That opened up a whole different batch of questions, but they weren't questions he could focus on at the moment. Now he needed to focus on getting back to his office. And, more pressing than that, to notify someone about what had happened to him.

If he could get police units or even agents to that business park within the next five minutes, there might be a chance of nabbing the bastards who had tried to kill him. Though, if they were professionals—and he assumed they were because they'd somehow known where he would be—he knew the chances were slim.

When he placed the call to the internal CIA line for prominent high-profile investigations, his heart was still hammering. But by the time he relayed what had happened, Roger also felt something else rising in his guts: he was pissed off, and he was going to get to the bottom of this with or without help from official channels.

15

When Roger arrived back at the Pentagon, there were several people waiting to meet with him. One was Henry Frederickson, who looked just about as angry as Roger was. Another was Hector Moreno, an Assistant Director with the CIA. There was one other agent with him, a man Roger had never seen before. Both Frederickson and Moreno came rushing toward him as Roger entered the lobby. He gave them a curt nod to the left, signaling for them to head over to the primary stairwell.

The agent accompanying Moreno stayed behind, surveilling the lobby. Roger assumed he was simply a level of protection for Moreno, which seemed like a bit much as far as Roger was concerned.

"Jesus, Commer," Frederickson said. "You know you've got cuts on your face, right? Dried blood too."

"I know," he said, heading to the men's restroom just shy of the stairwell.

He walked inside with the other two men following him. Roger looked himself over in the mirror while Moreno did a quick sweep of the stalls. He nodded and said, "We're alone. So what the hell happened?"

"Exactly what I told your people on the phone," Roger said. "Someone took a shot at me after I left the prison. Devante Abdul told me about a Nightwatch encampment in Pamplin, Virginia—I was going to see if he was telling me the truth." He yanked several paper towels from the dispenser by the sink closest to him, wetted them, and dabbed at the first of six minor cuts on his face. The deepest was one on his cheek that had bled enough to trickle down his face, splattering on the left shoulder of his shirt.

"And you're sure it was a gunshot? Not a rock or—"

"If someone chucked a rock at my car while I was doing at least fifty miles per hour and hit my window with that much accuracy, they're a fucking wizard." He realized how quickly he'd lost his temper, so he did his best to calm himself down when he added: "Ballistics will likely confirm it for me. When I got out of my car, I saw where the bullet tore into the passenger side door, right near the floor. The slug is still in it, I think. Based on your line of questions, can I assume your men found nothing on the scene?"

"Not yet, but they're still out there. Finding the shooter is pretty much impossible, but maybe they'll come across the casing."

"Roger, who knew you were going to the prison?" Frederickson asked.

"No one. No, wait…Everson knew. And then I checked in when I got there, so two different people at the front desk. But I trust Everson. And besides…the shooter knew my car. They knew what I was driving and where I was coming from. Whoever it was…I think they had me tagged even before I went to the prison."

"But how? How did they know you were headed to the prison?" Moreno asked.

"Maybe they followed me. Maybe they've been on me for a while. For all I know, they've had drones trailing me around. And I don't think it's beyond reason to assume that this is connected to my efforts to make the President aware of the intelligence emerging from Everson and Dean Page.And I don't think it's beyond reason to assume that this is connected to my efforts to make the President aware of the intelligence emerging from Everson and Dean Page.

"Jesus…." Moreno said.

"You've filled him in, I take it?" Roger asked Frederickson.

"I did. And he's one hundred percent on our side."

"The President is being a fool on the Nightwatch situation," Moreno said. "But I have to say…yes, I think it might be a stretch to connect this incident with the Nightwatch issue."

"Director Moreno, would you like to guess how many times people shot at me *before* I brought that intelligence to the President this morning?"" Roger wiped the last remaining cut free of blood and tossed it into the trash bin.

"Well, your position has you involved in some very peculiar and controversial things, right?" Moreno asked.

"Sometimes. But I've never been shot at, at least since I was promoted to this job." He then looked directly at Frederickson. "Has the President been notified of this?"

"No. But Vice President Warren has. In fact, he's sending a small security detail to escort you home."

"That's unnecessary."

"Really? You're the one that keeps reminding us you were just shot at."

"But a security detail is only going to—"

"Save your breath. It's happening. They're already on their way."

"Before you two start arguing," Moreno said, "I need to know how much air to give this thing. Am I sitting on it for a while, or do you want it to be public knowledge?"

"Sit on it," Roger said. "For now, at least. Until I've spoken to the President about it. And hopefully Dean Page as well."

Frederickson sighed and shook his head. "You know you'll have to be the one to inform the President. If I tell him, he's going to ask how I knew."

"No," Moreno said. "I'll tell Deputy Director Gleason. Standard protocols would have me report something like this to him, anyway. And because Mr. Commer believes it has direct ties to his interest in potential terrorist activities, Gleason has to tell the President...or at least his National Security Advisor. So I'll handle that. And I'll ask my colleagues at Homeland to check out Abdul's tip about a Nightwatch outpost in Pamplin."

"Fine," Roger said. And then, looking to both men, he said: "What now?"

"What now," Frederickson said, "is you wait on that security detail and go home."

"Someone just took a shot at me, dammit! How am I supposed to just go home and wait for something to be done?"

"Well, what do you think you're going to get done here?"

Roger recognized it was a good point and, really, Moreno's men were better suited to handle anything that could be done to find the shooter. He eyed the Assistant Director with as much authority as he could muster—which was difficult because he felt rather helpless at that moment.

"Fine. But I need you to call me if you get any updates. I need your word on that. You call me even if it's after the President has heard and is in the loop. I need to be the first to know."

Moreno shifted uneasily and then looked at Frederickson. He was clearly uncomfortable with the idea of keeping secrets from the President.

"He's right," Frederickson said. "For now, Roger has to be the head of this. Any information about the shooter needs to come to him first."

"There's no need for the President to know you were involved in this part of things," Roger said. "I mean, if that's what you're worried about."

Moreno nodded and started for the door. "Fine. But...are you both certain Nightwatch is on the move?"

"Any doubts I had were just erased when someone tried to blow my head off as I was driving down a public highway," Roger said. "And it also tells me that not only are they on the move, but they have moles in DC, and they already know I'm looking into them."

He was pretty sure this convinced Moreno, but he still looked very uncomfortable as he gave both men a parting nod and made his way out of the restroom.

"Roger, do you have a change of clothes in your office?" Frederickson asked.

"Yeah, why?"

"Because there's blood on your shirt."

Roger looked back into the mirror, completely forgetting about the blood on his shoulder. Jesus, how had things gotten this bad so quickly? The bullet had nearly plastered his brains all over the passenger side of his car. And because the shooter knew they'd failed when Roger made his getaway, there was no telling what else they might do in the coming days.

"Tell me," Roger said, now also heading for the door. "This security detail...will they stay parked in front of my house?"

"Probably. Well, until the President finds out about it. After that, who knows? Do you...do you think they'll still come after you?"

"I do."

It was a daunting prospect but; he wondered if his life being in danger might make the President open his eyes to the genuine threat. But as he made his way up to his office to change into a clean shirt, he already sensed that it was going to be a long shot.

16

Roger was shocked to discover that he wasn't nervous to be stepping back out into the streets again. Someone clearly wanted him dead and was willing to make a public spectacle of it. He'd been around enough to know the inner workings of so-called public hits. Whoever had tried taking him out had failed. That meant they'd wait a while before making another attempt. Right now, there was too much of a risk, and they were likely regrouping.

For now, he was confident it was safe to move about. The security detail that escorted him out of the building didn't seem to agree, though. He was flanked by two men in suits, one in front of him and one behind, as he made his way across the small, open lot behind the building. They remained in this position until they reached the parking garage. There, Roger headed for one of several federal loaner sedans because his car was currently shot up.

Nearly three hours had passed, and there was still no ID on the shooter—or *shooters*, for all he knew. Moreno's men had also not yet found casings, residue of any kind, or any other traces of evidence left behind. This didn't really surprise Roger, though. The men who'd attempted to take his life were pros. And even if they weren't, whoever sent them was. People like that didn't do sloppy work.

As Roger made his way out of the parking garage in the sedan, the suited men followed him in an identical car. Roger rolled his eyes as he peered at them through the rearview. Yes, he understood the necessity of it, but it made him feel like he was being babysat.

It wasn't until he was back out in traffic that Roger felt threatened. He glanced nervously over to every parking lot and shopping center he passed. There was a noticeable spike in his anxiety, mixed with a rush of sharp adrenaline as he fully expected a gunshot to sound at any moment.

But nothing of the sort happened as he made his way home. And all the while, Moreno's men stayed right behind him—and it remained that way the entire trip: leaving DC, onto I-395, and all the way out to the coast.

Roger was just ten minutes from pulling into his driveway when his cellphone rang. The caller display read UNKNOWN, which wasn't irregular in his line of work. He accepted the call via Bluetooth on his stereo system, now very much aware that every phone call he got until this entire Nightwatch mess was cleared up could be detrimental. Someone wanted him dead, and he had some very serious levels of protection assigned to him; he was drawing more unnecessary attention.

"Hello?"

A slightly robotic male voice said, "Is this Roger Commer?"

"It is."

"Please hold for the President."

It wasn't the first time he'd received this call. In fact, it was one he'd taken five or six times over the past decade. But it became no less nerve-shredding. He felt the weight of the entire day settle down on him as he waited for the transfer.

There was an audible click over the speakers, and then President Seibert's voice filled the car. "Mr. Commer?"

"Yes, Mr. President."

"I heard about your incident on the road today. Are you okay?"

"Yes, sir. I'm fine. Just a little shaken."

"Vice President Warren tells me he doesn't have much information to share just yet, so I thought I'd call you directly. Have you touched base with the CIA on this yet?"

"I spoke directly with Hector Moreno. He assures me he has his best working on it. He also has me being tailed by a pair of goons."

"There's no word on who might be responsible?"

"No *official* word. But if I'm being honest, I have a pretty good idea *why*."

The few seconds of silence made it clear that the President knew where he was headed with this. Roger also knew the President wasn't about to speak it out loud and encourage it, so Roger took control of the conversation.

"There were about ten people at that meeting this morning, Mr. President. And we both know more than half of them agreed with your stance on my updates concerning Nightwatch. If word got out that I—"

"Please be careful with that you say next."

Roger sighed and gripped the steering wheel tighter. It was odd to be hearing the President of the United States' voice in his car while driving through the city he lived in, but he didn't let the absurdity of it detour him.

"I'm looking at it with the eyes of someone with an intelligence background, sir. I am one of a few who knew about the information coming from Dean Page. I shared that information for the first time at the meeting this morning. I then begin looking deeper into it and then someone takes a shot at me. Surely you can see what this suggests."

After another moment of tense silence, President Seibert spoke up once more. His voice sounded calm but considerably calculated as well...almost as if he were trying to convince a child that yes, he really was listening to this long and rambling story.

"Let's say you're right, Mr. Commer. What do you suppose this so-called attack you're anticipating would look like?"

Roger wasted no time, even sidestepping the insulting tone in the President's voice. "If it's being done *on* the base, I'd assume it's coming in with deliveries...food, weapons, medical and maintenance supplies...things like that. And if that *is* what's happening, at least two people on the base would have to be in on it because it involves so many departments: deliveries, loading tracking, and drivers. And if the attack is coming from outside of the base—an assault or rocket of some kind, for instance—there's no way to know for sure how or when it would happen. It would be stupid of someone like Nightwatch to pull off such a feat, but they could. And rather easily because of lightened security protocols in the area. It would indeed be an act of war, but perhaps that's what they want."

"And why is that?"

"They're a terrorist body, sir. War is good for business."

"I have to say, Mr. Commer...you came up with that very fast."

"It's my job to think that way, Mr. President."

Roger turned onto his street, sensing the conversation ending. As he pointed the car to his house, he checked the rearview and saw the other sedan right behind him, Moreno's men blurred through the windshield.

"When do you expect to speak with this spy? Dean Page, right?"

"Right. And I don't know, sir. If I haven't heard anything in the next several hours, I'll reach out to Everson. I should know something by tomorrow morning."

"You're certain?"

"No. We're talking about a spy that, if his story checks out, might be running for his life right now."

"Very well. Contact my office as soon as you hear something. You know to make sure it comes directly to me, correct?" President Seibert sounded exasperated, maybe even disappointed. And it occurred to Roger in that moment, as he pulled the car into his driveway, that the President was looking for something—for some specific piece of information.

Maybe trying to find a crack in all of this so he can instruct me to stop looking into it without the order coming off as suspicious, Roger thought.

"Yes, Mr. President."

And then without so much as a goodbye, the call was ended, and Roger was once again left in a silent car. He sat in the driveway for a moment, watching as the agency sedan made no attempt at subtlety while parking at the edge of his driveway. Roger considered the conversation with the President for a while and then wondered how he was supposed to explain to Maggie that he'd come a few inches away from being killed today.

17

Maggie stared at him from across the dining room table, eyes wide and glistening with tears. "I'm sorry," she said. "I'm going to need you to explain this to me again. And Roger...I know there are certain things you can't tell me, classified details. But your life is at risk...you almost died today. I'm your wife, and I think for just these next five minutes, you can lay it all on the table."

"Maggie, you know I ca—"

"Someone tried to kill you today!" she nearly screamed it at him, and the tears that had been forming now came pouring down her cheeks.

So, with their dinner on the table between them, Roger did his best to tell her the entire story. The only part he left out was Dean, the spy that was working closely with Everson. Maggie knew Everson; she'd even met him a few times over the years at work functions, galas, and parties. And because Nightwatch was a well-known group, he didn't see the harm in telling her about his suspicions and the current predicament he found himself in.

Honestly, getting it all out felt good. Knowing that a caring and compassionate set of ears was taking it all in made the burden of it lighter. And when he was done, Maggie thought it over, dabbing at her tears with a napkin from the table. She poked at an asparagus spear for a moment before looking back up at him.

"So right now, you just need to hear from Everson to make sure the information is accurate, right?" she asked.

"Right."

"So what's the hold-up?"

"Everson is still waiting on verified confirmation from his sources overseas." This was the closest he'd come to stating that Everson was working with a spy—a spy that was really little more than a ghost for the CIA, NSA, and all other manner of intelligence agencies. How was he supposed to explain to Maggie that there were some agents in the field who moved in the shadows and held no real anchors to any reputable and recognized government agencies? It was the stuff of conspiracy theories, and he wasn't trying to make her even more worried.

"And do you think the President will come around to reason if he can get verification from Everson?"

"Honestly...no. But I think that sort of verification will get a few people in his close circles to take it more seriously. And hopefully that will trickle down into his Cabinet."

"How long?" she asked, still prodding at the food on her plate, though it was clear she'd lost her appetite. "If there *is* going to be an attack on Bagram, when will it be?"

"I have no idea. It could be five minutes from now, or it could be five months. That's what makes it so volatile. And, I think, it's also one reason President Seibert is unwilling to accept it."

Maggie nodded and finally started eating her dinner again. Roger did as well, also taking a sip from his glass of wine. Telling Maggie about what was going on made him feel better, but he also thought this might be one of those nights where he had three or four glasses of wine just to make sure he could get some sleep.

"I have to admit," Maggie said, giving him a slight smile, "that the cuts on your face look sort of rugged."

"Well, at least something came out of my near-death experience."

"Those men outside in that sedan...have they bugged the house?" Maggie asked.

"No."

"Good. Maybe after dinner, we'll head upstairs for a bit."

It seemed slightly out of character for her. Maggie was never one to openly express that she was feeling amorous. Roger supposed knowing her husband had nearly died earlier in the day had her feeling sentimental and maybe even sad. Maybe, he guessed, she just wanted to be close. And that was fine with him.

They finished up their dinner, talking about other things—namely about how this entire ordeal with the shooting and Nightwatch was likely going to result in canceling their plans to visit Thomas at college in Williamsburg over the weekend. It wasn't *nearly* the first time Roger's job had caused them to cancel family plans, and he was sure it wouldn't be the last. It was simply one of the many inconveniences his job brought with it.

Roger and Maggie finished up dinner, and Roger had one extra glass of wine as they cleaned up. Maggie then wasted no time leading him upstairs and taking him to bed. And when they were done, lying side by side with the light of dusk just barely peeking in through the blinds, Roger thought about his near-shooting again. He thought about how someone had sent a gunman to kill him just because he was working on a tip from a spy...a tip that no one was supposed to know about.

That made him focus on two specific questions. First, how did the shooter and their bosses know he was looking into potential Nightwatch movement? And second, if they were willing to attempt to kill him in such an open environment, what else might they be willing to do?

18

Roger could not finish the fourth glass of wine. It had made his stomach feel sour, likely because of how it was interacting with his nerves. As he readied himself for bed at 10:30, he walked over to the bedroom window. He was brushing his teeth as he did so, a habit Maggie always teased him about. According to her, he had an issue sitting still, even when he was brushing his teeth or just talking on the phone.

Brushing his teeth with one hand, Roger pushed aside the blinds with the other. The sedan was still parked outside, in the same place it had been when he'd finished up the call in his car with President Seibert. He wondered if another pair would come in to relieve them later in the night. He considered calling Moreno to ask, but didn't see the point. It would just be one more bit of information for his mind to process as he tried to get some sleep.

He and Maggie were both in bed with the lights out by 11:00. Roger traditionally woke up at five and had long ago become accustomed to functioning on six hours of sleep, while snagging a solid nine on Sundays. And though it took him longer than usual to fall asleep, the wine seemed to help.

This was the first thought that came to his mind when he stirred awake sometime later. With bleary eyes, he looked over to the bedside table. The soft blue numbers of the alarm clock told him it was 2:24 in the morning.

He slowly sat up, tense. Had he heard something in the house? Movement downstairs, maybe? He'd always been a light sleeper and given the day he'd had yesterday, he supposed it made sense that even asleep, his mind would be on high alert.

He got out of bed quietly and, wearing only boxers and a tee shirt, went to the window. He moved like a ghost, so as not to wake up Maggie. Pulling the blinds back, he saw the sedan still down below. If the original goons had swapped with another pair, he had no way of knowing. He slowly let the blinds fall back into place and, as he took a single step away from it, he heard the noise again.

It was slight and barely there, but definitely coming from downstairs. Roger moved quickly and with practiced precision. In three quick strides, he was out of the bedroom and pulling the door closed behind him, though not so far that it would click closed in the frame and wake Maggie. He then took a single step out into the upstairs hall before stopping and opening the small linen closet just off of their bedroom. Here, he hid one of his four weapons for home protection. He shoved his hand between the stacks of towels and an extra comforter, pulling out the FBI standard-issue Sig Sauer.

When he stepped away from the closet, the hardwood floor groaned under his weight just the slightest bit—but hopefully not enough to alert whoever was downstairs.

As Roger made his way to the stairs, the handgun held stiffly out in front of him; it occurred to him he could be overreacting. The sound he'd heard could be nothing more than one of the fridge's random, occasional noises. Because he was on such high alert from the day's events, maybe he was making more out of it than he needed to.

But his gut told him this wasn't the case. And the vast majority of the time, his gut was right.

He came to the stairway, pivoted around to look down to the first floor, and found the stairway empty. A soft blue glow radiated from down below, from the stove clock in the kitchen. *Well, of course no one is there,* he scolded himself. *If someone broke into your house, the alarm would have gone off.*

But his gut—the instincts he'd honed over his storied career—said otherwise. Even now, as he made his way down the stairs one by one, he could sense a presence downstairs—not so much movement, but a disruption to the air, as if someone had just passed by.

He made his way down to the bottom of the stairs, fully aware that if there was someone down there, he'd be completely exposed when he reached the bottom step. Once he was there, he'd have three different directions to check: the entrance to the dining room, the hallway into the front of the house, and the opened backside of the living room. As for his intruder, they'd only be focusing on the stairs.

He wasn't sure how to approach this. He could either hurry down and hope to catch them by surprise or announce that he was there, and he was armed.

In the end, he didn't have to decide. A voice spoke up in little more than a whisper from the right, coming from the dining room.

"I know you're armed," the male voice said. "I am too. But I don't intend to use mine. You can trust me."

"Bullshit," Roger whispered back.

He heard a bit of movement, and then the figure slowly stepped into view at the junction where the dining room met the hallway just eight feet from the bottom of the stairs. Roger swung his Sig Sauer in that direction and saw a Black man of about forty standing with his own gun held out grip-first toward Roger. He was wearing a black tee shirt and dark jeans. His hair was black and slicked back, revealing an angular face with a bit of five o'clock shadow darkening the edges.

"See?" the man said. "I'm a friend."

"Then why did you break into my house? *How* did you break into my house?" And then he asked what was perhaps the most important question. "Who the hell are you?"

The man grinned and holstered his gun at his back, pulling his black tee shirt down over it. "I'm Dean Page," he said. "And I think you and I need to talk."

19

They sat across from one another at the dining room table, illuminated only by the ambient blue glow of the stovetop clock and the small amount of moonlight that came in through the kitchen windows behind them.

"You asked why I snuck into your house," Dean said, keeping his voice low. "And rightfully so. But based on all I've heard since I got back into the country, it seems you may be in some trouble because of this Nightwatch business. I figured here was the best place you and I could speak…more secure and all."

"How did you even get in?" Roger asked, perplexed.

"Are you referring to the men out in the sedan or the alarm system on your doors? Which, by the way, is sorely out of date."

"Both."

Dean shrugged and said, "It's sort of my job to get around obstacles like that. I can go into detail with you if you'd like, but I think we have more pressing matters."

"Yeah, we do."

"Everson says the President isn't buying into the Nightwatch updates."

"That's putting it lightly. And look…anything you have that I can take to him is going to speed this along."

"I have plenty. But you know as well as I do, it's going to take a threat of war written in the sky by an airplane for Seibert to open his eyes to this. He's too sold on his own line of crap. He's in deep with President Shahin and Minister Daraa."

"Then forget him. I can show it to Frederickson and Vice President Warren, who's on my side in this. He just needs the right approach...and ammunition. If members of his Cabinet can see what you have and *their* knowledge makes it to the press, there would be immense public pressure for the President to take this seriously—to at least address it."

Dean seemed to ponder his reasoning for a moment and, as he did, Roger did his best to get a read on him. Given that he had snuck into a stranger's house by somehow slipping past two federal guards and an electronic security system, he didn't seem to be in a particular hurry. He honestly didn't seem all that bothered about anything. Roger assumed that after the ordeal he'd had in Afghanistan, Dean just felt fortunate to be in a safe home on American soil.

"I see your point," Dean said. "So what are the best channels to use to get this done?"

"That depends on a variety of things."

"What things?" Dean asked.

"First of all, the nature of the material you have. What are we looking at? How much is it?"

"Well, regrettably, the audio conversations I had were lost during an attempt on my life. And *that* would have nailed this whole thing shut right away. I've got photographs of secret sites all around the desert where Nightwatch has been setting up small camps. This includes pictures of individuals, two of which have formerly been on terrorist watch lists for years.

"But the real knock-out blow is from encrypted emails between two different men within Nightwatch and Minister Daraa."

"What are they discussing in the emails?"

"Well, Bagram is called out specifically...though it's in code. There are a few names I'm unfamiliar with as well."

"Any date as to when it will happen?" Roger asked.

"The only reference to a date I got out of those emails at all was 'in the coming weeks.' And the last of those was sent about six days ago."

"Okay, soon."

"Yeah, that's what I'm thinking. And there's one other thing…something that probably links all of this directly to whoever took a shot at you yesterday."

"You heard about that?"

"Yeah, Everson told me. Look, I have no proof other than a thinly veiled reference in one of those emails, but I am almost certain there are Nightwatch agents active in DC. And according to the lost audio I had, they've been here for at least two years."

"What have they been doing in DC?"

"Well, they may move around. There are little camps set up here and there around the country. It's not too dissimilar from those terrorists that engaged in typical flight training before flying planes into the Twin Towers on 9/11. But my guess is that someone's feeding them information. I don't know if there's a mole in Washington or if they're just somehow hacking our internal communications."

"Either possibility is terrible," Roger said. "If they find out just how passive Seibert is being about this—"

"Then the attack on Bagram would come sooner rather than later," Dean finished for him. "And you know…I fear it may go beyond that. If they get a good picture as to just how all-in the President is on his new relationships with people in power in that area, I don't see why they'd limit it to bases in Afghanistan. If they have agents here, why not pull off an attack on American soil?"

Roger considered all of this and with every second that passed, both threats seemed more likely…more real. "They have to have ears *somewhere*," he said. "How else would they have known where I was and where I was going when they took that shot at me?"

"No clue. Where were you coming from when they made the attempt?"

"Prison. I'd gone to speak with Devante Abdul to see if he could tell me anything about Nightwatch movement stateside."

"Well, I doubt they have ears in the prison. I know Abdul saw himself as a big deal over here, but no one in Nightwatch ever did. I doubt they're keeping tabs on him."

"So, from somewhere else."

"Maybe."

"Do you think...Jesus, I can't believe I'm even suggesting it. But do you think it might be Seibert himself?"

"I doubt it. But I wouldn't totally eliminate the idea that he has someone doing it *for* him...passing along information here and there. But again, I'd say that even *that's* pushing it.

Both men went quiet for a moment. Dean looked at his watch and quietly got up from his chair. "I shouldn't stay too long. I'll make sure you have everything I've got tomorrow. Maybe email, maybe copies delivered to your office. I don't know yet."

"How would you even know where to—"

Dean waved the question off. "Mr. Commer, you know what we have on our hands, right?"

"Yes."

"Tell me, then. Just so I know we're on the same page."

"We have a very real terrorist threat on an American base that could claim the lives of Americans and Afghanis alike. And here in the States, we have a President who is choosing to be blind to it because of good-will policies he forced into place with the country the terrorists are coming out of."

Dean nodded and said, "Yeah, that sums it up perfectly. And what do you think we need to do?"

"Convince him," Roger said. But even as he said that, another solution came to mind, but it was dark and dangerous, and he couldn't bring himself to say it.

Fortunately, this was another point he and Dean were on the same page about. And Dean had no problem stating it out loud.

"That," Dean said, his voice like that of a ghost in the dimly lit dining room. "Or we figure out a way to get him out of office."

20

Roger knew what he needed to do the following day and because of that, he was unable to go back to sleep once Dean had gone. As he lay in bed, he ran the scenarios through his head, one by one. He did this until he gave up trying to get more sleep. He then went downstairs, brewed a cup of tea and went to his study where he fired up his laptop.

He had no immediate access to the database he used at the Pentagon, but he had an unauthorized secondary system he could access from his home computer. He used an onion server, almost in the same way folks who surfed the dark web accessed their disreputable websites.

It wasn't nearly as thorough as what he had at the Pentagon, but it was a few steps above most standard police databases. He wasn't even sure what to look for. He ran a quick search on Dean but found nothing new—just his exemplary military record and a ding from eleven years ago when he'd been involved in a trial involving a closed-circuit monitoring case where he'd been forced to kill a foreign spy.

Giving up on trying to find something wrong with Dean and his work, Roger opened up his personal email. He put a quick filtering protocol in place and then a re-routing directive. He understood very little about how it all worked. Everson had set him up with an IT guy a few years back, making sure he could send private information from home from time to time. Essentially, with these protocols in place, no one could track back the email to him...even though he was sending a message to the Vice President of the United States.

He made sure his message to Warren was brief and to the point. He needed to meet with him as soon as possible. He'd spoken to their "person of interest"—even in an encrypted email he didn't want to be *too* careless by dropping names—and needed to relay some information.

With that email sent, he nearly logged out of everything, but then he saw he had an email waiting in his inbox. Given that it was only his personal Gmail account, it was family, friends, or spam.

This one was from Thomas. The subject read: *Just a heads up!* The email was brief yet informative, the usual trademarks of an email or text from Thomas. In it, he explained that he and two of his friends were currently at a buddy's beach house not too far away from Newport News. Yes, they'd be missing a single day of classes, but planned to be back on campus by Sunday night.

Roger was actually happy about this. Thomas was a very hard-working kid and rarely allowed himself to take breaks or have fun. Roger wasn't naïve enough to think that Thomas would go to college and never drink or party a bit. He knew he just had to trust his youngest son the same way he'd trusted Bret, their oldest. Bret was currently living in Texas, working with one of the nation's largest IT companies. And while his kids differed greatly from one another, Roger knew they each had good, balanced heads on their shoulders.

He sent a quick email back that simply read: *Sounds fun! Have a good time and let us know when you get back.*

Roger nearly stepped away from his laptop after that, but a sudden thought struck him. Sure it was nothing, and wanting to just play it safe, he pulled up the weather forecast. As he'd expected, the tropical storm was bearing down on North Carolina. Tropical Storm Louise still looked to make landfall as a hurricane along the Outer Banks around eight in the evening tomorrow, but it appeared to have made a slight eastern shift sometime in the last six hours.

He clicked on the live radar link and saw that the new trajectory would still have it hitting northeastern North Carolina, but it was being pushed farther east, where it was also going to clip coastal Virginia. Depending on whether it maintained its course, he and Maggie would be safe in Occoquan. The Williamsburg and Newport News area, though...well, that was a different story.

He nearly emailed Thomas back to ask if maybe he and his friends should turn back and head inland. But it felt a bit too protective. Thomas had always rebelled when being told what not to do. He was eighteen now, old enough to make these decisions for himself. Besides, there was no clear sign yet that the hurricane would directly affect him. He may just experience some hard rain and a few gusts of stronger-than-normal wind.

He finally stepped away from his laptop. When he returned to his kitchen, he looked to where he and Dean had spoken less than four hours ago. When he looked at the clock and saw that it was now 5:05, he figured it was time to start the day. He rinsed out his mug and started brewing a cup of coffee. With no real rest to speak of and burdened with all this new information from Dean, the day was going to call for a strong brew.

21

Vice President Warren emailed back just before Roger was on the way out the door. He checked it as he stood in the kitchen. Maggie was setting up her own workspace in the kitchen as she prepared for her day. She worked from home as a part-time research assistant for a chemical manufacturing company. It was something she'd always been passionate about, making sure household cleaners and pesticides were as healthy as possible. Roger had tried talking her into retirement, but she simply couldn't sit still.

Warren's email consisted of just a few words: *Meet F at Candlers. 8:10.*

That was just an hour from now. He had plenty of time, but the set-up had him worried. Why not meet at the Nest? Were they afraid that his base of operations had been compromised because of the shooting yesterday? Despite the safety measures of Moreno's men, did Vice President Warren still think he was in danger?

Ah hell, Moreno's men, he thought. He'd been so wrapped up in the visit from Dean and the information that had netted that he'd forgotten about the security detail parked in front of his house. He certainly didn't need them tailing him when he met with Frederickson.

Slowly, Roger started to feel overwhelmed. He was keeping secret meetings from the President. He was working with the Vice President and Everson to build a case that would put a huge dent in the President's relationships overseas. There might be an actual threat against an American base on foreign soil. And he also had CIA spooks shadowing him—for his own good, sure, but it was already a nuisance.

"Something wrong?" Maggie asked him from the table.

"Nope. Just...a lot of moving parts for so early in the morning."

She frowned and nodded her sympathy. "And did you see the email from Thomas? About Newport News?"

"I did."

"If that storm keeps tilting eastward, Newport News might get hit pretty bad. Do you think we should call him?"

"No. I trust him. And Louise's course doesn't seem fully set yet."

She frowned again, this time in disagreement. "I'm going to keep an eye on it. Don't be surprised or angry with me if I call an audible and reach out to him."

He really wished she wouldn't do that, but he didn't have the time to argue with her right now. "Okay, that's fine." He walked over to give her a kiss goodbye as he pocketed his phone.

He took the phone right back out when he got outside. As expected, a black federal sedan was still sitting there. Not that they were doing an exceptional job or anything. Dean Page had gotten right past them last night without raising any alarm.

He gave them a perfunctory wave as he got into his car. He pulled up Moreno's number as he got behind the wheel. Moreno answered on the second ring.

"Hey, Roger. Everything okay?"

"For now. But listen...you need to call your men off. For just a few hours. I'm about to go into a meeting that no one else knows about and I can't have extra ears around. Not even your men."

Moreno sighed. "You sure about this?"

"Yes. You can sic them back on me around nine o'clock if you really want to, but I don't think it's necessary."

"Yeah, I'll give it some thought. For now, I'll tell them to come on in. But...everything is okay?"

"Not sure. I'll fill you in later."

They ended the call and when Roger backed out of his parking spot and cut out into the road, he grinned at the sight of the man behind the wheel of the federal car. He was speaking into a cellphone as Roger passed, likely conversing with Moreno and being given their new orders.

He checked his rearview as he passed out of Occoquan and saw that they were still back there. But since they were likely heading in the same direction he was, he thought nothing of it. As he drove towards DC, he tuned the radio to a local news station. He doubted there would be a word of his incident yesterday even though it had included a shooting on a packed highway and in a very public place. On that note, he was right. But honestly, he was listening in for updates on Hurricane Louise. He still wasn't truly worried about Thomas but felt the need to stay as updated as possible.

What he found out was the hurricane was still on its newly projected course, where it was not only going to slam into North Carolina's Outer Banks, but much of Virginia's southern coast as well. This included Norfolk, Virginia Beach, and Newport News. At the moment, the coastal communities in Carolina were lightly evacuating, and people expected a similar announcement to be made in Virginia within a few hours.

Already, the skies above the nation's capital were showing signs of gray as the storm neared land. Of course, DC wouldn't see much of it. Maybe some overdue rain and mild wind gusts, but that was about it.

But as he neared Hyte Park, Roger forced thoughts of the hurricane out of his mind. He had to focus on the task at hand. Because if today turned out to be nearly as stressful and treacherous as yesterday, it was sure as hell going to be a long one.

22

Hyte Park was predictably quiet at 8:05 in the morning. And though the Vice President's message had said nothing about Hyte Park, the coding of it had been simple enough to decode. The *F* he'd referred to was Frederickson. And the Candler location referred to a spot along the western rim of the small duck pond.

Roger had used this same location about a dozen times in the past, often for clandestine meetings that only a handful of people knew about. Finding the "Candler" code was fairly easy for anyone who knew where to look. It was just confusing enough to keep any prying ears and eyes from guessing, though. The *Candler* in question was Derik Candler, a deceased man who had donated two antique benches to the park. They were at the edge of the small duck pond. Roger had no idea who Derik Candler was—just that he'd died in 2015, a fact given by little brass plates embedded along the top of both benches.

After parking his car in the lot to the left of the duck pond, he could see the benches. Frederickson was already sitting on one of them, hunched over in an attempt to not stand out. Roger didn't hurry or rush, not wanting to draw attention to himself...not that he would, really. To his right, across a wide expanse of grass and a small playground and a set of swings, he saw two people on a morning run and an older lady walking her dog. To his left, a small group of people were sitting on mats and facing an instructor for a morning yoga session. No one was paying attention to him or the duck pond.

As he joined Frederickson on one of the Candler benches, two ducks skittered off from the bank and into the water. Per usual, Frederickson wasted no time getting to the point.

"I don't have much time. If I don't at least check in soon, the Protective Services Battalion will come looking. And that's a group we don't need sniffing around in the midst of all of this."

Roger understood perfectly. The U.S Protective Services Battalion was the group in charge of looking after people like Frederickson and other Cabinet members. The President and Vice President got the Secret Service; Cabinet members got the Protective Services Battalion.

"I met with Dean Page last night," Roger said.

"And?"

"And I believe him. Nightwatch is on the move and has the capability to stage an attack on Bagram. He got photos of sites, some emails, and he had audio as well, but it was destroyed when he made a run for it. He also says he's pretty sure Nightwatch has ears in DC...which makes sense, given that person who tried to shoot me knew where I was while I was on the road."

"So what do we do?" Frederickson asked. He hadn't looked at Roger for a single moment. His focus was on the pond and the ducks, trying to look as inconspicuous as possible.

"The simple answer is trying to convince the President. He's not going to listen to me unless I have solid, irrefutable proof."

"He might listen to the Vice President," Frederickson said. "But even that's doubtful."

"Okay...so who do we know we can get on our bandwagon but also tend to always be on the president's side on most things?"

"I'm not sure. I mean, there are a few Senators we might wrangle. But if you think there are truly Nightwatch spies or representatives hidden in our midst, that could be risky."

Roger thought this over and hated to admit that he was right. Other than the handful of people who already knew what was going on, it could be dangerous for anyone else to know about it. He wasn't prepared to claim that the President knew very well he *was* telling the truth and might have a hand in whatever Nightwatch was up to—that was borderline ridiculous. But he wasn't about to rule out the possibility that someone close to the President had their hands in what was becoming a tight-knit mess.

"When will the President be back on Pennsylvania Avenue today?" Roger asked.

"Two o'clock this afternoon, according to the VP. It was supposed to be later, but he's bumped some stuff up and canceled a few meetings because of the storm that's about to hit North Carolina. Why?"

"Well, he wanted to know when I spoke to Dean Page. So, I think I'll just try to get some time with him again today…make one last pitch. It can't hurt."

"It could piss him off."

Roger shrugged and said, "He's already mad at me about this whole thing."

"Good point." Frederickson sighed and got to his feet. "I'll reach out to the Vice President and see what I can do to make sure you get some face time. It won't be a direct request from him, though. That would be too suspect."

"So he'll ask someone else to do it? That sounds like a really risky game of telephone."

"It'll be fine, I think. I'll ask Claire Montgomery."

"The Press Secretary? Isn't that a little dangerous? Sort of like poking the hornet's nest?"

"I don't think so. I get the sense that she stayed silent at yesterday's meeting for a reason. She's never been a huge fan of the President's foreign policies—though she'd never admit it. And she's the President's golden child at the moment because of how she smoothed things over when the media tried taking him to task for those missing campaign funds."

"Yeah, I forgot about that. As long as you think she'd lean more toward our side than his policy of denial, maybe she *would* be a good ally in all of this."

"Maybe not an ally just yet," Frederickson said. "But she could maybe move a few pieces around for us for now...namely getting you a meeting today."

"Okay. That'll work."

"You heading to the office after this?"

"I am."

Frederickson nodded and turned his back, heading for the lot opposite the one Roger had parked in. "I'll drop you an email as soon as I get an okay."

Roger took a moment to look out over the pond. There were four ducks there now, making their rounds. And as the weight of the Nightwatch situation settled on him all over again, Roger envied them. Swimming around, without a care in the world. No knowledge of terrorism or political scandals.

And oddly enough, as he watched the ducks drift listlessly about on the water, Roger had an idea. He nodded to the ducks as if thanking them for the inspiration and then left the benches behind.

23

As Roger drove to the Pentagon, he was thinking about his father—which was odd because it wasn't something he did very often. His father had left him and his mother when Roger was twelve. He'd cheated on Roger's mother with a younger woman and when confronted about making a choice, he'd left his family behind.

The ducks back at the pond made him think of his father. For the few years he and his dad had been close, his father had done his best to get Roger interested in duck hunting. Roger had found it pointless because the dogs really did all the work. The dogs went out into the brush and fields to flush the ducks out and then a man with a gun, hiding a suitable distance away, blasted them out of the air, and the dogs retrieved the kill. Roger had simply never seen the sport in it.

But he thought of those ducks now, particularly how the dogs had flushed them out. It made him wonder if he could flush the President out of office. It was easy enough to picture Seibert as a duck. But who—or *what*—would serve as the dogs?

It was a concept that nagged at him until he was in his office in the underground level of the Pentagon. He instantly started thinking of all the dirt that people had thrown at the President during the previous election. As was typically the case during any election cycle, the vast majority of it had all been bullshit. But there had been a few nuggets that had stuck due to the abstract nature of the truth.

For instance, there were allegations that the First Lady was deeply involved in insider trading. Besides having a few notable acquaintances in Silicon Valley and Wall Street, no one had ever made definitive links. On the other hand, there was also no proof to the contrary. But even so, that was the First Lady, not the President.

Sitting in his office by himself, staring at the ceiling and trying to think of ways to smear the President...he didn't think his job would ever come to that. It felt almost ridiculous because even if he could think of something, it needed to be implemented quickly. He thought of Nixon and Watergate, and every other Presidential scandal that had hit the papers and airwaves. After Nixon, there were a few moments in history that had *almost* gotten a sitting President booted from office. But *almost* wasn't going to work here.

The hell of it was that as hard as Roger thought, he couldn't think of anything...no skeletons in Seibert's closet. Every controversial topic from his past that had been thrown at him was always knocked down immediately. He'd done his time in the military and had seen actual combat. There were records of donations from Seibert's personal accounts to worthwhile, respected charities. Ironically, the only thing Roger could think of to really hold against Seibert was his blind allegiance to these threats overseas—a blind allegiance that was giving Nightwatch an open and unobstructed playing field.

And as difficult as it would be, he knew that was where this entire strategy would have to be played. If he wanted to make the President look bad, it might very well come down to reminding the public of all the nasty things Minister Daraa or even President Shahin had done while in power: the authorization of public beheadings, sending troops into villages with toxic gases to search for traitors who didn't exist, blatant election fraud, and in Shahin's case, a son who had been linked to a child-trafficking outfit.

But again, it all came back to the matter of time. Even if Roger could somehow orchestrate the most elaborate and effective smear job of all time, it would take months for any actual damage to be done. And they didn't have months. Hell, they may not even have weeks.

His stomach's rumbling told him it was nearly lunchtime. Just as he thought about this, his phone rang. The display told him it was May. He picked up right away, wondering if Claire Montgomery had played her part and managed to get him a meeting with the President.

"Hey, May. What's going on?"

"I just got off the phone with the Oval Office."

"Don't you feel special?"

"Hardly," May scoffed. "Anyway, maybe *you* should feel special. You've got a meeting with President Seibert and some of his advisors at 1:45."

Roger checked the clock on his laptop and saw that it was noon. "Confirm it. I'll be there."

"They didn't exactly give me the choice to confirm. I think you're just expected to be there. Speaking of which, if you're going to be rubbing shoulders with the President on a more consistent basis, I think we need to discuss a raise."

"Yeah, I think I've earned it."

"I meant for me!"

"I know, May. Thanks!"

He ended the call and tried to think of how to spin this meeting. A lot of whether Seibert would actually listen depended on who else would be in that meeting. He hoped Frederickson would be there, along with the Vice President. If both of them were there, maybe he'd have a chance.

On the other hand, he'd been working around Washington long enough to know that sometimes, when a plan was set into motion, there was no stopping it. If Seibert had already made up his mind about plans and allies in that region, all of this may be for nothing.

But Roger couldn't think like that. He had to at least try. And if it turned out Seibert was still going to be stubborn and not budge, then Roger knew he would just have to get creative.

24

Roger wasn't sure if it had been Claire Montgomery who had set the wheels in motion for the meeting, but it just so happened that she was one of the first people he saw when he arrived at the White House. She was standing outside the library as Roger made his way through the Visitor Entrance. A slim, middle-aged African American woman, Claire Montgomery always carried herself with poise and a quiet, stern quality. Roger had seen fire in her eyes many times during press briefings, and he didn't envy anyone who crossed her or asked an errant question while the cameras were running.

Roger didn't exactly head in her direction, but he slowed a bit as he passed by her on his way to the meeting in the Cabinet Room.

"Do I have you to thank for this?" he asked without stopping.

Montgomery kept her lips thin and pursed, no sign of a smile, and barely parting them at all to answer. "Maybe. Now make it count."

It helped to know that he had one other person in the President's circle on his side. In the grand scheme of things, the Press Secretary would not carry much weight, but it still made him feel more confident.

Roger was no stranger to the White House. While he didn't keep count of trivial tidbits, he figured he'd probably stepped through that same Visitor's Entrance at least thirty times in the past ten years in an official capacity. And another four or five for private parties and functions. So, as he passed through the hallways, he nodded to the familiar faces and subtly showed his badge to anyone who gave him a suspicious look.

When he came to the Cabinet Room, he found the door partially open. He knew that some Presidents had been perfectly fine to hold smaller meetings in the Oval Office, but President Seibert was a man of routine and formality. Any meeting that may contain even a nugget of confrontation would not be held in his inner sanctum.

Roger knocked on the door and stepped inside. There were three people at the large table where he'd first presented his findings concerning Nightwatch. The President was at the head of the table, sitting down and looking over what looked like blueprints. When he realized who the other two men were, Roger felt an immense weight slide off of his shoulders. This might be easier than he thought.

First, there was Secretary of Defense Frederickson. He was standing by the President's left shoulder, pointing something out on the blueprints, or whatever it was Seibert had spread out before him. Sitting to the right and closer to the door was Hector Moreno. If this was going to be the entire audience, luck might finally be on his side.

Everyone looked up as Roger entered the room. He noticed right away that Moreno did his best to not look him right in the eyes, not wanting to give himself away. Roger assumed the President knew Moreno had been in charge of trying to find his shooter from yesterday. But he wasn't sure if the President knew Moreno was just as convinced as Roger was that if Dean Page said Nightwatch was on the move, it should be taken seriously.

"Is this it?" Roger asked as he settled down in the chair across from Moreno.

"Seems that way," President Seibert said. "Koontz was supposed to be here, but he's been held up in Williamsburg over preparations for the hurricane.

Kevin Koontz was the President's Senior Advisor. Roger wasn't sure why he would have been in Williamsburg, and he didn't much care. Had Koontz been here, he would have trashed any idea of Nightwatch being active again. He was just as sold on President Seibert's goals in Afghanistan as Seibert himself was. For him to not be here might be an enormous advantage.

"What are you looking at, sir?" Roger asked.

"Security schematics for Bagram," Frederickson said. He was playing his part well, not seeming at all bothered that Roger was there. Roger wondered if he'd be able to remain cool and calm if the conversation got heated. How adamant would he be that Roger was right...that the President needed to take this Nightwatch threat seriously?

"Does this mean you're going to look into it?" Roger realized how over-eager he sounded right away; he wished he could take the question back.

"That's what I'm doing right now," Seibert said. "Secretary Frederickson and I have come up with a series of questions we will send to the heads of security and operations at Bagram. He is going to relay your concerns to them."

"Mr. President, I've already done that."

"I'm aware of that. But, with all due respect, it's going to hold more weight coming from him. They *are* aware that your intel is coming from a spy, correct?"

"No. But I'm telling you, Everson and Page can be trusted."

"He's right, Mr. President," Moreno said. "Dean Page risked his life to get us this intelligence."

"Yet he comes with no hard, irrefutable proof."

"Mr. President—" Roger began.

"I need all three of you to just dish it all out right here and now," Seibert said. "Assistant Director Moreno, you're first. I know that this asset working under your man Everson has a bit of a past. Some psychiatric issues, I believe?"

Roger saw the stunned look on Moreno's face. For one single moment, Moreno looked pissed. He quickly gathered his wits, though, pulling himself together.

"After several active tours, one in which he was shot twice while pulling three children out from a pile of rubble in Kuwait, he required counseling and medication for a while. But that's been almost a decade ago."

"But he was kept away from all CIA, FBI, and private projects, correct?"

"Yes, sir," Moreno snapped.

Roger's stomach sank. Was the bastard really going to sink this low?

"Sir, Page has encoded emails with names and strategies. We could—"

"And how did he get them?"

"I don't know, sir."

"Assistant Director Moreno, how about you?"

Moreno took a moment to answer. As he did, Roger saw that Frederickson also looked a bit shocked at the jarring nature of the President's line of questioning.

"Well, Mr. President," Moreno finally said, "I'd have to check with Walter Everson, but I'd assume he exploited vulnerabilities in their systems. Much of the communications systems for terrorist networks are a hodge-podge of secondary systems."

"So, in other words, if questions were raised, he could be considered a hacker?""

Words started coming out of Roger's mouth before he was aware of it. "If questions were raised by whom? I'm sorry, sir, but questioning the legitimacy of Dean Page right now isn't a priority. You asked to know when he was in the country, and he's now in the country. You wanted me to share whatever information he had with you, and that's what I'm here to do."

"That's correct. And you have done all of those things. However, see it from my point of view, Mr. Commer. Let's say I reach out to Minister Daraa or even President Shahin and ask them questions about Nightwatch—an organization they have vowed to have gone after and dismantled. If I tell them we have intelligence that suggests they are still on the move and even planning an attack, they'll want to know how we came across such intelligence. And if I tell them it came from a spy in the area, do you have any idea how much damage that will do to the relations I have worked so hard to establish between our regions?"

Roger figured that if he'd already crossed a line, there was really no point in letting up now. "Then why do we have spy programs over there in the first place?"

He saw a bit of fury flickering in the President's face. Behind the President, even Frederickson now looked stunned at Roger's reaction. But Roger could also see the man thinking quickly, his panicked eyes darting all around the room as if searching for an answer.

"Those programs are now useless and antiquated," the President said. "And though I don't think they are currently needed over there, I understand the necessity of them."

"If I may, Mr. President?" Frederickson said, angling to the side of the table and sitting down beside Moreno. "We are getting intelligence from such programs all the time. And sometimes, when we receive such information, it's already outdated. I believe you could play this off in a way that makes you seem very concerned about the standing of President Shahin's promises."

"I'm listening...."

"Tell them that the Department of Defense received a memo from last year...previously classified. Say that there was mention of new Nightwatch movement. You can simply ask for clarification and spin it in a way that makes it seem like you fear Nightwatch may move without Shahin's knowledge."

"So...lie?"

"Yes," Roger said. "Hell, you could even go a step further. Tell them that if they'll look into this then, as another sign of goodwill, you want to make sure the folks being held in Bagram's prisons from previous terrorist movements aren't being held unfairly. If Shahin and Daraa think they can free even one or two of their people from Bagram prisons, doing something as simple as sending some hounds to sniff out Nightwatch activity won't bother them in the slightest."

Roger could tell he had the President hooked; he could see it in the man's eyes. Still, Seibert looked back to Frederickson. "If it comes down to it, would that work?"

"That's not for me to say, Mr. President. That's up to the heads who run Bagram. But...yeah, it's a square deal that I don't think anyone from either side would disagree with."

"Fine," President Seibert said. "I'll make some calls and see if I can get Shahin and Daraa on the line. But Mr. Commer...if I go this route and this blows up in my face, you're going to have a rough road ahead of you."

Roger knew it wasn't an empty threat, but he wasn't scared. He was actually quite pleased with the plan they'd come up with. The only remaining question, of course, was if Seibert would actually do it. But with such a win-win situation, Roger didn't see how he'd be able to refuse.

"Then that'll be it," the President said, getting up from his chair. "I have two calls to make before I can tackle this, but I'll have it taken care of within three or four hours."

As everyone got up and left, Roger noted the sour expression on Moreno's face. Apparently, he wasn't too pleased with the way things had gone—likely because President Seibert had scrutinized Everson and Page so closely. As for Frederickson, he seemed just as pleased as Roger felt as the four men made their way into the hallway.

Roger wasted no time with pleasantries or goodbyes. He started back the way he had come, heading past the library and toward the visitor's exit. He made for the doors when his cell phone buzzed in his pocket—a quick, momentary burst indicating a text rather than a call.

He checked it right away and found that the message was from an unlisted number. Still, he read the text and afterwards, he hurried his step through the doors and back toward his car.

The text read: **It's Dean. Meet me at the parking garage behind the downtown Arts Center ASAP. Urgent.**

25

It had been a very long time since Roger had been anywhere near the downtown Arts Center. The last time he'd visited had been six Christmases ago when he, Maggie, and Thomas had all watched a performance of *The Nutcracker*. The Arts Center parking garage seemed like a very bizarre place to meet with a government spy...which, Roger assumed, was exactly why Dean had chosen it.

Locating Dean's car took more time than he would have preferred. It was, after all, the middle of the day, and the garage was located in a rather busy part of town. But he eventually found Dean on the third of four levels. He was driving a Tesla and was parked directly beside the little corridor that led to stair access. Roger parked in the next available spot, three spaces down, hurried over to Dean's car, and got in on the passenger side.

"So, what's urgent?" Roger asked, not wanting to waste any time. Based on President Seibert's endless stream of questions regarding Dean, Roger assumed any meetings between them should be kept short and sweet, just in case anyone might see them.

"What's urgent is that all our plays are being conducted in behind-closed-door meetings while Nightwatch is out there doing what they damn well please."

"What? Look, I don't know how fast you expected this to happen, but Seibert is being very bull-headed about this."

"Can you convince him?"

Roger considered it for a moment and then answered as honestly as he could. "Alone, probably not. But the Secretary of Defense is on our side. Assistant Director Moreno over at the CIA too."

"He was to look for your shooter, right?"

"Right."

"Any luck on that?" Dean asked.

"No, not yct."

"How long do you think it will take for Seibert to come around?"

"That's a loaded question," Roger said. He then recounted everything that had been discussed just half an hour earlier in the White House Cabinet Room. And with each bit he shared, he could see Dean getting more and more agitated.

"You probably already know this," Dean said when Roger was done. "But there's only one reason anyone in power would want to discredit an asset who is coming in with this sort of information?"

"Because he fears what you might bring to the table."

"Exactly."

"So the question is...why would he fear a spy sent by his own government? A spy bringing back information that might save the lives of thousands of Americans overseas?"

"I think I know the answer to that," Dean said. "But it's not pretty."

"Try me."

Dean sighed and looked out of the window in a paranoid manner. It was, Roger assumed, the habit of a man who was used to sneaking around and always having to watch his back.

"Let's say he gets this information and believes it. If he doesn't act on it and doesn't even breathe a word to the enemy about it, he keeps the enemy friendly. And we know how hard he's worked to keep things stable between our two countries. That's no secret. So he keeps those overseas friends by not ruffling their feathers. But he knows just what sort of trouble he's sitting on...a powder keg just waiting for that spark, if you will. And for a President with an election year coming up, that can work as a sort of insurance."

Dean looked at Roger knowingly, waiting for him to finish the equation. Roger knew exactly where he was headed with it but was afraid to actually say it. Still, he knew he had to. Because in a situation like this, every angle had to be explored...no matter how dangerous it seemed.

"If he goes into an election year with the threat of war hanging over the head of the country, he stands a better chance of re-election...especially after he's the one that tried working so hard to re-build bridges that had formerly been burned over there."

"Bingo," Dean said. "The threat of a looming overseas conflict is always beneficial to the President because, despite what popular opinion and Joe Schmo on the street says, the chances of a change in the Presidency during such a time is very small."

"This is...this is all a big stretch, you know that?"

"Oh, for sure. I have zero evidence for any of this. But if Seibert is pushing so hard against this and trying to discredit me, I think it's something that needs to be considered."

"You think...wait...do you think he maybe even *knows* it's true? Do you think he knew about Nightwatch movement and the Bagram threat before you even heard about it?"

"It's crossed my mind. But listen...if there's nothing set in motion by tomorrow morning, I'm afraid it might be too late. There are things I can do...emails and phone records I am pretty sure I can get my hands on that could smear him. Nothing awful. Just pardons of known criminals, loosely linked ties to men that have been arrested for naughty stuff with underage girls. Seibert isn't directly tied to any of it, but he's close enough to get burned. Everson would shit if he knew I had access to it, but...well, it's an option."

It was tempting, but Roger knew it might be messy. He never thought he'd be in a position where he had to legitimately weigh the option of possibly smearing someone publicly, especially a sitting president. "I don't know. Let's say we go that route. Who do you think he's going to suspect right away if information like that comes out?"

"Not for me to worry about." Dean smirked and said, "I've made a pretty good living off of making myself hard to find."

"No. Let's wait to see if he comes through with his phone call to Daraa and Shahin. Let's not make any huge move we'll regret later."

Roger could tell that Dean was conflicted over this. He understood the caution but also knew it might be deadly to wait. If all of the intel he'd gathered had even a kernel of truth to it, Bagram might be attacked two months from now...or it might be attacked tomorrow. There was just no way of knowing.

"Fine. But if things aren't different by tomorrow...."

"Then we'll cross that bridge when we get there."

Roger could tell that Dean wanted to say something else. Deep down he knew that if Dean wanted to, he could go rogue and make a play himself. If he did indeed have incriminating information against Seibert, there was nothing Roger could do to keep him from using it.

He just had to trust the man. To stay any longer and drag the conversation out would be useless. Roger opened the door and got out.

"Mr. Commer, be careful. I'm sure I don't have to tell you that if someone took a shot at you once, they'll have no problem doing it again."

Roger only nodded as he closed the door. He started for his own car, trying his best to process the absurd reality of the conversation he'd just had. He couldn't believe that he—

The revving of an engine from behind him broke his concentration. At first, he thought it was Dean, but then he remembered the man drove an electric car, which had no transmission. When Roger turned, he saw a black sedan blazing forward. It was coming from around the turn that led to the ramp down to the second level.

It must have followed me, and I didn't see it, he thought. *It was waiting for me to get out, to—*

He didn't have time to carefully think it out. His fight or flight instincts kicked in and the most sensible thing to do, he thought, was make a run for his car. It was less than twenty feet away. He had his holstered Sig Sauer at his back, but he didn't want to draw it and fire in a public place unless it was absolutely necessary.

So he ran as hard as he could for his car. He could see the reflection of the oncoming car in his windows, and it was closing quickly.

He reached his car and swiveled hard to the left, pivoting into the space between his car and the one beside it. As he did, the sedan veered hard to the left. At the very last moment, it barely clipped Roger high up on the right leg. As he spun around and caught himself against his car, the front of the sedan collided with the back bumper of his own sedan—not even *his* car but a loaner from the CIA.

The slight impact to his leg hadn't hurt all that much, but a wave of panic went spiraling through him. He instantly reached for his gun, drawing it expertly out of its holster. At the same time, he studied the sedan, looking through the windows. There was a driver and a passenger, and as Roger drew his weapon, the man on the passenger side was raising his own gun.

Time seemed to freeze or Roger as he leveled his gun at the sedan, his gaze drawn to the barrel of the gun that was pointed directly at him.

26

It would occur to Roger later on that the main thing that spared him in those moments was that the man in the sedan hesitated for just a moment. Roger, on the other hand, did not.

He fired off a shot that took the passenger in the shoulder. The passenger fired back out of sheer necessity and instinct, but the jolt of Roger's shot threw his aim off. The shot went slightly wide, pinging into the side of Roger's car, missing him by less than six inches.

Roger knew that he was trapped. He was literally boxed in, with his own car to his left, the neighboring car to his right, and the attackers' car in front of him. He was going to have to shoot his way out of this and if that meant he had to kill someone, then so be it. But even as he dropped to a knee into a shooter's stance, he knew his chances were slim.

He fired another shot and wasn't sure if it had hit its target or not. He barely had time to figure this out, though, because there was another gunshot at the same time. Oddly enough, it didn't come from either of the men in the sedan.

Roger turned his head for just a moment, just quick enough to see that Dean had come out of his car. He was perched between the doorframe and the door's hinges. His shooter stance was firm, but his posture was a bit sloppy as he leaned back against the door for support.

Still, when he fired off his shot, he did so with ease. Following the initial shot, he popped off three more, one right behind the other. Roger turned back to the car and saw three holes in the back glass, in a nearly perfect arc. One of the men inside began to scream and the car began to churn forward. It pushed against the back of Roger's car for a moment before the driver jerked the wheel hard to the left, freeing it.

It moved forward for just a moment, long enough for Roger to understand that he and Dean working together had thwarted whatever attack the men in the car had in mind. With no possible escape ahead of them other than the fourth and final level of the parking garage—where they would be trapped—the driver switched to reverse. The tires squealed as the car rocketed backwards, the men inside apparently no longer interested in their original plans.

But Roger had no intention of letting the bastards get away so easily. He stood up, took a long stride to the ruined back end of his car, and aimed at the wheels. He fired twice, taking out the front driver-side tire. The car jerked a bit as the tire went out. At roughly the same time, the driver did his best to cut a hard turn, directing the front of the car to the ramp that would take them down to the lower levels.

Both Roger and Dean fired at the car, but Roger only got off two shots before he realized how stupid he was being. He'd taken out a tire and at least one man in the car was wounded. He could easily chase them down in his own car and call for an assist.

He opened his door quickly and was prepared to do that very thing. But Dean called out to him, shaking his head.

"You can't chase them."

"What?"

"It's kill them or let them go."

Already irritated that he was wasting time as he heard the engine revving below and the blow tire shrieking against the pavement, Roger was quickly losing his temper. "How do you figure *that?*"

"If you chase them down and make some sort of arrest, how the hell are you going to explain that? You can explain it to Everson or Moreno, maybe even Frederickson. But how do you think the President is going to handle the fact that you were out here meeting with me in secret?"

"He doesn't have to know."

Dean shook his head again. "Do you come to the Performing Arts Center regularly, right in the middle of a workday?"

He was right, and Roger knew it. He sneered as he holstered his gun. "Fuck! So they're just going to get away with this?"

"Maybe not. We got at least one of them pretty good. And did you see them?"

"I saw the passenger. White guy, maybe forty. Dressed in a tee shirt. Clean-shaven. That fits the description of about ten thousand people in the immediate area."

"The passenger might have been Hispanic," Dean said. "Hard to tell. But it's pretty clear they wanted you dead."

"Apparently they'll have to get in line."

"Chances are it was the same crew that tried to take you out yesterday."

"And I can't report it."

"Well, you can report it…you'll just need to come up with an *excelle*nt story to work around it. And you know, Roger…before I caught my plane to make it back home, I was attacked before heading into the airport." he chuckled nervously and said, "Oddly enough, *that* was in a parking garage, too."

"One attempt on your life, and two on mine. What the hell, Page?"

"If you count the one in the desert after I came across the information, there have been two attempts on my life too," Dean said. "Not that it's a competition."

Roger suddenly felt very trapped, and he didn't like it. Maybe he couldn't share the full details of this encounter with Seibert, but he could sure as hell use this new anger and frustration to drive his point home.

"Get out of here, Page," Roger said. "Someone will have reported those gunshots, and we don't need to be seen together. *Especially* not at the scene of a gunfight."

Dean nodded. As he slid back into his car, he said, "I'll be in touch."

Roger got back into his car, realizing that it now had a bullet hole in it. He was about to head back into town with his car sporting a bullet hole for the second day in a row. It was almost funny. He figured at some point he'd have to answer for it, but he wasn't going to volunteer to tell the true story unless he had no other choice. Because for right now, he thought Dean Page might be the stealthiest and best-equipped ally he had. To make it known that they were closer than Seibert was aware could be dangerous.

He didn't realize just how much adrenaline had been pumping through him until he pulled out of his parking spot. His hands were trembling with both anger and anticipation. No...he couldn't tell Seibert what had happened, but he could tell Frederickson. Maybe he could think of some sort of work-around to help explain the situation.

One way or the other, the President had to know the scale of events that were taking place on people for simply trying to bring attention to Nightwatch movements. As far as he was concerned, if he continued to openly stick his big presidential head in the sand, that would tell Roger all he needed to know.

And if that was the case, then Roger wondered if he may end up having to do something drastic at the end of all of this.

27

Roger felt a slight fatigue come over him as he raced back toward Pennsylvania Avenue. Having been in a few gunfights before, he was well accustomed to the symptoms of an adrenaline crash. As it pumped through the body, it caused the individual to feel a surge of energy and, sometimes, heightened senses. However, not too long after the exciting event ended, it usually caused people to come down quickly.

But Roger had far too much to do, so he did his best to push back the crash. As he neared the White House, he switched on the radio to listen to the local news. As he'd expected, there was chatter about Hurricane Louise. He listened intently, wondering how the hurricane's landfall might upset some of the President's already-scheduled plans.

"…won't see much here in the nation's capital other than a few inches of rain and some angry gusts of wind," a monotone newscaster reported. "However, folks on the North Carolina coasts all along the Outer Banks are already feeling the effects. Although landfall isn't expected for another hour and a half, evacuations have been underway for most of the day. They're getting wind gusts of up to forty miles per hour and the rain started coming in this morning. Currently, it's still coming down with up to three inches being reported in some areas.

"It's also worth noting that the last-minute shift in direction seems to have completely spared South Carolina. They'll be getting some wind and showers, but that's about it. It's now the Hampton Roads area of Virginia that suddenly finds itself in danger. Virginia Beach residents are currently in the midst of evacuations, with predictions of the storm affecting daily life throughout the area."

Roger ruminated on this. Thomas would be directly affected by the storm whether he was at school in Williamsburg or at the little get-away place at the beach. He wasn't too worried about Thomas because he was a smart kid. It was the boys he was hanging around with that Roger was worried about. He knew none of them but, having once been a college kid himself, he was sure there was at least one idiot among them.

At a red light, he picked up his cellphone to place a call to Thomas but then realized that in the wake of the garage shootout, he'd completely overlooked protocols. Speaking of *idiots,* was he really expecting to just roll up to the White House and have an impromptu meeting with the President?

"Damn," he muttered, pulling up Vice President Warren's number. He wasn't entirely sure he'd be able to get Warren, but he had to try. The line rang once before going to an automated voicemail. He then tried Secretary Frederickson. It was a long shot, but Frederickson would be easier to get in touch with—but the chances of him knowing exactly where the President was or what he was doing would be smaller.

He got the same result with Frederickson: a single ring, a click, and then automated voicemail. Frustrated, he hung up as the light turned green, and soon he saw the gates of the White House coming into view. The afternoon sky was darkening a bit as gray clouds were pushed in from the south, an extension of Hurricane Louise.

Out of options, he figured he'd do his best to get as close to Seibert as he could. Hell, the President wouldn't be at the White House, anyway. Yes, he'd promised to call Minister Daraa or even President Shahin, but there was no guarantee he'd told the truth.

When his phone rang in his hand, he jumped a bit. He hated he was so easily startled now. Surely, it was nothing more than an after-effect of the parking garage shoot-out and his frayed nerves. Throw in a college-aged son who was currently in the middle of hurricane conditions, and anyone would be jumpy, he supposed.

He was relieved when he saw the caller ID display Frederickson's name and number. Roger answered the call right away, trying to hide the jitteriness in his voice.

"Hey, Mr. Secretary. Sorry for the call."

"No worries, but I don't have long. Anything new on your end?"

"Yes. I met with Dean and then a pair of men in a sedan nearly killed me.

"What?"

"Someone was onto us. Somebody knew we were going to be there."

"Are you okay?"

"Yeah, but it was close. Damned close. For Dean too. We're good, though I'm coming to the White House with another car with a bullet hole in it."

"You're on the way right now?"

"I am. I'm on Pennsylvania, coming up on the gates. I need to speak with the President."

"Good. Listen…you did *not* hear this from me, but he's literally about to get into his limo, on his way to a charity dinner. If you can get around to the West Wing in the next five minutes, you can probably get a word in with him. But once the Presidential caravan is on the move, you can forget about it."

"Got it. Thanks."

And wouldn't that be a little too convenient? Roger thought. *Seibert knew he had this dinner lined up when he vowed to make the call to Daraa and Shahin. He knew there was a very small chance I'd get to speak with him.*

Roger came to the western entrance of the White House, pulled in, and showed his credentials to the man at the gate. A small part of him actually thought he'd be turned away—that the President had put the word out to not allow Roger Commer onto the grounds. But the slightly plump man at the security gate gave him a nod and allowed him to pass through.

It had been a while since he'd been on this side of the White House, but he remembered the structure of it well enough. To the left, the thin, paved entryway veered off into a very small parking lot for esteemed visitors and staffers. But the exit the Presidential limo would come out of was to the left.

Roger had never actually been over that way before, so he had to do his best on assumptions. For all he knew, Secret Service and any number of security guards could come running at him as soon as he pulled his car in that direction.

As he veered to the right, the driveway curved along a curb. Coming up to it, he spotted three limousines, all identical. He also saw three members of the Secret Service standing outside of them. One of them looked to be roughly the size of an oak tree. They all turned in his direction. One of them started speaking to the man beside him. The third lowered his hand to his hip, clearly ready to draw his sidearm if it came to that.

Getting a little nervous, Roger stopped the car and placed the same credentials the security guard had approved in his right hand. He slowly opened the door, raised both hands, and stepped out.

"Stay right there," the oak-tree sized Secret Service member said.

"Of course. I have my credentials in my right hand. Roger Commer, CIA and Special Ops. I had a meeting with the President this morning and was hoping to follow up before he left."

The large man approached him and yanked the ID out of Roger's hand. He glanced at it for about three seconds before glaring at Roger and then looking back to the other two men. He gave a curt nod to them and then faced Roger.

"Whether or not you have business with the President is up to him. We'll let him know you're here. But for now, I need you to turn your car around and—"

"It's okay!" a voice called out from behind him. Roger could see President Seibert and the First Lady coming out of a set of double doors off of the West Wing. The First Lady looked both modern and regal, dressed to impress. Seibert, as usual, looked debonair in his suit.

"Sorry, sir," the Oak Tree said. He handed Roger his credentials and stepped aside.

"No need to apologize," the President said. He was smiling as he helped the First Lady into the last limo in the line of three, but Roger could tell the expression was fake. He was pissed off that Roger was here and was doing everything he could to keep his composure.

As he covered the twenty feet between the limos and where Roger stood, he whispered something to one of the other Secret Service men. The man nodded and instantly went to stand guard by the last limo. Then, without any of the men shadowing him, President Seibert took Roger gently by the arm and led him several steps away from the limos, closer to Roger's car.

"Mr. Commer," he said in a gentle yet grave tone, "are you out of your damned mind?"

"Maybe a bit," Roger said. "For the second day in a row, there was an attempt made on my life. It was planned and deliberate and only a fool could look past the fact that both events took place when I began pushing for you to seriously look into this Nightwatch business."

"When did this happen?" Seibert said. Roger thought he looked legitimately concerned, but his mind was clearly elsewhere.

"About an hour ago."

"And where did it—"

"Why does it even matter?" Roger interrupted. He hated to sound as if he was trying to hide something, but he didn't want the President to know about his secret meeting with Dean Page. That might raise far too many alarms.

However, President Seibert leaned forward and lowered his voice even more. "Maybe it happened when you were meeting with your spy friend, Dean Page."

Roger hadn't been expecting this at all. His shock apparently showed on his face because Seibert smirked and nodded.

"I'm the President of the United States," he said. "I know just about everything that happens in DC. So my advice to you is to be more careful who you keep company with. Perhaps the danger you found yourself in was intended for Mr. Page…and you were just in the wrong place at the wrong time."

Roger didn't like the President's tone. It almost seemed as if he insinuated that he may have had something to do with the attack…and maybe it *had* only been intended for Dean. But if that were the case, that meant Seibert was willing to kill in order to keep a lid on Nightwatch movement overseas…and here, in the States. Roger didn't hold a very high opinion of President Seibert, but he was pretty sure the man wouldn't stoop to having someone killed.

At the same time, Roger couldn't help but wonder…if Seibert knew about his meeting with Dean, did he also know about the covert meeting he had with Frederickson at the duck pond? Did he know about the phone calls with Frederickson and Vice President Warren?

The sad truth of the matter was that Roger had no idea. As it stood, he could only assume the worst. Still, he wasn't going to be sidelined. Not yet. Not after all he'd been through.

"Sir, were you able to make the call to Daraa and Sh—"

"I was. I wrapped it up no less than twenty minutes ago. I have assurances from both men *and* members of their cabinets that oversee terrorist activities in the area that your threat is dead. There is nothing to pursue."

"Of course they'd say that. You can't just be—"

"With all due respect, Mr. Commer, I'm done with this. I've entertained the idea long enough…perhaps a bit too much. There is no story here, no threat."

"Mr., President, if you—"

"This matter is closed, Mr. Commer. If you'll excuse me, I have a charity dinner to get to. Now, please get your car out of my way."

He turned his back to Roger and marched back to the limos. On his way to the one he'd helped the First Lady into, he stopped for a moment to speak to one of the Secret Service agents. The agent nodded and took several steps in Roger's direction.

"Yeah, I'm going," Roger said.

He was furious that Seibert had so easily dismissed him. But he was also slightly terrified over how Seibert had known about the meeting with Dean. More than that, the man had seemed almost entertained over shocking Roger with the information while not seeming to care that their lives had been in danger.

As far as Roger was concerned, the entire conversation was proof that Seibert was up to something—that he may even be purposefully hiding information pertaining to Nightwatch. As he got into his car and backed out, Dean understood that there was very little he could do.

If he had any hope of stopping whatever plans Nightwatch had, he was going to have to do something drastic.

28

Roger's mind was going in a million different directions as he returned to his office. When he finally settled down at his desk, he saw that he'd somehow missed a call from Moreno shortly after speaking with President Seibert. He'd left no message, so Roger grabbed his phone to call him back.

Before he did so, though, his mind seemed to slip into a little nook—a thin place he reserved for his family and personal life among the crazy pressures and stress of his job. For a moment, as thoughts of Thomas and the hurricane crossed his mind, he felt like a terrible father.

He skipped the call to Moreno and pulled up Thomas's number first. When Thomas answered on the second ring with a simple "Hey, Dad!", Roger noticed two things right away. First, he was in a good mood; he could hear his son's smile and warmth in his voice. Secondly, the reception was bad. It wasn't *poor* by any means, but there was definitely a disturbance in the cell service because of the storm.

"Hey, Thomas. Sorry it's taken me so long to call. I got your email about being at the beach for a bit. Are you still there?"

"Yeah. But this place...it's not like *right on the beach*. We're about half a mile away."

"Have they not evacuated the area yet?"

"No. You know, Mom already called to check in on me."

"As she should. This is pretty serious, Thomas."

"I know. But I think we're safe. We did think about getting on the road and heading back to campus, but there was just so much traffic."

"Well, I think it's too late to change your mind on that now, anyway."

"Oh, for sure. I don't think the worst of it is here just yet, but it's getting nasty out."

"Please, just stay inside and be smart."

"I will, Dad."

"Love you, kid. Take care."

He felt much better as he ended the call. He understood the mentality, he supposed. Of course a bunch of college kids would find a thrill in riding out a hurricane. It was irresponsible of course, but he had to trust Thomas's judgement.

With that call made, he sent a text to Maggie. *Gonna be late tonight. Don't wait up.*

Because she loathed texting, all he got in response was a thumbs-up emoji.

Feeling that he had the family end of things settled, Roger could finally turn his attention back to his Seibert problem. He felt tempted to call Moreno back but, based on his conversation with the President, he wasn't sure how safe that might be. Besides, he assumed Dean had told Everson about the day's events and Everson had sent the message up the chain to Moreno.

Assuming this was the case, he decided it would be safest to send an inconspicuous text. He pulled up Moreno's number and texted a very simple message: *I'm safe. Updates later.*

With that done, Roger sat behind his desk and stared at the ceiling. He slowly swiveled in his chair, trying to think of a solution. He took every facet of his problem and compiled it into a case, as if it were something he was going to take to court.

At the core, it was quite simple. He had a spy who reported that there was movement and planning taking place by Nightwatch, a terrorist organization in Afghanistan that was supposed to have been dissolved and no longer operating. The President of the United States was refusing to listen to such news because of the work he'd put into brokering partnerships and allies with the leaders of that geographic area. In addition, there was now the possibility the President may very well be interfering with any attempts to continue to learn more about these planned attacks.

Dean claimed to have emails with names and proposed plans in them. Bagram Air Force Base had been specifically called out. To Roger, these essentially served as a smoking gun—proof that the President should take the threats seriously. But he also knew how easy it was for professionals to doctor such emails.

And *that* was going to be the one big hang-up in getting things handled in a civilized and professional matter. Roger knew that there were a few ways to go around the President in matters of national security. There were a few ways he could play it. He and Frederickson could work together to present the information to the House of Representatives, or certain members of Congress. If they thought the case was daunting enough, they would bring it to the President's attention. And if he still refused to listen, things would get a lot more difficult for him. At that stage, it would then make its way to the media through press debriefings and other wide-reaching platforms.

And if it became too much of a mess, things could even roll toward impeachment by the House and conviction by the Senate.

That, of course, would include a lot of luck and risk. Even if they had a solid case, it would take months for anything to happen. And perhaps the most dangerous element of this entire ordeal was the fact that no one knew when Nightwatch planned to strike.

With no real avenue to investigate, Roger went to the database. He looked up the names of known terrorists who had been part of Nightwatch and then tried linking them to Seibert, his friends and family, or even campaign donors. As he suspected, there was nothing. The closest he could find was an elderly Texas Congressman who had invested millions in an oil racket in Afghanistan. He discovered his links to the oil fields through a man who was later found to be in charge of a Nightwatch compound. The elderly man in question abandoned the project when this came out, though. Also, because the gentleman had died four years ago, it wasn't as if he could be questioned or used as a witness.

Roger then tried a similar search for Minister Daraa and President Shahin. Their files were quite bare. Both men were highly protected and the only intel the CIA, NSA, or Homeland Security had ever collected about any of them was all speculative at best. There were several links to members of Nightwatch, Al Qaeda, and other terrorist organizations, but given that the entire Afghani government was currently trying to distance themselves from all such activity, it was all dead history and useless to him.

However, as he read up on a now-deceased terrorist leader by the name of Bahiri Marwan, he saw another name. It was a name he was familiar with but hadn't thought of in a very long time. And rightfully so...it was the name of a woman who had become something of a hushed legend within most American intelligence agencies. Anyone who knew about her—and the number was small—called her Amber. No last name...which was fitting because Roger was sure Amber wasn't *really* her first name.

"Amber," he whispered in the otherwise silent office.

It was tempting in a terrifying sort of way. All he knew for sure about Amber was that she was of French origin and had moved to America sometime around the age of seventeen. Based on what he knew, she'd enlisted in the military at eighteen, was a Navy Seal by the age of twenty, and then she'd more or less gone off the grid and was accessible only via special military projects. Some called her the president's assassin, others simply "an asset." She was sort of a dirty little secret...the tool that was sent in to wrap a job no one else could do. Sometimes this meant the deaths of America's enemies, and sometimes it resulted in the exchanging of information that most would be scared to even talk about.

Her name was tied to now-dead terrorist Bahiri Marwan because it was highly suspected by counter-intelligence organizations that she'd not only assassinated him but also killed the four other members of his group who were found dead alongside him. A few documents and a single wire transfer were the only evidence, and she had never been properly sought. She'd returned to the shadows, nothing more than a whispered legend.

Roger sighed and pushed himself away from his desk. "You're nuts," he told himself. This was true. Even if he wanted to go chasing after the ghost that was Amber, he wasn't even sure how to make such a request. Especially not if the President was on to him. Amber was much more likely to do Seibert's bidding and take Roger out rather than the other way around.

But as he thought harder on it, the President's death seemed like the easiest solution. With Seibert out and Warren ushered into office, they would handle the Nightwatch issue the right way and with extreme force.

He checked his watch and saw that it had somehow become 8:15. He had no answers, and any ideas he had were absolutely ludicrous.

Yet as he left the office and headed out into the chilly DC night, he worried that a quick and succinct solution was going to be the only way. And whether or not he wanted to admit it, maybe thinking of things like assassinations or exaggerated scandals were all he had left.

29

Dean pulled his car into the ratty little garage of his Chantilly, Virginia home. It was a quaint, cottage-style house just outside of the city. A small screened-in back-porch looked out over a stretch of overgrown forest while the front porch faced a two-lane road that boasted several similar homes. Because of its simple design and proximity to DC, it was the favorite of his three houses down the East Coast.

The runner-up was the one in Morehead City, North Carolina but depending on the time of year, the beach crowds could be a bit much to handle. The third was a condo in Florida, where he only stayed about a month year. In addition, he made a small fortune by renting it out to tourists for the rest of the time. Each abode was under a different name, none of which was his *real* name.

He spent the most time in Chantilly, though. It was close enough to DC to stay comfortably in the know, allowing him to meet with Everson and other secret contacts, but it was also just far enough away from the center of power to have a nice head start if he suddenly needed to leave—whether it be on a new mission or if he caught wind that someone was on to him.

He'd owned the house for nearly a decade now, and so far, no one had figured out who he was. The name on the mortgage was Earl Ambrose. And because it was paid for and there were no longer any bank affiliations, it was *that much* easier to stay hidden.

Parking in the garage and killing the engine, he removed both of his guns from their hiding places within the car. One was a standard Glock 16, which he'd used to help Roger in the parking garage, and the other was a Sig Sauer MPX.

He closed the automatic garage door and carried the guns into the house. He'd come here for just a few hours a day ago and before that, it had been nearly five months since he'd stepped inside. He had a cleaning lady come once every two weeks just to make sure the place never smelled stale when he came back home and to stock the kitchen with some groceries. Some traces of the cleaning products she used still hung in the air.

Dean walked into his bedroom and placed the Sig in his bedside table drawer. He carried the Glock into the kitchen where he left it on the counter. He'd learned long ago that in his line of work, it was important to always have a gun within easy reach. He would, of course, hide it whenever he had company over, but he rarely *had* company. On the rare occasion when he dated, he did everything he could to turn the tide of a night's events toward going to the woman's place rather than his house.

But Dean hadn't had time to date in the last year and a half. And until this Nightwatch trouble blew over, it would remain on the back burner. For now, he'd be perfectly content to have a sandwich for dinner, watch a bit of TV, and maybe even get some solid sleep in his own bed while he waited for updates on Seibert and the Nightwatch situation.

He threw a turkey and cheese sandwich together, sliced up an apple, and took his meal into the living room. When he switched on the TV, the news was showing footage of the Outer Banks in North Carolina as Hurricane Louise was due to make landfall within the next half an hour. A dedicated weatherman was standing on one of the beach avenues, knees braced and raincoat up like a suit of armor as he did his best to give an accurate report to an equally struggling camera operator.

Dean spent the next ten minutes flipping back and forth between news channels, wondering if some intrepid reporter had heard minor blips on the radar about the Nightwatch rumblings in the capital. He wasn't at all surprised when he came across nothing.

He was fully prepared to just tune to a station that showed old sitcom reruns, put it at low volume, and get some sleep on the couch. Yes, he knew he *needed* a good night's sleep in his bed, but he also knew he wouldn't sleep soundly until this Nightwatch mess with Seibert was all tied up. Besides, it wasn't even six o'clock yet, so even if he fell asleep, he'd be up in another hour or two...nothing more than an evening nap.

He reached for the remote control, but his hand froze just before grabbing it. He'd heard something from the back of the house. A slight creaking noise, not quite a full footstep but certainly not as innocuous as a natural, settling noise of the house.

Quietly and with practiced stealth, Dean stood up from the couch. He cursed at himself when he realized he'd left his Glock on the kitchen counter. So, unarmed, Dean moved quietly into the hallway that connected the living room and kitchen. Three rooms lined the hallway, two bedrooms on the left, and a bathroom on the right. Because the noise he'd heard had come from the back of the house, he knew those rooms were safe. Maybe the entire house was safe. Maybe he was just overreacting to every little thing because of the way the last few days had gone.

As he neared the kitchen, he heard the noise again. This time, it was more prominent. He was hearing footsteps, soft and measured, out on the screened porch. Now that he knew he wasn't just imagining the sound *and* had its location, he hurried his pace. He strode into the kitchen, his eyes on the Glock sitting on the counter.

He passed by the door that led to the garage in the back left corner of the kitchen, then the kitchen table. He extended his arm to grab up the Glock but another noise from directly behind him made him hesitate for a split second.

The door to the garage blasted inward with a clatter of cracking wood and busted hinges. It jarred Dean, but he had been at this job long enough to push through such a distraction. Even when he saw not one but two dark-skinned men in ski masks hurry through the garage door, Dean grabbed his gun. The man in front of was carrying a crowbar. The second was carrying Dean's own shovel, which was usually propped up in a bucket out in the garage.

Dean was about to pivot toward them when the back door was also blown open. In his haste to protect himself from the two men coming out of the garage, he'd momentarily forgotten about the footsteps on the screened-in porch. A third man came rushing into the kitchen through the door to the back porch. He carried an AK-47, the barrel trained on Dean.

Still, Dean turned the Glock in the armed man's direction. As soon as they were in a stand-off, Dean realized he had made a mistake.

In the second it took him to swing his concentration to the man with the AK, the lead man coming in from the garage threw the crowbar. He knew rushing across the kitchen would take too much time—that Dean would get off a shot before he reached him. So the assailant chucked the crowbar at him, tossing it so that it spiraled end over end. Dean heard it whistling through the air, before one end clipped his shoulder and the other end slammed into his head. His shoulder went momentarily numb, but that was drowned out by the sudden, roaring pain that encompassed the left side of his skull.

As Dean stumbled hard into the kitchen wall, he tried to right himself and keep his aim on the man with the AK, only to realize that his vision was blurred. He was seeing fuzzy-edged doubles of everything. Still, he knew he had to prevent all three of them from getting to him at the same time. He fired off a round.

He didn't have time to see if his shot landed, though. Just as he pulled the trigger, the man who'd thrown the crowbar was on him. He came at Dean in a powerful tackle-stance. Dean tried to level his gun to blast him in the head, but he wasn't quite fast enough. The man's shoulder slammed into Dean's stomach. The wind went racing out of him as his back was driven against the kitchen wall. There was a bit of give behind Dean as the sheetrock cracked and broke.

Acting on instinct, Dean brought his hands together and sent them down in a clubbing motion right between the man's shoulders. He followed this up by driving an elbow hard into the same place. The attacker stumbled, releasing his grip, but Dean had no time to take advantage of this. Instead, he had to lean backwards as the second man came forward, swinging the shovel around like a baseball bat. Dean tried to dodge, but the spade-end of the shovel caught him in the jaw.

The pain was immense. He spun around slightly; the pistol flying from his hands as he tried to catch himself. The man with the AK wasn't moving. He simply stood on the other side of the counter, the gun trained on him while the other two attacked.

So they aren't here to kill me, Dean thought. *If that was the case, he would have already put a few holes in me.*

This calmed him a bit, but it didn't change the fact that he was getting his ass beat. The shovel-wielding man was drawing back for another blow, and that's when Dean finally got a chance. He drew back his right fist and, still seeing double, simply aimed for a spot in the middle. His vicious jab connected, smashing into the man's mouth. But the crowbar-thrower had gotten back to his feet and delivered a similar jab. Only this one was right into one of Dean's kidneys. His legs went out, and he hit the floor.

As soon as he was down, one man kicked him in the ribs. The other landed a kick right to his balls. The world was nothing more than a kaleidoscope of pain: his jaw, the left side of his head, his groin, his kidney. He groaned but nothing more. He bit the rest back, determined not to scream out in front of these men.

Slowly, as bits of the world seeped back in beyond the agony, Dean noticed the man with the AK-47 again. He'd finally come over to the other side of the kitchen counter to join the other two. He was no longer brandishing the gun at him. Instead, he kneeled down, planting his knee directly into Dean's chest.

"Dean Page," the man said. His eyes were just as black as the fabric of the ski masks the trio was wearing. "It's about damn time we finally met."

"Who…" Dean tried to say. But as he got the single word out, the man planted his knee harder into his chest. It added a whole new level of pain to the whirlwind.

"No questions out of you," the man said. "All you need to know is that we've been on to you for about a week now. Had we been out in that desert when you were listening in to conversations you had no business hearing, you would have never made it back to the States."

The man leaned in, his masked face just a foot away from Dean's nose. "We're not going to kill you. Well...maybe not. That depends on the choices you make from here on out. See, we know about your buddy in the CIA...the rogue fellow with the phantom job...Mr. Roger Commer. We know all about him. About his job. About his lovely wife. About his son. And we know he's been working with you. We know about Everson and what all of you are trying to push through to our idiot President. So...not only are you going to put that shit to rest, but you're also going to make sure we speak with Commer. Because of his job, we can't very well just roll up to his house and take him out. So we're going to have you make a call for us. You're going to tell him you want to meet again. Do you understand?"

Dean said nothing. After speaking the single word moments ago and feeling the pain and effort it had taken, he wasn't sure he could even if he wanted to. His head was a maelstrom of torment, and his groin felt like it was on fire.

"I said, *do you understand?*"

"I..." Dean managed, his voice weak. "I..."

Through the mouth hole in the man's mask, Dean saw him smile. The man then leaned forward, as if mocking him, and said "What was that?"

With their faces now only six inches apart, Dean couldn't help himself.

He spit directly into the man's face. The masked man chuckled and removed his knee from Dean's chest. He then looked to the man with the shovel and nodded.

The shovel-wielder stepped forward and drew back with the shovel as if it were a golf club. Oddly, it was the sound the shovel made when it struck his head that Dean noticed first. Hollow and almost musical, it filled the world.

The pain came barreling in a second later, but it was brief.

After that, there was only darkness. As Dean blacked out, his final thought was just how much trouble Roger Commer and his family might be in.

30

When Roger arrived at the White House the following morning to join the morning briefing, he already had an uneasy feeling in his stomach. Even if Seibert allowed him in, there was no way he was going to candidly discuss the Nightwatch issue. As Roger parked in his usual spot, he wasn't at all surprised to see a large man dressed in a Secret Service-style suit coming across the lot to meet him. The man dressed in a Secret Service-style suit was clean-shaven and had his eyes hidden behind a pair of dark sunglasses.

"Shit," Roger muttered.

Apparently, President Seibert had been one hundred percent serious yesterday afternoon. Roger could still hear the man's bitter voice in his head, the words rather plain but coming out as a warning. *"With all due respect, Mr. Commer, I'm done with this. I've entertained the idea long enough...there is no story here, no threat...this matter is closed."*

The man in the suit who was currently marching toward him was apparently proof of this. And if Roger was being completely cut out of all White House communications, that essentially meant he was on his own, save for a handful of others who understood how dangerous the President was acting.

Roger had barely even stepped out of his car before the large man had closed the distance between them. He was pretty sure the man *was* Secret Service; Roger didn't think Seibert would send a typical security guard to handle such a detail.

"Good morning, Mr. Commer," the man said. He moved with the intimidating fluidity of someone capable of switching from pleasant to hostile in the blink of an eye, and Roger knew the man was packing at least one gun. If Seibert had given him the authority, Roger knew this man would engage if necessary.

"Good morning to you too."

"President Seibert has asked me to let you know that your presence is not required at this morning's meeting, or any future meetings for the foreseeable future."

"I see," Roger said, trying to decide if it was worth arguing over. In the end, he figured it was smarter to not make even more trouble. Maybe if he simply gave the appearance of being a good little boy, Seibert might assume he'd finally tucked his tail and run. "Well, I guess it was nice of him to save me the walk inside, huh?"

The agent said nothing. He stood his ground, though, making it apparent that he had no intention of moving until Roger was on his way out of the lot. Roger wasted no time, already getting back into his car. He even gave the Secret Service agent a sarcastic wave as he drove off.

He hated the feeling of knowing his only means of staying in the know was to wait for either Frederickson or Warren to call him. But if he was being cut out of all White House communications, he assumed it would be harder than ever for Frederickson to reach out to him.

In the farthest reaches of his mind, he thought about the name he'd come across in his research last night—Amber. He wondered if Moreno would know how to get in touch with her.

Are you seriously considering that? Roger asked himself. *Are you seriously contemplating the assassination of the President of the United States?*

He was. It sent a feeling of disgust and sickness through him, but he couldn't deny it. The sad thing about American politics was even if someone found something deeply incriminating against Seibert in the next few days, it would get tied up in court—worse yet, a politically driven D.C. court. People would use words like *impeachment* and *conviction,* but regardless of the decision, it would be too late. Based on what he knew about the planned attacks on Bagram, there wasn't much more time to lose.

When he was three miles away from the White House, Roger pulled his car into the lot of a small park that looked out over the Washington Monument. He wasn't quite ready to head to his office at the Pentagon yet because he didn't know what the day had in store.

The thought of calling Moreno to inquire about Amber just wouldn't leave his head. The only reason he didn't was because he knew making such a request would cross a line that there was no coming back from. And if it all went badly, his career and maybe even his life would be in jeopardy.

As he considered all of this, his phone rang. When he saw Thomas's name on the caller display, that sick feeling he'd been wrestling with increased. He'd been so wrapped up in how Seibert was going to respond this morning, he'd totally forgotten to call Thomas to check on him. Hurricane Louise had made landfall later yesterday evening and the coastal areas had been hammered pretty badly.

He answered the call, swallowing down his nerves and saying a quick prayer that Thomas was okay. "Hey, Thomas. You didn't get blown away, did you?"

"No. We're all good. There are some stray branches in the yard and a few trash cans got blown over, but I think that's the worst of it. I can't say the same for the folks out on the beach, though. Have you seen the news at all this morning?"

"No, not yet. Why? How bad is it?"

"From what I saw on television, it was pretty bad. A lot of people in Virginia Beach got flooded and there are tons of houses on the beach that were ruined. I'm surprised Mom didn't tell you about it yet."

"I got an early start this morning; I left before your mom was awake. Did you know anyone in the area that got hit hard?"

"No, not me. But one of my friends has an aunt and uncle that live right on the beach. He's trying to get in touch with them right now."

"But *you're* okay?" Roger asked. "Do you need anything?"

"No, I'm good. It looks like the roads are clogged up, so we're going to wait until that clears before we head out."

"Well, be careful. And thanks for calling to update me. You know, your mother and I are hoping to make it up there soon. The house isn't the same without you."

"Yeah, I hate to admit it, but I miss you guys...and home. Maybe I'll head down there this weekend."

Roger's heart lit up at this. He wondered if the hurricane had scared his son a bit and made him miss the security of a secure home. "That would be amazing," Roger said.

"Well, maybe I'll see you then. Bye, Dad."

They ended the call, and Roger was amazed at how just hearing from Thomas seemed to center him—to calm him and to help him think more rationally.

The idea of somehow reaching out to the woman known as Amber was still simmering, but now seemed like the last, desperate plans of a madman. All he'd needed was a moment to cool down, to re-orient his mind away from Seibert's dangerous foolishness.

Roger took a moment to think about the state of things. Yes, it would be much harder to be of any influence if Seibert was straight-out refusing to speak with him. But he still had a hand in this game. He just needed to get a clear picture of what his position looked like.

With no White House access, that likely meant Vice President Warren would not be able to assist any longer. Not unless he had a very subtle way of passing information to the outside without Seibert or any of those around him catching on. He supposed Frederickson was still on his team, as he wasn't so directly tied into the White House or Seibert's inner circle. He also had Moreno and Everson...and Dean Page. And as unofficial as it felt, he knew Dean was his best shot at getting anything done. It had been Dean, after all, who had uncovered the news of the danger. And Roger had watched Dean handle himself extremely well when they'd been attacked in the parking garage yesterday.

So maybe he should start with Dean. He could call Dean, tell him about how horribly Seibert was reacting, and see if they could come up with a plan. He understood that this was potentially dangerous; after arranging the meeting with Dean yesterday, someone had apparently known when and where. And he had no way of knowing which end of the line of communication had been compromised.

Still, he had to get in touch with him and had no idea where to look. He supposed he could try to be clever and crafty when he had Dean on the line. With a bit of nerves coming back, he called the same number he'd used the day before.

The phone rang just once before it went to an automated voice message request. He set the phone down and started the car again. He figured he may as well get to this office. It was the only sure place anyone would know where to get in touch with him. Of course, the President also knew where his office was, so he might have someone scouting the place out. Roger made a mental note of this and planned to look the entire hall over for anything suspicious when he arrived.

However, as he was about to pull onto the street, his phone dinged at him as a text came in. He saw it had come from Dean.

It was short and sweet but felt important: *New info. 331 Arbor Way, Chantilly.*

For Roger, it was a easy decision. Chantilly wasn't too far away, and it would give him something to do until Frederickson was freed up from whatever bullshit meeting Seibert was trying to orchestrate without Roger. So, with a new destination, he turned left, heading farther away from Pennsylvania Avenue and hopefully closer to a solution of how to stop a potentially massive terrorist attack.

31

Roger made the drive with a knot of worry tight in his stomach. Given the way the last several days had gone, he fully expected gunshots at any moment—maybe a sniper on top of a building or in a car he passed along the way. He could usually look past such worries, to compartmentalize things and focus on the here and now. But the way this worry continued to gnaw at him was yet another sign of just how serious the situation was becoming. If he didn't fix this Nightwatch business soon, he feared he may not just lose control of the situation, but of himself as well.

The drive to the Chantilly address took a little less than half an hour. The house was rather simple. very nondescript and unassuming. There was a quaint look about it, but it could use a good pressure washing of the vinyl siding. Still, it seemed like the perfect home for a government spy who was trying to remain in hiding.

Roger parked in the thin cement driveway. The garage door was closed, and there were no vehicles in sight. When he got out of his car, the sense of fear crept back in, but he did his best to shove it aside. Dean had invited him here and so far, he had no reason at all not to trust him.

He walked to the front door and knocked softly. When he took a single step back to wait, his hand instinctively went to the butt of his holstered Sig Sauer. After a second or two, he heard Dean call out from inside.

"Come on in. It's unlocked."

Roger reached out and grabbed the door handle. Then he stopped. Something didn't feel right. Dean had been through just as much shit as Roger had over the past few days. Would a government spy honestly leave his door unlocked and answer the door in such a lackadaisical fashion, even if he *was* expecting company?

Just as this notion registered in Roger's mind, he felt an immense jerking sensation as the knob was yanked out of his hand. The moment the door opened, he was attacked.

The first thing he saw was a short but well-built, dark-skinned man standing in the doorway...a man who was not Dean. And then, as soon as he saw this, he saw the figure lashing out with something, aiming for Roger's stomach. Before he could back away or sidestep, the attack landed. Something hard and unforgiving slammed into his gut. The wind went racing out of his lungs as he dropped to his knees.

But he never actually touched the porch. He was grabbed by the neck right away and pulled inside. Still not able to breathe and with a growing ache in his abdomen, everything went by in a blur. He could see the basic layout and corners of what appeared to be a living room and the entrance to a hallway in front of him. He was yanked into the house and immediately turned to face the man who had attacked him at the door. The man was coming forward with another attack. Roger could now see that he had been struck by a crowbar. And now it was aimed at his head as it sailed through the air.

He jumped back and nearly stumbled over his own feet. The moment the crowbar passed by his head, missing him by less than a foot, he reacted instinctively. Despite the pain in his stomach, he charged forward and threw his shoulder into the attacker's waist. At the moment of contact, he also delivered three rapid punches to the man's ribs.

The man cried out, and they both fell to the ground. Roger instantly did his best to throw his weight hard to the right, hoping to mount the man and deliver at least a few vicious blows. But just as he started trying to, he caught movement in the hallway to his right.

He turned just in time to see another man running at him. There were perhaps three feet between them when this new attacker dove forward slightly and raised up his knee. Roger was just barely able to block the blow. But the force of his defense sent him sprawling backward off the original attacker. As he hit the floor, he instantly reached for his Sig Sauer.

He unholstered it and had brought it up when the original attacker swung the crowbar around. There wasn't much force behind the blow, but it struck Roger directly on the back of the hand. A little burst of electric pain shot through his wrist, causing him to nearly drop his gun. The amount of time it took him to reclaim his grip was more than enough opportunity for both of the attackers to reorient themselves. The one who had attempted to use his knee as a weapon came charging at him with a right-handed punch, an old-school haymaker.

Roger did his best to avoid the blow, but it still landed on his neck, directly below his jaw. Instantly after this, the other man struck out with the crowbar again. This time the blow had more strength to it and struck Roger high in the back. When he fell to the floor, he tried to catch himself with his hands but one man was already delivering a kick to his side.

All of the blows had come with blinding speed and, for a moment, Roger's body couldn't quite decide what hurt the most. His wrist was still hurting but there was a fresh wave of pain cascading across his back from the most recent impact. Through it all, he was still having trouble collecting his breath from the initial pain from the crowbar while he'd been at the front door.

Things had gotten bad quickly. And somewhere behind all of this, a question flared like neon in darkness: *Where is Dean?*

This question was obliterated as one of the men stopped down on his right wrist. The pain was horrendous and caused him to unclasp his fingers from the butt of the pistol. The man with the crowbar kicked the gun to the other side of the room and even through the agony, Roger understood that this might be a good sign. While these men had no problem beating the hell out of him, it seemed that they had no interest in killing him. Not yet anyway.

As the pair of men worked together to pull Roger to his feet, he caught sight of a third figure standing in the hallway. Everything was quite blurry, but he could see the man advancing as he stepped into the living room. It was hard to place his nationality—maybe something Middle Eastern. He was well-shaven and handsome, his dark eyes boring into Roger.

"Bring him back here," this man said.

The two attackers pushed him toward the hallway. His side was aching, but he didn't think they had broken any ribs. His back was hurting as well, but based on the flexibility of his movements while he was pushed, he thought nothing was permanently wrong there, either. If anything had been soundly damaged, it was his wrist. He wasn't sure if it was broken or not, but for right now, that seemed to be the origin of most of his pain.

"Who are you?" Roger said.

As a response, he received a swift slap to the face by the third man. It really wasn't even all that hard, just the sort of slap to shut him up...to let Roger know he had no right to ask questions in this situation.

Roger had been in this sort of position before... rarely, but the one instance had been enough for him to think on it time and time again. He knew what to do, and he did his best to keep a rational mind as he was ushered into the house's kitchen. He made sure to study every inch of the house he passed through. He took note of where each door was, of how the men moved, of how wide the hallway was. And though he could do this with the practiced skill of a computer that had been programmed to do such a thing, it all fell apart when he saw what was waiting for him in the kitchen.

Dean was lashed to a kitchen chair. His waist and chest were tied to the back of the chair, and his arms had been pulled behind him with his wrists also tied. There was dried blood on the left side of his face, and a large bruise on the right that had nearly swollen his eye shut. He looked tired, horrified, and dazed. His face was very puffy, and his left eye looked hazed over, as if he wasn't sure what was going on.

The kitchen itself was also a wreck, with two doors blown off their hinges and propped against soot-stained walls.

The two men shoved Roger to the floor. He landed just a few feet in front of Dean, nearly colliding with the chair. There were little splotches of dried blood on the tile and scuff marks from where the chair had skittered back and forth.

"What do you want?" Roger asked. Suddenly, he wasn't sure if them not seeming to want him dead would play in his favor. Maybe they were going to do to him what they'd been doing to Dean.

"Answers," the third man said. Roger assumed this was the leader of the trio. "Answers and then silence."

"I don't underst—"

The leader slapped Roger hard across the face, with much more force this time. His ears rang, and the side of his face felt like it was on fire.

"Here's what we need to know," the man said. He had a very vague accent, slightly Afghani, but buried under years of living in America. "We need to know how much your friend here has told your President. We need to know what sort of plans and forces are being set into place to attack us."

"I don't even know who you are."

The leader stepped aside and allowed the man with the crowbar to come to the front.

"Don't be stupid, Mr. Commer. You will answer my questions, or we will shatter Mr. Page's knees. Am I understood?"

Roger looked at Dean and still wasn't sure he was fully coherent. He'd been through the ringer with these men, and Roger wondered if Dean would even feel it if they shattered his knees. Of course, he didn't want to be tested on that theory.

"Yes, I understand."

"Okay, so what has been passed on?"

"He had audio recordings, but those were lost in a fight as he was leaving the desert. All he has are emails with encoded messages."

"You're certain?"

"Yes."

"And has he gone directly to your President Seibert with this information?"

"He hasn't, no." Roger couldn't tell if they believed him or not. He certainly hoped so, as he was, after all, telling the truth. He also knew where this line of questioning was headed. So he tried to come up with a solution, a way he could tell as much of the truth as possible while also providing himself with a way out.

"Has anyone talked to Seibert?" the leader asked.

Roger studied the three men, taking in their features. The man with the crowbar did indeed look to be from Afghanistan. It was harder to place the initial attacker.

"I did. I passed on what Dean found."

"Well, that was a mistake," the leader said. He reached over to the kitchen counter and grabbed a knife. It was a large butcher's knife, like something out of a horror movie.

This next part would be tricky. There was no way Roger could tell them that none of it mattered—that Seibert wasn't moving on anything regarding Nightwatch. If they knew that, these men would report back to their superiors and have a field day with this sort of freedom. So he was going to have to lie and make it a good one.

"But no one is listening," he said. "If we had the audio Dean captured, it would be one thing. But it's just emails...emails no one can really even make sense of. A few names, and the mention of an attack on Bagram. But there's no hard evidence."

The leader chuckled and said, "So you mean to tell me that your government is doing nothing about this?"

"They're doing *something*," Roger said. "But I didn't know what. I'm not allowed in any of the meetings."

"Maybe..." the leader said thoughtfully. "But we're told you have been speaking with Secretary of Defense Frederickson in private. Is that correct?"

"No."

The leader moved aside again, and this time, when the man with the crowbar moved forward, there were no further warnings. He brought the bar down on Dean's knee. Dean shrieked out in pain, jerking so frantically that the chair nearly tipped over. He seethed and writhed, trying to swallow down further exclamations, which came out as pained grunts.

Roger did his best to keep calm as he said, "That's uncalled for. I don't know why you even have him as a prisoner. His part in this is done. Everything he knows, I now know. As does President Seibert."

"So you have no role in whatever the outcome might be?" the leader asked.

"None. I am behind the scenes and nobody really involves me in the inner circles where this stuff is discussed.

"And you, Mr. Page? Do you agree with this? You've said you can't help us, and now Mr. Commer is telling us the same. What do you say to this?"

The leader stepped forward and leaned down a bit to look Dean square in his one good eye. He grinned, as if teasing a child with a piece of candy.

Dean responded by spitting in the man's face. And then he smiled. He'd been beaten and tortured and looked to be nearly on the brink of death...but he *smiled* at the leader.

Without a word, the leader stood back up to his full height. He extended his hand to the man with the crowbar and took the weapon.

"Watch closely, Mr. Commer."

With the crowbar over his shoulder, he then turned slightly to the left. He took a batter's stance and by the time Roger knew what was about to happen, it was too late. He screamed out briefly but the sound of the crowbar striking Dean squarely on the side of the head was somehow louder. It was the worst thing Roger had ever heard.

It triggered something in him...a flight or fight response from the reptilian brain. And as the leader readjusted his grip on the crowbar and came out of the swinging motion, Roger could not help himself.

He sprang forward, roaring out in rage, both hands clenched into fists.

After that, the kitchen became a blur of shouts and motion, and everything happened incredibly fast.

32

When Roger began fighting back, two distinct sides divided his mind. One side realized how foolish this was...how it could very well mean that within a handful of minutes, he'd leave Maggie a widow and his sons without a father. But the other side of his mind was driven by his training and a need for justice. These were violent, evil men. And even if they had no intention of killing him just yet, Roger had no interest in going through whatever torturous hell they'd put Dean through.

So he fought because his life depended on it.

He went for the leader, mainly because he was currently holding the only weapon in the room. He resorted to the basics of attack, driving his right fist hard into the man's crotch. It was a crude yet effective strategy, crumpling him right away. He attempted to swing down with the crowbar, but it missed by a wide margin.

With the crowbar-wielder on the floor, Roger quickly pivoted from his knees and turned to the other two men. The leader was already charging forward, his right hand raised in a fist. As he brought it down, aimed directly for Roger's face, Roger went low. From his crouched position, he wheeled hard to the right, in a clumsy sort of half-roll. The punch missed, and Roger was able to trip him. The man went falling in an awkward tumble, slamming into Dean's refrigerator.

At the same time, though, the third attacker was coming, and Roger had no time to side-step the attack. The man threw himself fully on top of Roger, and they collided on the floor. Roger felt the man's hands go directly for his neck, the pressure immense—so tight and rigid that he was sure his neck would break. A moment later, as Roger was fighting for breath and trying to squirm his way out from under the man, the leader regained his feet. He delivered a swift and brutal kick to Roger's ribs.

"You made this so much harder than it had to be," the leader said in his slight accent. He then delivered another kick to his ribs and quickly shoved the other man off of him. "Now, you're going to replace your dead friend in the chair. And we *will* get our answers from you. We are—"

The sound of a soft gunshot interrupted him, almost like a puff of air. Just as Roger heard it, a neat red hole appeared in the man's forehead. His eyes glazed over, and he collapsed.

From his place on the floor, Roger scrambled to his feet as another gunshot sounded. This time, he heard it more clearly and saw where it was coming from. Someone was standing in the hallway, their posture locked and perfectly still. The second gunshot took out the man who had been attempting to strangle Roger. He didn't see where this shot landed, but he could tell the man was dead instantly.

The third man was still recovering from the collision with the refrigerator. Wincing and near tears, he raised his hands in surrender, staring at the figure in the hallway.

"Please...no...I beg..."

The figure fired another shot, moving the silencer-equipped pistol slightly to the right before they did so. The shot took the man high in the right arm. Stepping into the kitchen, the figure then came forward. They were dressed in all black: jeans, a long-sleeved tee shirt, and gloves. But the plain yet elegant face overshadowed all of that and the short-cropped blonde hair that was pulled slightly back into a ponytail.

It was a woman. Her eyes were like steel as she stepped further into the kitchen. The one remaining attacker was groaning on the floor, his right arm bleeding. Approaching him, she kicked him in the chest and proceeded to stomp on the area where she had shot him. The man screamed in agony.

Without even looking in Roger's direction, she said: "Are you okay, Mr. Commer?"

"Don't know yet," Roger groaned. "My ribs are banged up, and my wrist is numb but...but I think I might be okay."

"*Please...*" the man on the floor said.

The woman angled her gun down to the man she was still stepping on. "Who sent you here?"

The man groaned and shook his head. "I can't tell y—"

The woman fired off another shot. It was just a warning shot, though. Chipped tile from the kitchen floor sprang up in a little cloud about an inch away from the man's head.

"Sure you can," she said.

The man was wailing now, his breath coming in huge, panicked gulps. "No," he gasped. "Can't...I don't even know who. Just got paid to come make Dean Page talk."

"And Mr. Commer?"

"Yeah, him too."

"Who paid you?"

"I don't know!" the man screamed. "I got the call from Sav."

"Who's Sav?" the woman asked. Her questions were coming as if on an automatic loop.

"Him!" the man screamed, nodding over toward his dead leader.

"Are you a Nightwatch member?"

"No..no...but I knew...I..." He stopped here and screamed again, nothing but pain.

"Answer me or your knees are next," the woman said. And then, looking to Roger full on for the first time, she added: "You're free to go, Mr. Commer."

"No," Roger said, getting to his feet and realizing that his ribs were actually hurting much more than he'd realized. "I need to know when the attacks are supposed to happen."

"You heard him," the woman said. She stepped down on his gunshot arm again. "When?"

"*I don't know!*" he screamed. "Sav had all of that information, and you killed him!"

Roger watched the woman think for a moment. Before she could say anything else, another voice spoke up from the hallway.

"Roger?"

He turned at the sound of his name and was shocked to see Everson standing there. The man looked like a ghost in the hallway, especially when his eyes found Dean, motionless and dead in the chair.

"Everson? What are you doing here?"

"Leave her to it," he said, not answering me. "Come with me and just let her do her thing."

"But—"

"Listen to him," the woman said. "Go outside to your car. I'll be there in a few minutes."

He didn't like the idea of so willingly walking away from a source of information, but he also had no intention of getting on this woman's bad side. And as he limped over to Everson, it occurred to him who this woman was.

Roger followed Everson down the hallway and retrieved his Sig Sauer. Before they reached the front door, he heard the woman whisper something, almost sweetly, to the remaining attacker. He responded with panic and fear. He was almost glad when he and Everson were outside.

"That's Amber, isn't it?" he asked as he hobbled over to his car. Maybe they'd cracked a rib or two after all.

"It is," Everson said. He seemed profoundly sad—whether over Dean's death or that they were in the presence of a rumored, deadly assassin, Roger wasn't sure.

"Who called her?"

"I did. But with Frederickson's blessing."

The weight of what this might mean silenced Roger for a moment and all he could do in the meantime was slide painfully into the driver's seat of his car and wait for Amber to come out.

33

When Amber came out of Dean's front door three minutes later, she looked completely emotionless. To a passerby, she might appear like nothing more than a housewife about to run an errand. Her appearance and demeanor didn't hint at all about the horrors that had been left behind in Dean's kitchen. She wasted no time, coming directly to Roger's car, opening the passenger side door, and getting in.

"Unless something changes," she said, "the attack on Bagram will occur in five days. And while everyone in charge is blinded by that, the intention is to have a similar attack on a base here in the States. But he didn't know where and even said that part was really just a rumor—maybe even just shit-talking by the guy in charge trying to amp them up."

"Is he still alive?" Everson asked. He was standing outside of the car, leaning slightly forward and peering in through Roger's opened window.

"No."

"Do you think he was telling the truth?"

"Yes."

"How do you know for sure?" Roger asked, not sure he really even wanted to know.

"I've done this quite a lot, Mr. Commer," Amber said. "When a man knows his life is in your hands and that you can take it at any moment, they become very easy to read...especially with truths and lies."

This woman had just killed three men Roger assumed were linked to Nightwatch. The information she'd gathered as a result was really only a confirmation of things he already knew, but these things were serious enough for Nightwatch reps—whether abroad or hidden in Washington— to come after anyone who might work toward putting a stop to their plans.

"This is all confusing as hell to me," Roger said. "How did you even know where I was?"

Everson frowned a bit and looked nervously around the yard, as if he thought there might be other enemies lurking about. "I don't know all the specifics," he said. "But it started with Frederickson. When he got word that Seibert was going to bar you from the morning briefing, he knew things could get bad. He knew Seibert was no longer entertaining your warnings. And after the shootout in the parking garage yesterday, he didn't see the point in taking any chances. He contacted me and asked for a meeting with Dean. I tried calling Dean, but there was no answer. So I tried on an emergency line he and I have and when he didn't answer *that*, I knew something was wrong. I relayed that to Frederickson, and he panicked. He reached out to someone on his end and asked them to locate you. When he found you were headed to Chantilly, I put two-and-two together."

"But how did he know where I was going?"

Everson chuckled nervously. "He's the Secretary of Defense. It's not all that hard."

"Okay...and what about her?" Roger asked, nodding toward Amber. She, too, was looking out the window and all around the yard.

"Dean *never* misses a call from the emergency line we share. The one time he was unable to answer it was because he was in Russia, in the middle of an information exchange three years ago. So it means bad news when he doesn't answer. Again...I put it all together. The shootout yesterday, someone taking a shot at your car before then, and both of you in the same location again...I wasn't taking chances. I gave Amber a call."

Roger wondered if Amber had been on Everson's mind lately too. He didn't think Everson had any direct oversight over her. Based on what Roger knew of her, she was more of a freelancer for anyone in need...so long as their interests were a match with her own.

"What have you heard about Nightwatch?" Roger asked Amber.

"Not much. But I did know Dean. I knew him fairly well, actually. And if he believed there is a credible threat on the way, then that's the truth. I just confirmed that truth in his kitchen."

"Will you stay on board?" Everson asked. "Do you think you can help us until this is all wrapped up?"

"I can make myself available, yes," she said. Her eyes were icy, and her jaw was set. She was all business, not the least bit affected by what she'd just done in Dean's house. "But it seems to me, the success of what you're trying to do comes down to convincing the President — or at least those in his circle - that this threat is indeed credible. And I don't know that I'll be much help in that regard."

"I'm pretty sure he *knows* it's credible," Roger said. "And he either doesn't care or he..." He stopped himself, not sure if he should say such a thing in front of Everson. He knew Everson was on his side, but to state that the President knew about the planned attack and was choosing to *let* it happen bordered on treason.

But apparently, Everson had already crossed that mental line himself. "Or he knows it, and he's allowing it to happen."

The comment even grabbed Amber's attention. She eyed them both suspiciously and seemed to read their minds. Roger felt especially vulnerable, given how he'd thought of her last night and whether she would be an option.

She shook her head slowly, her icy eyes showing the slightest bit of an emotion that looked like nervousness. "No," she said. "Absolutely not. I personally don't like the man and disagree with lots of his policies, but there's no amount of money I'd take to eliminate the President of the United States."

"No one is asking you to," Everson said. "But we need to figure *something* out. You said yourself...five days, and Bagram is going to be attacked. What can we do?"

"I can try warning the higher-ups over there," Roger said. "But if Seibert finds out, it's going to be bad. And he'd override those warnings anyway...he'd claim I was being paranoid."

"For now," Everson said, "I'd like you both out of here. I need to find out how these fuckers knew where Dean was living and who sent them...and I doubt the Pentagon or the CIA is going to lend a hand. If Seibert says this is all nonsense, they're going to agree."

"Count me out for now," Amber said. "I just shot three men connected to a terrorist ring. I'll touch base later, but for right now, I need to become a ghost."

And with that, she got out of the car. She didn't say another word; she simply walked to the end of the driveway, looked to the right, and started walking quickly in that direction.

"So, that's Amber," Roger said.

"Yeah...that's Amber."

"I was sort of hoping she'd be all for taking Seibert out. Is that wrong of me?"

"No," Everson said, laughing. "It was in my head, too. Now...I need you to follow me."

"Where?"

"A place just outside of Alexandria no one knows about. Well, no one other than Dean. We'll be able to speak freely."

"I wonder if they're tracking our cars."

"They?" Everson said.

Roger understood what he meant. Was he unknowingly accusing Seibert of keeping tabs on us? Did he have a team making sure he stayed in line? And worse yet, his thoughts turned back to the very unsettling idea that Seibert or some of his minions may have somehow set up the events that led to Dean's death...and nearly Roger's as well.

Roger was struck then by just how much of a loss Everson had been dealt. As far as Roger knew, Dean had been close to Everson for about a decade. But there was no time to dwell on such things right now. Grieving could come later. As would addressing his many wounds.

For now, they needed to work together to figure out a way to shut down this Nightwatch effort. And with their access to people and resources in Washington slowly being choked out, it was going to be even harder than before.

"Here's what we'll do," Everson said. "Meet me ten miles up the road. There's an Exxon station just before you get to the stoplight at the intersection. Park your car there. I don't *know if* they'd have your car bugged or being tracked, but then again, you *are* using a bureau loaner right now. From the gas station, you and I will go to Alexandria, and I'll get you back to your car as quickly as possible."

"Yeah, that sounds fine. There's a lot of wasted time bunched up in there, though."

"Alexandria is only half an hour away. We should be fine. While you're heading to the Exxon, I'll follow to make sure you're safe and make a call to an outfit that will scrub Dean's place clean. No bodies, blood, fingerprints, anything."

"What will happen to Dean?"

"I'll see that he gets a proper—but discreet—funeral."

"And the other three?"

"Gone, as if they never existed."

It occurred to Roger that now Dean was dead, Everson might be his most reliable ally. Based on the events that just took place in Dean's house, they were playing an entirely different game now. And even if it seemed the table might be tilted against them, they had to keep fighting.

As Roger backed out of Dean's driveway, he wondered if he should pay a visit to the emergency room after Everson was through with him. His ribs ached fiercely, but not enough to think one or two might be cracked. His wrist was hurting quite a bit and a bruise had formed along the top of it. He was pretty sure the wrist would need some attention...but not today. He could grip the steering wheel and *almost* make a complete fist with it. He'd get it looked at whenever all of this was over. If his ribs were seriously injured, it would be a different story, but he could live with a subpar wrist for a few days.

One last realization occurred to him: up to this point, his irritation and anger stemmed from Seibert's refusal to listen to him. But now, as a result of how the last few days had gone and how each new day seemed to be getting progressively more deadly, he was actually starting to be scared. He'd never felt out of his depth before, but as he drove toward the gas station with Everson's car trailing behind him, Roger felt like he was drowning.

34

"There's something I need to tell you about the place we're headed," Everson said. They'd dropped Roger's car off at the gas station twenty minutes ago, and they were just now getting into Alexandria. Everson was driving a bit faster, and Roger shared the man's urgency.

"Yeah, what's that?"

"The reason only Dean and I know about the place and no one else does is because we used it as a sort of base of operations now and then."

"A base of operations for what, exactly?" Roger asked.

Everson sighed, and Roger could tell he was nervous about whatever he was on the verge of saying. "This stays between us, right?"

"Of course. Everson. You may be the only real ally I have right now…the only one that could actually help, that is."

"Well, with Dean's job, he was never really any member of an actual department. Everyone used him on a sort of freelance basis. Sort of like Amber, just on a more profession- and government-mandated scale. But because of that freelance schedule, he often found himself with large chunks of time when there was nothing to do. So he and I got into a little side-hustle that no one other than my wife ever knew about."

"Intelligence gathering?" Roger guessed.

"In a sense. We did our very best to keep it all legal, but it was essentially what Dean did for government agencies, only we were doing it for corporations and big businesses."

"And you kept it quiet?"

"We did. For about four years. Do you remember about six or seven years ago when that pharmaceutical company out of Switzerland bought out Jones-Briggs Pharma?"

"Yeah." He recalled it had resulted in a decrease in the cost of almost every heart-related medicine in the country.

"That only happened because Dean and I could find proof of price tampering and the fudging of results from clinical trials. Once we found all of this out, we provided the information to bigwigs in the industry. Two days later, Jones-Briggs knew they had only two choices: face the consequences and suffer bankruptcy and a public revolt or sell the company before any of it happened. And that's all because of the private work Dean and I were doing from this place I'm about to take you to."

Roger was certainly a lot more interested in where Everson was taking him. He'd assumed it would be an office setting in a secluded building, or maybe even some back room in an old house somewhere. Instead, the scenery outside of his window suggested Everson was taking him to the outskirts of Alexandria. As the highway branched to the east, out toward the city, Everson had veered right and was working his way into a more rural-looking area. There were still strip malls and fast-food restaurants, but they became fewer and fewer by the minute.

Then, slightly over half an hour after they'd left Dean's house, Everson turned off the two-lane road and into a paved driveway that cut through a gorgeous expanse of fields. The path branched off two ways after a quarter of a mile—to the right the paved surface continued, and to the left there was a gravel road Everson turned onto, which lead farther into the field.

A large barn sat at the back edge of the field, bordered by a horse pen that looked as if it hadn't been in use for quite some time. The barn was one of the largest Roger had ever seen, the sort that was usually found on big cattle farms. Two large doors sat up front, large enough for tractors and hay bailers to enter.

Everson pulled his car up in front of the barn and parked. When he got out, Roger followed. They entered through a secondary door along the left side of the barn. Inside, the floor was concrete and showed few signs of its former purpose. Instead, the interior was split in half. A half-wall separated the concrete floor with the back half, which still contained a few large horse pens and stalls. But Everson was walking to another door on the opposite side of the building—one that led into another room rather than back outside.

He unlocked this door with a key from a ring he pulled from the pocket of his pants. When he opened the door, the overhead lights switched on automatically, revealing a staircase that led down into a cellar.

"This all seems very covert," Roger joked.

"It sort of has to be," Everson responded as he led Roger down the stairs.

The staircase was short, ending in a room that had no resemblance to the barn over their heads at all. The room was about thirty feet by fifty feet. A large table sat in the center of a floor adorned with large, simple tiles. Three workstations were set up along the walls, all with laptops, monitors, and an abundance of tech that was way over Roger's head.

"Okay, so what now?" Roger asked.

"Now," Everson said, taking one laptop from a workstation and bringing it to the large table. "We're going to do our best to rally the troops. All calls and communications in and out of here are private and secure thanks to about twenty different safety measures Dean had installed. You and I are going to figure out who's on our side and who can actually help. Because after today, I think it's become pretty clear..."

Roger knew what Everson was going to say and couldn't agree more. He interrupted, finishing the statement for him.

"...that Seibert has to be stopped somehow."

35

Moreno was the easiest to get in touch with. A simple call to his secretary, and Everson had Moreno on the line within ten minutes. Frederickson was quite a different story. And as Everson worked toward trying to get Frederickson on the line, Roger began to get a good picture of how the communications down in Everson's hidden bunker worked.

He was using a landline phone with some sort of sophisticated blocker on it. It was an attachment to the cradle of the phone, roughly the size of a man's wallet that caused any attempt at bugging or eavesdropping to instantly disconnect. Beyond that, Everson had also explained to him that as a secondary measure of defense, there was a special insulation between the barn floor and the ceiling of this office that was partially concrete, making it almost impossible for anyone with radar or high-tech listening devices to home in on any activity going on below the barn.

It took another twenty minutes, but Frederickson eventually came on the line. He wasted no time getting to the point, and he sounded instantly irritated.

"Everson, stop calling me so casually," he barked. "I have to keep using this dummy phone and every time I use it, I get more and more paranoid. If you think I—,"

"With all due respect," Everson said. "It's extremely necessary this time."

"How so? And make it quick. I might have three minutes before anyone notices I'm gone. I'm currently standing in a vestibule in the J. Edgar Hoover Building."

"First," Everson said, "you should know that Roger Commer is with me, and AD Moreno is also on the line. Things have gotten infinitely worse. Dean is dead. Men I strongly believe were hired by Nightwatch insiders killed him. They spoofed a text from Dean's phone, causing Mr. Commer to drive to the house where he was being held and tortured, and Mr. Commer was nearly killed as well."

"Jesus," Moreno said.

"Are you one hundred percent certain they were affiliated with Nightwatch?" Frederickson asked.

"Fairly certain. If I provide the address where the bodies are being moved, could one of you send someone out to profile them?"

"I'll send a team over, sure," Moreno said.

"Did *you* kill them, Everson?" Frederickson asked.

"No."

"Then who? Commer?"

"No, sir. It was...it was Amber."

"Oh for fuck's sake!" Frederickson said.

"Sir, we're running out of options. What was I *supposed* to do?"

Frederickson's sigh was so loud that Roger could feel the slight vibration of it through the table. "I suppose you're right. And based on this morning's meeting, it may get worse. Vice President Warren asked about the rumors of Nightwatch movement, and President Seibert said the matter had been handled and was no longer worth investigating. When I asked for his source and evidence, he cut me off and moved on to other things. He used the hurricane on the Virginia coast as a distraction from it and...."

"Sir?" Roger said.

"I have to go." He blurted it and with no explanation. His line went dead, leaving Roger and Everson to stare at one another.

"You still there, Moreno?" Everson asked.

"Yeah, I'm here. Let me know where your cleanup crew has secured the bodies. I assume Dean's will be there as well?"

"Yeah...."

Everson cradled his head in his hand as he looked to the table, struggling with emotion.

"And hey, Roger?" Moreno said.

"Sir?"

"I'm here for whatever you need. I don't know if I can get much pushed through, but I can try. Right now, I'm working with a small team that's coordinating with a few folks on the ground over in Bagram, but we can't put much manpower behind it without attracting unnecessary attention."

"I appreciate it."

"Okay, guys. We'll wrap for now. Moreno, I'll send you the address where the bodies are being taken. Do you think you can maybe get back on this same line in about two hours or so, just to—"

There was a small clicking noise, and then Frederickson's voice was on the line again. "Guys? Are all of you still there?"

"Yeah," Moreno said.

"Still here," Everson confirmed. "Is everything okay?"

"No. No, it's not. Vice President Warren is currently being rushed to the hospital. Some details are murky right now, but everyone is guessing it's a heart attack."

"But he's still alive?" Roger asked.

"That's what I hear. But...shit...the timing is highly suspect. I...I shouldn't tell you this, but I think it has to be said considering Warren's current state. This morning after the meeting at the White House, I met with Vice President Warren and two others whom I will not name at this point. We started putting a plan in motion to unseat the President."

"Unseat or *eliminate?*" Everson asked.

"Ultimately? Eliminate. A series of staged events would take place that would keep agencies like the FBI and CIA in something of a mad scramble. And during that time, actions would be taken to remove the President. Along the way, over several weeks, they would strategically place breadcrumbs in the form of falsified emails, financial records, and so on, pointing to the culprits coming from somewhere in Nightwatch territory. Two birds with one stone."

There was a moment of stunned silence around the table as Roger, Everson, and Moreno let this sink in. The idea of getting Seibert out of the picture had become more than just talk and speculation; the Vice President and some allies had actively started putting a plan together. And now, on the same day those discussions had begun, Vice President Warren was being rushed to the hospital. A man of sixty-eight years and in decent health, it seemed highly suspect.

"Hold on," Roger said, trying to find the thread of the plan in the midst of his shock. "You said over the course of several weeks?"

"Yeah. We figure maybe about two months."

"Mr. Secretary ...we have five days. According to the men who killed Dean and nearly killed me, the attack on Bagram is supposed to take place in five days. And following that, there may be one on a base here, on American soil."

"Maybe they were just screwing with you, tying to flex their muscles."

"Doubtful, sir. From the very start, Dean was saying we didn't have very long."

"Gentlemen, this is going to get bad," Frederickson said. "All of you need to destroy your phones and start using new burners. Especially you, Mr. Commer. Adding in today, this has been the third attempt on your life in the past three days."

Roger knew this, of course, but it felt so much heavier hearing someone else speak the fact out loud.

"I need to go...for good this time," Frederickson said. "Moreno, seeing as how you're the least likely to be followed or suspected, I'll send you updates on the Vice President as I get them."

"Got it."

Frederickson left the line for the second time, leaving the other three men in shocked silence.

"You still there, Hector?" Roger asked.

"Yeah. I'm here. And honestly...look, I don't know what I can do. I'm happy to help however we can, but barring some unseen Hand of God moment, I'm clueless."

"Wait, hold on," Roger said. "Hand of God…Frederickson said that Seibert focused on Hurricane Louise when he changed the subject at the meeting this morning, right?"

"Yeah," Everson said. "Yeah, he did."

"I wonder if we could somehow use that to our advantage. I mean, at some point, he's likely to head out to the coast to make an appearance, right?"

"I'd assume so," Everson said. "But how would that help us?"

Roger had an answer, but wasn't sure if he wanted to state it so plainly in front of Everson and Moreno. If Seibert went out to the coast, he'd be away from the usual protections and security of the White House. Sure, there would be Secret Service there, but he'd be much more vulnerable than normal. He tucked this information away and focused on the conversation.

"So if Vice President Warren dies in the hospital," he said, "the president will likely nominate Pelingra to fill the VP seat."

"What are your thoughts on him?" Everson asked, looking at Roger.

Roger thought of what he knew about Speaker of the House James Pelingra. He was loyal to a fault when it came to Seibert, and usually one of the more vocal members of Seibert's circle when the President needed defending. But it was no secret that they didn't exactly see eye-to-eye on everything.

"He's a wild card. I think if we go to him with our concerns, there's a very good chance he'd stonewall us. Hell, he already knows my concerns, come to think of it. He was in the last briefing I sat in on. He didn't seem all that alarmed."

"So Warren would be a better pick if we can get Seibert removed?" Moreno asked on the phone.

"Yeah, as far as I can tell. But again…none of this matters. We have five days. And that's no time to put together some huge political strategy. No conspiracies, no blackmail. That shit takes time."

"So where does that leave us?" Moreno asked.

"We all know the answer to that," Everson said. And God, Roger was thrilled that someone else answered the question instead of him.

"Yeah, I guess we do," Moreno agreed.

"So what we have to ask ourselves," Roger said, his voice tight and worried, "is if the lives of a few thousand people in a terrorist attack on an American base overseas is worth more than the life of the President and the chaos his death would cause."

"This is...Jesus, we don't have the authority to make that call," Everson said.

"That means...what exactly?" Moreno asked.

Looking anxiously at Roger and with deep concern in his eyes, Everson said: "It means we have to hope for a miracle, that President Seibert will stop being stubborn about this."

Again, the line went quiet because all three men knew it was not going to happen. And with that knowledge, Roger felt completely helpless.

36

About halfway back to DC, Roger wondered again about medical treatment for his wrist and ribs but decided he couldn't afford the delay. He needed to get back to his office. Half the afternoon was gone. As he parked in the garage at the Pentagon and made his way to his office, he had a very hard time accepting the fact that he'd almost been killed—that his morning essentially started with a life or death situation, and he was now heading to work as if it were any other day.

It made him wonder what, exactly, might happen if the story of what occurred at Dean's went public. What would happen if the CIA report fell into the wrong hands...if Moreno handed it off to a third party before filing it away through proper channels? He made a mental note to check in with Moreno that evening to see if they'd come up with any positive IDs on the three dead men from Dean's house.

For now, as he sat down behind his laptop with his ribs still aching and his wrist swollen, Roger's main concern was getting an accurate picture of Vice President Warren's condition...and how it had happened in the first place. He didn't want to just *assume* Seibert had something to do with it, but that's where his mind tried to take him.

And you'd better get that in check, he warned himself. *You're going to get overly paranoid, jump to some very dangerous assumptions, and end up getting into more trouble than you can handle.*

But his injuries suggested that maybe he was already at that point.

Roger checked his email, certain that there would be a few internal messages regarding Vice President Warren. But there was one from the Press Secretary's office that caught his eye. It gave a play-by-play of the details as everyone at the White House understood it. Vice President Warren had been on his way to a call with the Canadian Prime Minister when, according to a White House aide, he made an emergency run to the restroom. When he came back out, he looked pale and shaken according to at least two staffers who saw him. He then spoke briefly with a White House intern and started toward the conference room where he was to make the call. However, just before he reached the office, he stumbled and nearly fell to the floor. White House security assisted him to the nearest available office and, fearing a heart attack based on the symptoms, he was rushed to the hospital. For now, he was in stable condition and there appeared to be no signs of secondary concerns.

It was a very detailed retelling of events, but Roger learned nothing he wanted to know. The last of the three emails to come in arrived just eleven minutes ago. It was an update on the Vice President's condition. It was confirmed that he'd had a heart attack, though it had been a minor one. He'd be kept overnight for observation but should be released tomorrow. The email, again coming from the office of the Press Secretary, stated it may be as much as a week before he would return to his duties.

That, Roger supposed, was good. If Seibert somehow had a hand in whatever happened to Warren, it hadn't been very effective. Roger desperately wanted to shake the idea that the President of the United States may have done something like this to his VP. But the timing *did* seem odd...especially if the attack on Bagram was indeed going to take place in five days.

"Yeah, but what if..." Roger muttered to himself as he sat behind his desk, feeling aimless and at his wit's end.

What if?

He decided in that moment to allow himself to assume the worst for just a few minutes. Assuming that Seibert had attempted to get Warren out of the picture presented an entirely new lens to view this mess through. Why *would* Seibert want Warren out of the way? Sure, Warren had been vocal in private settings about his displeasure with the relationships Seibert was fostering overseas—particularly when it came to the rumored threats of Nightwatch movement. But to make an attempt on the man's life…that seemed a bit much.

Unless Warren had come across proof of his own. Unless Warren had been pestering the President behind closed doors to take this Nightwatch threat more seriously.

Again, Roger knew it was a stretch, but it made him wonder what other connections the Vice President might have had that Roger didn't know about. Did Warren have his own version of Everson…someone who worked in the shadows with people like Dean or even Amber?

Or had Seibert simply discovered that Warren had been very interested in all that Roger had to say? Had Seibert found out that Warren had been doing his best to be involved in all of the secretive meetings that Roger had been holding in regard to Nightwatch?

Maybe it was Frederickson. Maybe he's slipped up and said something near Seibert. Or maybe the entire fucking office was simply bugged, and Seibert was aware of everything that had been said in the last few days.

This idea seemed a bit far-fetched, but it wasn't one he was willing to dismiss. Curious, he grabbed a pen from the small cup on the side of his desk, then a scrap of paper from a drawer. He wrote a brief message on it and then exited his office. He took a right out of his door and stepped into the concave, square space by his office that served as May's office. She looked up at him and when she opened her mouth to speak, Roger placed a single finger in front of his lips to shush her.

He handed the note to her and watched as she read it. The message read: *Has anyone claiming to be from the WH or DoD been by to do anything in my office?*

May seemed alarmed at the question; her eyes wide as she looked up at him. She shook her head and gave him a puzzled look.

"Just checking," he said quietly. And then, still keeping his voice low, he asked: "No visitors of any kind?"

"None."

He knew this didn't necessarily mean his office wasn't somehow bugged. With the technological advances in spy equipment and surveillance, there were a multitude of ways to get it done remotely. Or a clandestine team could've done the work after hours.

"Thanks," he said. "If you see or hear anyone th—"

The sound of footsteps from the end of the cavernous hall interrupted him. He looked to the right and saw a woman walking toward them. She was the only other person in the hallway—which wasn't surprising, as this sub-floor didn't get much traffic—and she walked with scary confidence.

When Roger saw her face and understood who it was, he understood the confidence. It was Amber.

She didn't smile or nod as she approached them. Her eyes were just as stone-cold serious as when he'd seen her earlier in the day.

"We need to talk in private," she said. She stood very close to Roger, and her voice was low, nearly a whisper. "Not your office, if possible."

Something about her demeanor instantly placed her in total control of the situation. He was eager to please, nodding and waving to her to follow him as he left May's desk. He skipped his office and led Amber farther down the hallway to the same conference room he'd used yesterday for his call with Frederickson and Everson.

Through it all, Amber never said a word. She followed behind him, quiet and measured. It made him feel very uncomfortable and he couldn't help but wonder if her visit was going to help or make things even worse.

37

For a period of about five seconds, the conference room was dead silent once he closed the door behind them. He was always surprised just how isolated and cold the room seemed when the door was closed. The dark walls, black floor, and sleek table under the dim lights were almost intimidating. But once Amber started talking, none of that seemed to bother her.

"You're sure this room is secure?" she asked.

"I think so. Tests showed that even a parabolic dish from just down the hallway can't penetrate the walls. It's the same for just about every office down here on the sub-floors."

"Good."

"Do you mind me asking how you got in?"

She took a key card out of her pocket. It was a generic one, the sort that security sometimes used to get in and out of the Pentagon. There was only a string of numbers and a barcode, all without a picture. Which would obviously work well for Amber.

"I picked this up not long ago. I'd rather not say how."

"That's perfectly fine. Now...what can I do for you?"

"I've reconsidered my thoughts about what we discussed earlier," she said.

"What thoughts?"

"If it came down to it and there were no other options, I'd take the job."

Even in a room he'd assured her was safe, he noticed that she was still being a bit vague, and her voice remained in that low, raspy whisper. But he knew what she meant.

"Why?" I asked. "What made you change your mind?"

"I heard about the Veep." She hadn't sat down yet, choosing instead to slowly pace along the front wall of the room. "The timing is odd, that's all. And between you and me and these hopefully secure walls, I may have managed to get a look at the patient's latest medical records."

"How?" Roger asked, flabbergasted and a bit scared.

Amber shrugged nonchalantly. "Because I'm good at my job. Anyway...he had a check-up just a bit over three weeks ago. He's perfectly healthy for a sixty-three-year-old man. The only major concern was what looked to be a sizable kidney stone forming but the notes indicated it wasn't anything to be concerned about yet. There was *nothing* to indicate he was in danger of a cardiac episode."

"I know where you're headed with this because I've considered it too. But how would someone *cause* a heart attack?"

"Have you ever heard of succinylcholine?"

"Heard of it, yes. But I'm not sure what it does."

"It's a subtle poison, in liquid form. About five or six years ago, a Soviet spy was detained for killing off an American diplomat with it. He'd placed the succinylcholine into a pen—the sort that you have to click the top down to get the point to come out. He'd rigged the clicker with a hidden fine-point needle. Just like that, the succinylcholine entered the diplomat's bloodstream. And what succinylcholine does is quickly paralyze most of the muscles in your body...except the heart. And that means the heart starts working triple-time to make up for the rest of the body. If Warren were in worse shape, and this *was* what happened, it would have killed him. Of course, this is all just speculation. Just to prove a point that it *could* be done. And if there's even a chance that our man had something to do with anything like that just because his number two disagrees with him about things going on, he's too dangerous to remain in charge."

She'd obviously put some very deep thought into this. Which made Roger feel a bit more at ease. It meant he wasn't the only one thinking devious, paranoid thoughts.

"Did anyone actually *ask* if you'd do it?"

"No," she said at once. "But I know there has been talk about it. Removing him politically—even if it's done in a cut-throat way—would take weeks or months. And we don't have that."

"Well, I suppose you know that even if I was one hundred percent convinced that…that *this* is the way to go, I don't really have the approval to give the order. Shit…no one does."

"I'm not looking for an order. I came to you because I know you're the driving force behind trying to get something done about it. Everson is as well, but his hands are ultimately tied by CIA red tape and regulations. And I thought you should know that if no other option is found in the next few days…I may be available."

Roger nodded, finding it suddenly very hard to believe that they were actually having this conversation. "Okay," he said. His palms were sweating, and his stomach felt like it was doing barrel rolls. "And what would you need from me?"

"I don't know if it would be you or someone else, but I'd need seven million dollars plus expenses for moving out of the country…to an undisclosed location where I would remain for the rest of my life."

"And you could just pull up stakes and move, just like that?"

"I could. It's one of the many benefits of working in the shadows of this system we're currently trying to fix." She shrugged again, making Roger wonder if it was sort of a nervous habit for her. "Anyway, think it over and get back to me. I understand you'd have to look into my demands to see if it's even possible, but I would of course, prefer you not tell anyone we had this talk."

Roger wasn't sure if this would be possible. If he was seriously going to look into those details, he'd have to tell *someone* at some point. But that was a concern for another time, as Amber was already heading for the door.

"I assume you'll get back in touch with me?" he asked, still feeling dizzy from the conversation—from Amber's sudden appearance to the speedy nature of the conversation itself.

She offered a thin smile and said, "Yeah. I'll be in touch."

And just like that, she was gone. Roger remained in the conference room for a while longer, sitting at the empty table and feeling sick to his stomach. Things had escalated swiftly over the last few days but now, with Amber's visit, he truly felt the weight of the decision that needed to be made pressing down on him like a huge, invisible fist.

38

He felt almost guilty when he left the office at 6:30. But he knew that going home and being around Maggie would help to clear his mind. Sitting in his office and feeling trapped by the decision he needed to make would do nothing but stifle him. He could just as easily make the decision at home, where he at least felt more at ease.

As soon as he stepped through the back door and smelled Maggie's homemade tomato sauce on the stove, he knew he'd made the right decision.

Maggie was stirring a pot on the stove when he came in. Seeing her sent a flare of warmth through him. He supposed at some point he might tell her about the danger he'd faced today, about how he'd seen a man killed right in front of him...but not now. No, right now, he needed to unwind and try to feel normal if only for a fleeting second.

"It smells great in here," he said as he closed the door and walked to the stove.

"Good. I wasn't sure when you'd be in, so I thought I'd make those gnocchi you like...the kind you say tastes just as good reheated."

"Have I ever told you how amazing you are?" he asked, approaching her from behind and wrapping his arms around her waist.

"You have, on occasion," she said with a laugh. "But it never hurts to keep hearing it. Now back away. We can snuggle up all you want later. And, honestly, maybe without clothes if you have it in you."

"Yes, ma'am," he said dutifully. Though, really, he wasn't sure how his ribs would hold up to any physical activity, no matter how nice it might be. And, as he'd already decided, he wasn't ready to explain the events of his day to her just yet. He backed away and took a look around the kitchen. "Anything I can do to help?"

"Nope. We'll be eating in about ten minutes. You can get the dishes when we're done."

"Fair deal. I'll just go wash up, then."

He kissed her on the cheek and hurried down the hall to the bathroom. With the door closed behind him, he unbuttoned his shirt and slid it off. He looked at his left side in the mirror and saw that there were two bruises—one not so bad, but the other having already turned an angry shade of purple. Another deep bruise marred the back of his hand, and his wrist remained swollen.

"Damn," he muttered. There was no way to get around it; he was going to have to reveal at least some of the truth to Maggie over dinner. Especially if she planned to see him without clothes later on.

He buttoned his shirt back up and opened the medicine cabinet. He took out a bottle of ibuprofen and swallowed three and a handful of water from the sink. Then, trying his best to piece together how much he'd share with her, he headed back out to the kitchen. Just as he re-entered the room, Maggie's cellphone began to ring from the kitchen bar.

"Would you mind getting that?" Maggie asked him as she began adding the cooked gnocchi to her tomato sauce.

Roger walked over to the bar and saw that the call was coming from Thomas. He grabbed it right away, feeling incredibly guilty that he'd been so preoccupied with his own day that he'd almost forgotten about Thomas out on the coast after the hurricane.

"Hey, Thomas," he answered.

"Mom? You sound different," Thomas joked.

"I sound like this when I'm worried," Roger joked right back. "Your mom is finishing up dinner. Hold a sec...I'll put you on speaker mode." He placed the phone back on the counter, switched it to speaker mode, and said, "So how are things on your side of the state?"

"Messy. We're headed back to campus. We're nearly there, actually. But the amount of debris and wreckage in the road is sort of nuts. The college sent an email out about an hour or so ago and said all classes are canceled tomorrow. I don't think there was any damage, but they're concerned with traffic and safety measures, I guess."

"That's for the best," Maggie said. "What are you going to do with your day off?"

"Well, that's why I'm calling. I thought I might come in for a visit. Tomorrow's Friday, after all…so I figured I could make a long weekend of it."

"Oh, that would be wonderful!"

"Absolutely," Roger said. Though, as much as it pained him to think such a thing, it might be the absolute worst time for such a visit in terms of everything he was dealing with. He felt almost dizzy with the polarizing emotions—one side very happy at the idea of seeing his son, but the other wanting him to stay away until things were smoothed over.

"Great. I think I may drive in tonight, if that's okay."

"As long as you're not too tired," Roger said.

"Nope, I'll be fine. Is the security code the same as the last time I came home?"

"Yep, the same," Maggie said.

The mention of the security code made Roger think of the night Dean had showed up in his house, sitting right there at the kitchen table after easily getting past his security system.

"Awesome. Looks like I'll see you guys soon. Bye for now."

Roger could hear the excitement in his son's voice as he ended the call, looking forward to a long weekend at home. He wished he felt the same. And in a surge of anger that felt almost childish, he resented Seibert and the situation he was putting everyone in because of his refusal to move on the Nightwatch alerts.

"Roger?"

He blinked, his attention broken as Maggie called his name. She was moving dinner from the stove to the table, giving him a look of scrutiny.

"Yeah?"

"Are you okay?" she asked. "You're grimacing *and* you look deep in thought."

"Well…it was a day," he said. "I had to get rough with a suspect the CIA is dealing with."

"Rough?" she asked with concern. They sat down at the table together and her look of scrutiny never faltered. "How rough?"

Roger sighed and then proceeded to lie to his wife. Because of his job, it wasn't the first time he'd done it, and it certainly wouldn't be the last. He kept the details to a minimum. It was an easy enough task, and because Maggie was used to not being able to get full stories out of him because of clearance issues, she didn't ask questions.

As usual, Roger hated himself for it. Just once, he'd like to tell her what he was dealing with. Not only out of respect for her, but to unburden himself of the problems and decisions he could never discuss with anyone outside of a select few in Washington.

Instead, Maggie nodded through his fabrication, asking questions only when it pertained to his health. He explained the pain in his ribs away stating that the assailant had landed a knee and that he may have also tweaked his wrist when catching himself on the floor.

"If that pain lingers over the weekend, I want you to see a doctor on Monday."

"I can agree to that," Roger said. "But I think it's fine."

They left it at that, something that came as a bit of a skill from having been married for twenty-three years, twenty of which had been spent with Roger in secretive roles where he wasn't allowed to reveal certain information. They shifted the conversation to Thomas' visit, a topic that cheered Maggie considerably.

When they were done with their dinner, Roger did as he'd been asked and cleaned the dishes while Maggie answered a few final emails for work. As he washed and rinsed, his belly full from a good meal, his mind instantly wandered back to the situation with Seibert and Nightwatch. He wondered what information Moreno was gathering together about the dead men from Dean's house. He wondered how confident Amber truly was in her ability to take Seibert out if it came down to it.

Amber was the wild card. She was the solution he'd been looking for but now that the deadly solution was in his hands, he wasn't sure he could greenlight it. The heavy fact of the matter was that he really needed to speak to Frederickson about it. He needed a more rounded perspective on it, perhaps from someone who hadn't seen Amber in action today, a perspective that—

A well-rounded perspective, he thought. He lingered on that word: *perspective.* It made him think of the media, of journalists and news outlets. And just like that, another idea occurred to him.

Dean was gone. But where were the emails he'd been holding on to that contained names and dates? Where was the evidence of the entire scenario? Surely Everson would know. And if they could get those materials and send them to the press, it would make headline news right away—especially given a political climate in which roughly three quarters of the American population were skeptical about the President's foreign policies. And once it hit the media, Seibert would be forced to address it. Sure, he'd tell lies and dance around it, but he'd at least feel monumental pressure...not just the nuisance of a few government employees hounding him about it.

It was a tempting idea, and he mulled it over until he was done with the very last dish. But the longer he thought about it, the more he realized how reckless of an idea it really was. It wouldn't take much of an investigation to figure out where it came from, especially because he had told Seibert in the presence of several others than Dean had the emails.

But he couldn't help but wonder...would the news going live put a scare into the enemy? If Nightwatch leaders and whatever power mongers were driving them saw the news break around the world, would it change their plans?

Possibly...or it could provoke them into attacking, using the news as kindling. They could point to it as provocation for an attack, trying to shift the blame to the US. And in that circumstance, Seibert would get off free.

It was just another example of how there were no clear-cut solutions. And as extreme as assassination seemed, it looked to be the only option.

I could do it myself.

The thought landed in his head like a bomb. He stood at the kitchen sink, reeling from it. Today had changed so much for him—not just the battle at Dean's house but the speculation that Seibert or someone hired by Seibert may have made a very clever attempt on the Vice President's life. If Roger could know for absolutely certain that this was the case, maybe assassination wouldn't seem so extreme. Hell, it would almost seem justified. But there was no way he was going to be able to find out for sure. Even if a private investigation could be conducted, they'd not get the evidence in time.

So, then...maybe the doctor's records. Amber had been able to get a glimpse at Warren's medical history. Could she maybe be able to get information as it was fed into the database? Would there perhaps be traces of a drug in his system, as she'd suggested? If, of course, Seibert had been behind it.

It was all too much. And at the end of it all was the looming decision he needed to make. Should he give Amber the go-ahead? And if so, where would he get the funds? Surely Frederickson would be able to come up with it from somewhere. Government funds went mysteriously missing all of the time, after all.

With a deep and heavy sigh, he pushed himself away from the sink. He found Maggie in the living room, watching the evening news. It was on the local news now, about a bakery raising money for cancer research. But as Roger sat down beside her and gently took her hand in his, he couldn't help but imagine what might happen if the news headlines on the TV screen called out the President's refusal to take action against Nightwatch? How would it alter the shape of political power in Washington...and how might it impact the world?

39

I could do it myself.

The thought remained in his head, a rotten seed taking root after it had been accidentally planted. It blared in his mind throughout the night, and as it gnawed away at him, Roger knew he wouldn't be able to sleep. When he was certain Maggie was asleep, he slowly got out of bed. He glanced at the bedside clock as he left the room and saw that it was 12:47.

He walked downstairs, put on a kettle for tea, and stood in the darkness as he waited for the water to boil. The idea of taking Seibert out himself was appealing in a dark sort of way because he could think of several methods to get it done. The issue he kept stumbling over was a selfish one: there was no way to do it and not get caught. The easiest ways to get to him would be via the White House...and even if Seibert wasn't pissed at him and growing more and more suspicious, attacking the President *in the White House* was a suicide mission.

But if I could get my hands on his schedule...

The kettle whistled, and he poured water into his mug. The tea steeped as he walked quietly into his office. Thoughts of assassination and the ramifications of it followed him down the darkened hall like phantoms.

The difficult part for right now was that he needed to make some phone calls, but he'd already ditched his previous burner at Frederickson's suggestion and hadn't picked up another one yet. He wasn't about to risk making these difficult calls on his personal cell or his landline. He'd just have to wait until tomorrow, when he could get another burner.

In other words, he could do all the thinking he wanted tonight, but he couldn't risk making any of the calls he wanted to make—calls to Frederickson and Everson. Maybe to Moreno, to see of anything damning and definitive had been pulled on the three dead men yet.

The scariest part of all was that the idea of taking matters into his own hands continued to fester. It appalled him, but it was also starting to look like the simplest approach. He'd have full control over it. He'd be the only one involved, the only one to know. And really, if he focused on *only* that solution, he started to become more and more certain that he could maybe even do it and get away with it. It would all come down to the timing and location, to the—

A stifled noise broke his concentration. It was coming from the back of the house, by the kitchen. The back door. He instantly got to his feet and hurried over to the bookshelf on the right side of the office. He reached behind his plaque for Outstanding Service to the Country, presented to him by the FBI nearly twenty years ago, and grabbed the Beretta M9 he kept hidden there. He'd only ever used it for target practice, but his Sig Sauer was upstairs.

However, as soon as he removed it from its place on the shelf, Roger heard the familiar and almost warm electronic tone of the security alarm being reset to secure.

Thomas, he thought, remembering that his son had told them he'd come in as quietly as he could in the late hours. *You're so damned paranoid and all-consumed with this that you nearly went gunning for Thomas. Calm the hell down.*

With the pressure currently on his shoulders, that was much easier said than done. But he *was* able to momentarily put it to the side as he made his way out into the hallway to greet his son for the first time in about a month.

Thomas stepped into the hallway from the kitchen, a single backpack slung over his shoulders. He looked much more grown than he actually was in the poorly lit hallway. Roger's sudden presence in the hall startled him a bit; he gasped and took a shaken step back, quickly grinning as he understood the situation.

"You scared the crap out of me there for a second, Pops," Thomas said.

"Sorry."

"You didn't wait up for me, did you?"

"Nah," Roger said. "Not on purpose, anyway. I couldn't sleep."

"Work stuff?"

"Yeah. Is it that obvious?"

"That's the only reason you ever gave for not being able to sleep."

"Well, don't let me keep *you*," Roger said. "Your bedroom is all set up and ready."

"Thanks, but I might get a quick bite to eat before I get to bed."

Roger almost questioned this but then recalled his own college days. So what that it was 1:00 in the morning? The stomach of a college student without any real semblance of a sleep schedule was impossible to predict.

"Help yourself," Roger said.

"Oh, and do you or Mom happen to have an extra phone charger? We left the coast in such a hurry, I lost mine somewhere along the way."

"There's an extra one in the drawer to the console table in the living room." And as he answered his son's question, an idea came to him. It felt risky at first and made him feel slightly ashamed of himself, but he thought it might just serve as a solution to a lot of his problems. "Hey, Thomas...let me borrow your phone, would you? Just for like ten minutes?"

"Um, sure..." he said, digging it out of his pocket. He smirked a bit as he handed it over. "This isn't like when I was in high school and you're checking my texts and search history, right? Because I'm in college now, Dad...and I can guarantee that you'll see some questionable things."

"No, nothing like that. I just need to make some calls that...well, that might not be okay to make from home."

"Got it," Thomas said dutifully. "Say no more."

Roger figured this was the response he'd get. Thomas had always found the secretive aspects of his father's job fascinating. He'd always respected the fact that his dad couldn't share certain things about his work and had often gloated about the vast secrets of Roger's work to his friends.

"I'll give it right back," Roger said, turning back toward his office.

"Nothing's gonna blow back on me if someone traces that number, right?"

"Nope, scout's honor."

Again, as he entered his office, he felt like a miserable father. He should be out there with Thomas, catching up with him and asking him questions about the hurricane, and how classes were going. Instead, work was coming first...the same as it had been through most of Thomas's school years. Of course, this particular situation came down to more than just simple work. There was a great deal on the line here—namely the lives of thousands of people operating in and near Bagram and maybe that many on or near a base in America too.

He took his son's phone to his desk and then pulled up Frederickson's information on his own. With a look back to where he kept his gun hidden on the bookshelf, he typed Frederickson's number into Thomas's phone.

40

When Frederickson answered, the clarity of his voice made it apparent that he hadn't been sleeping, either. Honestly, Roger was surprised he'd answered a call from a number that wasn't stored in his phone.

"Who's this?" was how he answered. His voice was clear but quiet, tinged with a bit of urgency.

"It's Roger. Is it safe for you to talk at the moment?"

"As safe as it ever is, I suppose. But let me call you back at this number. Give me a few seconds."

Without waiting for a goodbye, Frederickson hung up. Roger assumed he was going to get a dummy phone. Though, honestly, if their houses were being bugged, all of this was a waste of time anyway. The idea of his house being bugged was disconcerting, but not out of the question. After all, *someone* had known Dean had been working with him, which he assumed meant there was a chance someone had known Dean paid a visit to his kitchen. Maybe he'd been under some sort of secret surveillance for longer than he suspected.

Or maybe he was just continuing to be paranoid.

Less than thirty seconds passed before Thomas's phone rang. Roger answered it right away. "Are you all good on your end?"

"Should be. It's sort of ridiculous that we're having to go to these lengths, huh?"

"Better safe than sorry, I suppose. Would you be more comfortable speaking off-line?"

"I really would. Can you do that at this hour?"

"I can." Again, he felt resentment toward the entire situation because his son was currently sitting in the kitchen. He'd also have to wake Maggie to let her know. And *that* was going to cause her to worry...especially after the paper-thin account he'd given her about how he'd gotten the bruises along his side.

"Candlers? At 3:00?"

Roger checked his watch. It was currently 1:12. "I can do that. And I'm reaching out to someone else as well. Maybe two others. You can guess who." He hoped so, anyway. Just out of precaution, he wasn't going to call out the names of Everson or Moreno.

"Yeah, I follow. I'll see you then."

They ended the call, and Roger wasted no time and called up Everson. With Everson, he wasn't quite as concerned about his phone potentially being bugged. Everson was a pro when it came to the knowledge of staying safe; Roger's glimpse of Everson's farm headquarters had served as even more proof of this.

Everson answered on the third ring, and in a surprising fashion. "Hey, Roger."

"How'd you know it was m—"

"Well, given our current predicament, I'm taking every precaution imaginable. I've got a geo-locator on this phone, linked up to a laptop. A call comes in, and I can detect where it's coming from to within a mile in just a matter of seconds."

"So we're safe to talk openly right now?"

"On this line, sure. But if you suspect your house might me bugged...I don't know. Probably not."

"Okay. I need to know if you can get your hands on the comings and goings of certain individuals."

"We are talking a big fish, here?"

"Yes. A great white, if you will."

"I don't know. The best means for that came and went today." Roger wasn't sure he meant Dean or Amber. It depended on Everson's definition of came and went. "I can do my very best, though."

"Any chance you could meet up later? Around 3:00?"

"No can do. I'm working on something over here, trying to figure some things out."

"So if you can find the information for me...?" He explained what he needed.

"I'll email it to you. Or, rather, I'll email you a link to a secure server. Make sure you turn your phone's notifications on, though. As soon as that link hits your inbox, an expiration countdown will start. You'll have about five minutes to grab it before the file will delete itself. Just a security precaution. No matter what you open the mail on, no one will be able to track it or ever prove you received it."

"I appreciate it."

"Are you okay, man? You sound...I don't know. Off."

"Yeah, just starting to buckle under the pressure. Our phantom friend visited me not long after you and I met. They offered to fill the role, and I...I'm not so sure."

God, it was difficult to talk in code. But Everson was a master at this sort of thing. Roger was sure the man knew what he meant: *Amber came to visit me today and said she'd be willing to take Seibert out if necessary.*

"Ah, I see." And he could hear the heaviness in his voice. He was also beginning to understand that the solutions we'd only been hinting about for the last two days were all of a sudden becoming very real. "Well, let me see what I can do about your request. If you don't get anything by sunrise, the answer is no."

"Thanks again."

With that, they ended the call. Roger thought things over, wondering if he had unknowingly set something in motion that could not be reversed. While he still felt confident that he would be able to do what was necessary, there was also a more rational part of him that wondered if literally killing Seibert to get him out of office and sabotage the plans of a terrorist organization was worth it. At the end of the day, he knew there were thousands of lives on the line.

And if Seibert wasn't going to make a move to keep those people safe, then yes...maybe taking him out was the most thorough solution to the problem.

He got to his feet and left the office, walking back down the hall to find Thomas sitting at the kitchen table. He was eating some of Maggie's leftover chicken salad with crackers. Roger sat down on the other side of the table and handed his phone back over. "Thanks."

"Sure thing. Are you okay? Looks like something's bothering you."

"Work stuff. And it's...well, it's a pressing matter. I hate to do it as soon as you get in, but I need to leave."

"Like...*now?*"

"Yeah."

"At this hour...man. Is it dangerous?"

Roger shrugged. "Could be. But it's being done at this hour *because* it's hopefully as safe as possible."

"Well, be careful." And then, because Thomas was just like his father and couldn't stand trying to wade through tension without offering up some humor, he added: "I came in for a long weekend to hang out with you guys. It would be a major drag to have to start planning a funeral instead."

"Ouch." But he had to admit...it *was* pretty funny. "I think I'll be okay. I love you, kid."

"Love you too."

"Now I just need to tell your mom."

"You're gonna wake her up and tell her you're leaving at one thirty in the morning?"

"I'm actually not leaving for another half an hour."

"Still...waking Mom up at this hour. Yikes. Looks like I'll be helping to plan a funeral no matter what."

***

"Mags, wake up."

Roger was sitting on the edge of their bed. He'd already gotten dressed and had his government-issued Sig Sauer once again in its holster. His ribs and wrist were aching, but they were dwarfed by the growing anxiousness that continued to bloom in his stomach.

Maggie groaned slightly and rolled over. When she opened her eyes, she was clearly still sleepy. But then she saw that he was in his suit, and her eyes opened wide. Alarm settled into her gaze as she quickly sat up.

"What is it? What's wrong?"

"Nothing, really. But I've just gotten off of the phone with the Secretary of Defense. I need to go to an emergency meeting in DC."

"Now?" She became even more awake at this and was growing scared.

"Yes. It's just a precautionary measure. No threat of national security or anything like that."

"Then why the urgency?"

"Sweetie, you know I can't tell you." The reply came far too easy, and he wondered how often Maggie secretly felt dishonored or dismissed when it was obvious he was keeping the truth from her.

"Fine," she said, nearly hissing the word. "Will you be back home, or are you just going straight to the office?"

Having no idea how the remainder of the night or the morning would go, he answered the safest way. "Probably to the office. But I'll call or text to let you know. By the way, Thomas is home."

"Good." The mention of Thomas being under their roof seemed to curb her frustration. "He's in his room?"

"Yeah, as of about ten minutes ago."

Maggie reached out and took his uninjured hand. "I'm used to being left in the dark about a lot of what you do, Roger. But, please...be careful. And text me just as soon as you can."

"I will. You have my word."

As he leaned it to kiss her on the forehead, he realized what her comment had meant to reveal. *Be careful.* He was pretty sure she saw right through the lie about the meeting. Maybe he was getting worse at covering his tracks as he got older.

"Love you," she said as she settled her head back down on her pillow.

"And I love you too."

He walked to the door and glanced back at her shape in the bed, her face toward him and her eyes closing. There hadn't been many moments in his career where he'd feared he may not return home, but the feeling descended heavily upon him as he looked at her. And when he finally managed to walk away, it took far too much effort. On his way down the hall, he looked at Thomas's bedroom door. It was closed, and all was quiet inside.

He stood there for only a moment, breathing in the absolute silence of his house—his peaceful home. And he vowed to himself that no matter what happened—no matter what decisions he was forced to make in the coming hours—that he'd find a way to come back… whatever it took.

41

The irony of meeting in secret under the cover of night was that it was to lessen the chances of being seen…but as Roger got out of his car and made his way across the shadow-strewn park, he felt more exposed than ever. The duck pond was somewhere in the darkness ahead of him and, hopefully, Frederickson.

Roger did his best not to think about the recent attempts on his life as he walked through the darkness. There was no way he could know if there were other people tracking him, no way to know how much Seibert already knew about what he was up to. So focusing on such things would only make him that much more paranoid.

Besides, the park was still and quiet. And within a few more seconds, the murky shape of the antique bench featuring the little engraving for Derrik Candler came into view. Frederickson was sitting there, hunched up a bit as if attempting to remain hidden. Hearing Roger approach, Frederickson turned in his direction.

"We clear?" Roger asked as he came to the bench.

"As far as I can tell, yeah. But let's make it quick, okay? I did recon, but a drone with IR and a parabolic mic would capture all of this. What's going on?"

"I got a visit from Amber this evening."

"What? At your house?"

"No. I was still at the office. She...she said she changed her mind. She said based on what she suspects about Vice President Warren's condition, she could be convinced to carry out the hit."

He felt childish, but he looked around wildly as he said the last word, sure that it was some sort of magic-triggered word that would bring armed men out of the shadows to take him out.

Frederickson looked shocked but only for a moment. "Convinced how?"

"Seven million dollars, plus help getting set up with a home out of the country."

"Well, that's less than I would have thought, actually. I could get that to her within a few hours. But think about the situation, Roger...think about the way the stage has been set. If he goes down and someone notices *when* those funds were taken, we will have to deal with an absolute avalanche of shit that will come right down on our heads. They wouldn't even have to do much digging to trace it back to us. Given the fuss that's been made the last few days about Nightwatch and foreign interests, you've pretty much put signs up along the way that would point them directly to you."

Roger felt almost embarrassed that he hadn't thought of this. He'd been so focused on getting the task done—and wresting with the reality of taking care of it himself—that he'd overlooked some of the more pressing details.

"So she'd be a dead end, anyway," Roger said. It wasn't until the words were out of his mouth that he understood just how much he'd been hoping it would work—that he'd been viewing Amber's involvement as an easy way out.

"Yeah, I'd say so."

"Any news on Warren?"

"The last thing I heard was that he was resting in stable condition. He'd had some sort of unexpected cardiac episode that came out of nowhere."

"No foul play?"

"None that I'm aware of."

Roger ruminated on this for a moment, wondering if he should tell him about the theory Amber had shared with him. But maybe that would stir a pot that was better left alone.

"Well, I feel foolish now," Roger said. "That's literally all I had. I was just wondering about the Amber approach, hoping there would be some way…"

"There are ways, sure. But it would only endanger you."

So, Roger thought as he stared out to the dark reflection of night along the duck pond, *it's another sign that maybe I should just do it myself.*

Just as he was about to say goodbye to Frederickson and take his leave, his phone dinged. It was a strange sound at first because he usually had his notifications silenced. But then he recalled the conversation he'd had with Everson about the time sensitive email that would be coming in.

"One second," he said as he quickly fished his phone out of his pocket. He opened his email app and saw the new email waiting for him, from an email address that was marked as private. He opened it up and saw only a link, just as Everson had indicated. Roger clicked the link and waited as he was connected to what he assumed was a private, secure server only accessible to Everson.

It took only seconds. The link took him to a page that had four viewable sheets. He tapped on the first one and saw that it was indeed President Seibert's itinerary for the day ahead. A very sophisticated bit of software seemed to have assembled it, revealing that the President's day began at 5:30 in the morning with a call to the US Embassy in London.

The second item listed was unexpected, though it did make sense. And as Roger read it, a simple yet dangerous idea formed in his head. His heart seemed to shudder as he read it again and started putting the pieces together.

"Roger?" Frederickson asked. "What is it? Are you okay?"

"Yeah." He nearly told Frederickson what he was looking at…and what the second entry on President Seibert's itinerary said. But he kept it to himself. If, at the end of all of this, things went terribly wrong, *not* knowing certain information might help to keep Frederickson in the clear.

"No," Frederickson said. "Something's up. What is it?"

Roger knew if he said anything at all, even anything that could be construed as a clue or hint, he could put not only himself but Frederickson at risk as well. So all he did was turn away and said, "I've got to go. You should get out of here too."

Roger turned and hurried back across the dark strip of grass and sidewalk that led back toward the parking lot. When he got into his car, he could just barely catch the shadow of Frederickson in the night, moving along toward his own car.

Roger took a moment to think. He'd closed out the email and the link, the sheets showing Seibert's itinerary now gone. Roger had seen all he needed to see. He thought briefly of Maggie and Thomas...hoping they'd understand. Hoping, honestly, that he could somehow get away with what he was about to do.

"I'm sorry, guys," he whispered in the car.

Then, with an ice-cold certainty of what needed to be done and how to do it, Roger started his car, backed out of the lot, and started driving toward the Pentagon.

42

When Roger pulled the car into the lower level of the Pentagon's underground parking garage, he thought of the trip ahead of him. He thought of the itinerary Everson had sent him, and of what President Seibert would be doing in the next two hours.

The parking garage wasn't a widely known location. It consisted of just one sub-level that was accessed via a highly restricted key card that only fifty or so people had access to—one of them being Roger. However, when he came to the security scanner that would read his card, he hesitated. Rather than scan his card and leave proof of what he'd been up to, he punched in the code for a manual override. When it asked him for his name, he typed in *Page, Dean.*

As the gate slid up on its runner, Roger said, "Good luck tracing that." With the gate raised up, he drove his current government loaner into the dark and secret spaces of the parking garage. He drove all the way to the end, parking the car a few spaces away from a perfectly lined up section of cars. There were eight in all, each one identical to the one beside it. They were very similar to the car Roger was currently parking, only newer models and equipped with bulletproof glass. Known as Last Resort cars—or LR cars— they were specifically set aside for agents and a select handful of local law enforcement who needed an untraceable car for any number of reasons.

Roger got out of his car and hurried over to the row of LR cars. He wondered what Seibert was doing at this very moment. His call to London wasn't for another forty-five minutes. He was probably just now waking up and thinking about the day ahead. Nightwatch and the attacks planned overseas were probably not even on his radar…not unless he was making calls in private to help make sure they'd be taking place. But even despite what he was about to do, Roger found it hard to think Seibert was actually *taking part* in the plans. Turning a blind eye was one thing…but having hands in the mess was something completely different.

Well, none of it is going to matter soon.

The second item on the President's itinerary had given Roger the opening he needed; it had more or less decided for him. Seibert was due to speak with the media at 8:00 in the morning, from a location in Virginia Beach that Hurricane Louise had hit particularly hard. He'd be away from Washington and the multiple layers of security the city provided. Sure, he'd be traveling with Secret Service personnel and there would be many local law enforcement on the scene, but Roger could easily avoid such obstacles.

So, you're really going to do this? He asked himself even as he approached one of the LR cars.

"Yeah," he whispered into the empty garage. "Yeah, I think so…"

At the trunk of the car, he tapped his security card against the emblem just above the hidden, concave trunk handle. There was an almost inaudible *beep* and then the trunk quietly popped open. A small interior light shone down on what at first appeared to be an empty and nondescript trunk. There was a small pouch in the rear right corner. Roger grabbed it up, unzipped it and grabbed the only item inside—the key to the car.

He then reached down into the trunk, finding a groove on the left edge of the floor. He located the small switch that was hidden there and pushed it down. The false floor of the trunk popped up and revealed the actual floor. There was the standard well for the spare tire, but it was pushed slightly to the left. The remaining space to the right revealed four different guns, all bolted down. One of them was a disassembled M24 rifle with a sniper scope. Each of the LR cars contained the same arsenal. Roger had used one of the cars when there had been an active shooter reported near the Lincoln Memorial not long after 9/11.

It was the sniper rifle he was most interested in. He was highly trained on the weapon, though he'd not fired one in a life-threatening situation in nearly fifteen years. However, he knew that if he could find the right vantage point, he could not only take out Seibert, but maybe even get away with no one on his tail. He wouldn't know until he got on the scene—which was exactly where he was headed.

Knowing that his weapon of choice was safely stored in the trunk, Roger used the same security card to unlock the driver's side door. There was a subtle *click* as the door unlocked, and Roger slid in behind the wheel. He wasted no time, though his nerves were now on fire. He was so jittery that his fingers were trembling when he once again typed in Dean's name to exit the garage.

Distantly, somewhere in the back of his mind, he knew his face was likely going to show up on the security feeds. And while that fact sent a spike of dread through his heart, it wasn't something he could focus on right now. If it came to that, and this whole thing played out to the end, he knew certain people within the White House and its more secret cabals might choose to overlook such evidence.

That was his hope, anyway.

Because as he pulled the car out onto the street and, at the end of the block, pointed it to the south, he knew there was no going back now. Virginia Beach was a little over three hours away. He could get there and do his reconnaissance before Seibert's security showed up in force, but it would be tight. There was no time for second thoughts or distractions.

So, with DC still quiet and mostly asleep all around him, Roger headed out of the nation's capital, fully prepared to do something so drastic that it could very well turn out to be one of the more controversial and impactful moments in American history.

43

Amber—as even she sometimes thought of herself after so long—sat on the couch in her small Georgetown apartment, drinking a cup of Moroccan green tea. She'd only managed two hours of sleep, between eleven and one, and she knew she'd be unable to get any more rest. There was just too much on her mind. But that was okay; she'd long ago grown accustomed to sleeping just a few hours here and there.

Roger Commer was on her mind, as was the President. She'd meant what she told Roger earlier—that for the right price and under the right circumstances, she would carry out the job. It had been a hard thing to accept—that she would pull the trigger on the President. But the more she thought about the situation and the people over at Bagram Air Force Base, the more certain she became that this was the only option.

If the President got away with this, what else would he attempt? She could recall how, at the beginning of his presidency, he'd come under fire for his aggressive policies overseas. But when those policies had garnered trust and worldwide attention from the media, it seemed President Seibert had known what he was doing. He'd made peace with men who had once been thought incapable of peace and diplomacy. Foreign relations seemed to be at a record level of cooperation in most places around the globe that tended to be rocky.

...if this attack from Nightwatch went down without a hitch, what others might come along? She wasn't sure if President Seibert was hiding anything, but she knew that inaction to stop such an attack was a welcome mat for other organizations to come in and do something similar.

After four in the morning, Amber paced around her living room. She would look out at the street and then to the living room rug. She wasn't sure why she was so stressed out. Roger had not called her, so she was off the hook. Apparently, he'd found another solution—maybe a better way to take care of the problem that didn't involve assassination.

So why the hell am I still fixating on it?

She didn't know. In fact, she'd never wrestled with a professional decision of this caliber before. She supposed it was because she knew there was a major issue out there. And her knowledge of it somehow held her slightly responsible for the outcome. Slowly, as if she still wasn't sure about what needed to be done, Amber walked into her bedroom and powered up one of her three laptops. This one was an older model, swiped from an old US Army reserve of tech equipment. She'd had it personalized several years ago by a Russian hacker living in the States. With the right passcodes and fake authorizations, she could get access to pretty much any system she wanted. So far, the only government system she'd not been able to crack into was the Jet Propulsion Laboratory. With a bit of patience, everything else was pretty much at her fingertips.

Amber sat on the edge of the bed and navigated to the nameless program the hacker had installed. She then selected from the list of forty-five databases and, with a bit more clicking, had every single detail about President Seibert's month—from a charity dinner four days ago to a meeting with the Russian President next week.

She scanned it, looking for weaknesses or areas where he might be vulnerable. It didn't take long. She found her answer within just thirty seconds. And as she closed out of the system, her mind was already back in the living room—back to the living room rug.

You don't need to do this, she told herself. You can let others handle it....

But, of course, she was concerned that others wouldn't be able to handle it. Maybe, she could just keep an eye on things... make sure she was around in case she was needed in a hurry. Sure, it made her feel a little pretentious and self-important but that was fine.

With adrenaline building and the reality of what she was about to do flooding through her, Amber walked back into the living room. She slid the coffee table off the rug and then nudged the small couch back, getting the feet off of the edge of the rug. She dropped to her knees and rolled it back, revealing the wood floor beneath.

She'd installed the false floor herself. The door was four-foot square, and the hinges were so thin that they hid beneath the rug with no problem at all. She hadn't had to open this secret compartment in nearly a year and even then, it had been a false alarm. Now, though...well, now things seemed more serious. She dug her fingers into the concave space where her hidden door met the boards of the rest of the floor and pulled it open.

The space inside was only a foot and a half deep; the construction of the apartment complex didn't allow for it to go any deeper. But that was all the space she needed.

She looked into the hidden space, her eyes trailing over the collection of weapons and black-market communication devices. She knew right away what she wanted, what she needed to take with her if she was really going to do this.

I don't know what I'm going to do yet; she reminded herself. *This is just in case....*

But when she reached into the space and pulled out the hard, black case that contained a Navy Seal-issued sniper rifle, she wasn't so sure. When she considered those poor people over in Bagram and the potential consequences if nothing was done about Seibert, she wasn't so sure she remained interested in *just in case* any longer.

44

It was 6:42 when Roger turned onto one of the central thoroughfares of the coastal region of Virginia Beach. It was a bit of a mess and a headache to navigate because so many of the primary roads near the ocean were closed off because of the damage that had been done.

The damage was truly significant in some areas. Closer to the beach, Roger spotted two hotels that had suffered the loss of ocean walkways and portions of patios. Despite the clear indications that there had been a lot of cleaning up by the city crews and state agencies, there was still a significant amount of scattered debris along the roadsides: piles of lumber and heaps of trash that had blown against the sides of buildings, the occasional banner or newspaper.

The schedule that Everson sent him hadn't called out a specific location, so Roger was just going to have to find it for himself. He thought about Seibert, and of how the media worked. He thought about ratings and headlines. All of that told him that the broadcast would probably *not* show too much of the storm damage, to not disturb morning viewers while they got ready for work. But they'd want to also provide a powerful reminder that this was at the beach, where the hurricane had forced the ocean to rage. But they'd also need enough room, and conducting a press conference on the sand, though picturesque, would be quite difficult.

All of this helped Roger to speculate that there was a very good chance the interview and speech would be held on a pier—one of the larger, tourist-geared ones. It would give a beautiful shot of the ocean behind the President. There was plenty of room to move around, and it would prevent sand from getting everywhere.

Roger worked his way around through a maze of closed side roads in the early morning hours. He didn't rush, telling himself he still had an hour to find the location of the interview and then a place to get a good view of it.

He got his first sign that he was on the right track when he came to his first closed road that also came with a blockade of two police cars. The bubble light on top of each was on, but only a single officer stood out to direct traffic. He lazily waved Roger on to the right, to a neat little side street bordered with small vacation homes and decorative landscaping. This street came to a T-intersection in front of a well-to-do resort.

As he came to the stop sign, a news van was pulling out of a side street by the resort. As it turned onto the street, a second one followed. News station logos were on the sides of both. Roger pulled out behind the second one and followed them down a rather cluttered two-lane road that shot directly through rows of hotels and restaurants, souvenir shops and strip malls. Two stoplights farther down, several cop cars were parked in the center of the intersection, making sure traffic was well-handled. He looked beyond the two news vans directly ahead of him and saw several more in the line of traffic. He also saw that a news van was at the front of the line and the driver had let their window down to show their press credentials.

Roger knew he could simply show his government ID and be allowed to follow behind the reporters. But that was just one more way he could be directly attached to what was about to happen. And the smaller the footprint he left behind, the better. Besides, with this little roadblock and the direction all the press was headed, he had a very good idea of where they were going to hold the interview and speech. As he inched closer and closer to the intersection, he saw a sign that confirmed his earlier theory.

A blue sign just a few feet away from the intersection read MILLER PIER, with a white arrow under it. The arrow was pointing to the left, the same direction in which the cops were allowing the news vans to advance.

Roger gave his right turn signal and turned off of the main stretch as soon as he could, avoiding the roadblock altogether. He went up two blocks and then turned left, looking down each side street he passed to make sure he was still lined up in the correct direction and location. When he saw the cop roadblock two streets down, he went one more block and turned left.

There was no parking on the sides of the street. He assumed it was all related to the President being in town. Still, he started looking for the perfect place. He passed a small bakery, a bookshop, and beach décor shop, and a real estate office. Nothing he could use. However, as he looked to the top of the book shop on the right, he saw a building that just might work—a building that was built exactly for what he needed.

He had to backtrack a bit, driving a block farther away from the coast, but it was worth it. The building in question was on a street corner that looked to be in the middle of some sort of renovation. A small, brick building was being restructured and directly beside it, there was an older building that almost looked like a church. An old, faded sign over the front door read Beachside Counseling and Support. But a secondary sign installed along the front door read FOR RENT OR LEASE.

The building was two stories tall, with a third level that looked condemned. Old, lopsided scaffolding hung to the right side of the building, jutting slightly out into the open space over the brick building that was being renovated. It would do.

He turned right at the corner and though parking was still sparse, he found a vacant spot just six spaces away from the corner. It was a tight fit and he dinged the corner of a small-bodied truck to get in straight, but that was the least of his concerns.

Roger got out of the car and was instantly aware of the smell of salt in the air. As he made his way to the back of the car, he inhaled deeply. He popped the trunk with his security card and moved around within the trunk as if he was simply running a normal, everyday errand. He lifted the false bottom and unscrewed the wing-bolts from the pieces of the rifle. When they were free, he grabbed the small, black case for the pieces, which was tucked between the side of the wheel well and the concave space for the rifle pieces. He placed the unassembled rifle into the case, which wasn't much larger than a standard briefcase. He then closed the trunk and turned back toward the building that had once been Beachside Counseling and Support.

He breathed in the ocean air as he listened to the hum and buzz of morning traffic, more congested than normal because of the high-profile guest in town. Roger passed by seven people on his way back to the white building and no one gave him a second glance. When he stepped off of the street and onto the dusty grounds of the lot holding the white building and the brick building undergoing renovation, he was certain no one saw him. Everyone in the vicinity was too focused on the excitement down by the coast, out on Miller Pier.

He walked to the back of the building that had once been Beachside Counseling and Support. The ground had been completely scraped, exposing the dirt and bits of old gravel below. A thick strand of beach grass and assorted weeds separated the lot from the next row of businesses behind Roger. He tried the back door—a simple little wooden door with an old, bronze knob. Someone had tacked a sign reading NO TRESPASSING to the door.

He looked around and, seeing that no one was around, kicked the back door. He kicked harder than he'd intended, and the door buckled and swung in with little problem, revealing a tidy yet completely abandoned office space. A few pieces of discarded lumber and old paint cans indicated that this building, like its brick neighbor, had been in the midst of being renovated at some point but it had never been finished.

None of that mattered to Roger. He hurried through the space until he came to a set of stairs on the right. With the rifle case clutched tightly in his hands, Roger continued up the stairs for a better view...for a clean shot.

45

The second floor was nothing more than a wide hallway with several rooms on each side. All the doors stood open, and the entire floor contained the odors of dust and mildew. Roger continued up the stairs. Even before he reached the third floor—which he was starting to suspect was some sort of late addition to the building—he had an idea of what to expect. He felt a draft of air, not entirely unpleasant.

The top of the stairway brought him to a space that had clearly been unfinished. And based on the amount of dust that had gathered on the floor, scattered boards, and sheets of unused insulation, Roger guessed the construction had stopped at least a year ago. The walls hadn't been finished, revealing hastily thrown-up insulation and support beams. A wood floor had been laid down but with no sort of finish or polish applied.

It was perfect...exactly what he's hoped to find. It was made even sweeter because there were windows along each wall. The window space to the left had actually been filled with glass, but the others were nothing more than empty squares with sheets of plywood used to cover them in order to keep the elements out.

Roger studied the room, gathered his bearings, and walked to the boarded over window on the right-hand side of the room. The plywood had been put in with screws but from what he could see, there were only six in all—enough to keep it up against the elements, but not enough to scar up the wall too badly.

Roger looked around the room and found a portion of a two-by-four that looked to have been used as part of a makeshift bench. The other pieces of the bench were in a small heap in the corner. He grabbed the chunk of wood and carried it over to the window on the right side of the room.

He had to chip away at the wall along the edges of the plywood in order to get the portion of board beneath the covering; it wasn't too difficult of a task because the wall was only basic sheetrock. What *was* difficult, though, was getting enough leverage under the board to pry up the plywood window covering. He dug his fingers between the chipped-away wall and the two-by-four, smashing his fingers. He gave a tremendous tug, but the plywood only creaked and groaned. Grimacing, Roger planted the point of his shoe against the baseboard along the floor and the wall. He dug in and pulled again.

A screw at the top of the covering gave way at once, popping out like a little rocket. At first, though, that was the only result. But as he gave one more violent tug, the entire bottom corner gave way, the screw tearing right out of the wall.

This allowed Roger to keep the covering up, partially covering the window, hanging at an angle from the other side of the frame. He peered out onto the criss-crossing streets, instantly spotting the whirling police lights a block farther down at the intersection he'd avoided. A block and a half past that, all the streets ended in rolling waves of crabgrass and sloppy little dunes as the beach took over.

In order to see Miller Pier, Roger had to stand directly in front of the window, keeping the plywood covering at an angle by nudging it with his shoulder. The area down by the pier, two and a half blocks away, was chaotic. Though traffic was not being allowed on the street, there were what appeared to be hundreds of people down there. The parking lots on both sides of the pier entrance were also packed with news vans and police cars. Beyond the building that served as the pier's entrance, the pier itself extended a good distance out into the ocean—about one hundred yards, Roger guessed.

As he'd suspected, there was a news crew out there, but it was more than a simple broadcast. There were special lamps and lights down there, with people scattered back and forth, running around like insects. One spot in particular had been blocked off from all of the commotion on the pier and *that* was where Roger assumed the President would be interviewed and give his speech.

He'd have a clear shot. The difficulty would be making sure he didn't hurt anyone because based on the state of things down there right now, he had no idea how many potential bystanders he was going to have to contend with.

Stepping away from the window, Roger looked at his watch. It was 7:39. He then walked over to where he'd set the case down and sat on the floor in front of it. He unsnapped the latches slowly and opened it. One by one, he took the pieces out and assembled the rifle. It was surprisingly relaxing, despite the absolute war taking place in his heart.

You can't do this…you can't do this…

Yes, I can. His one life is worth trading for what might be thousands at Bagram. And maybe still more stateside.

The back and forth in his mind carried on as he assembled the rifle. He was quite adept at it, and it took him no time at all. After putting it together, he looked at the rifle as if he had never seen anything stranger. He picked it up, tested its weight, and felt slightly sickened by how comfortable it felt in his grip.

He looked at the window he'd be standing at when he pulled the trigger. He listened to the morning commotion outside and looked at his watch again. It was now 7:46, and the rifle was ready to go.

He had nothing left to do but wait.

Or maybe you should call Maggie, he thought. *Don't tell her what you're about to do, but let her know you'll need to lay low for a while. And ask for her forgiveness in advance.*

The thought brought tears to his eyes, but he blinked them back. The last thing he needed was compromised vision. Still, he dug his phone from his pocket and scrolled to her number. But he couldn't bring himself to place the call. What the hell was he supposed to say anyway?

When the phone rang in his hand, he dropped it out of fear and surprise. There was no number on the caller display, though it read UNKNOWN.

His first impulse was to ignore it, but he also knew that anyone who was on his side in all of this would likely call from a blocked number.

Shaking slightly, he picked his phone back up and answered the call with the sniper rifle still perched across his lap.

"Hello?"

Everson's voice came through, stern and with an edge of terror to it. "Roger…would you like to tell me what the fuck you're doing in Virginia Beach?"

"Are you tracking me?"

"You're damned right I am. Roger…what are you doing?"

"Just monitoring things."

"Are you going to make me regret getting you that itinerary?"

Roger looked down at the rifle and didn't answer.

"I have something you need to hear," Everson went on. "I got the latest medical reports on the Vice President. He's currently alert and fully responsive. He has no recollection of any sort of foul play and from what I can see, there are no red flags in his records. No poison, no trauma…just a cardiac event."

"Would all poisons show up so clearly in basic medical tests?" Roger asked.

"All? I don't know. And I don't care right now. I need you to tell me you aren't about to do what I think you're about to do."

It took Roger far too much effort to get out this response. His heart was slamming hard in his chest, and it was becoming difficult to breathe. "Something has to be done. Even if Warren wasn't poisoned, what about the people at Bagram? What about the three attempts on my life? What about Seibert's refusal to listen to anyone?"

"I know, Roger. I know. But I—"

"What about Moreno? Is there any new information on those dead men from Dean's house?"

"Yes, actually. He called at about five thirty. One man has a definitive link to Nightwatch. Two of his brothers were killed in an attack four years ago, led by a secret American group. And another of the men is the son of a man who was detained in a Bagram prison until his death last year."

"So there are definite links?"

Roger could tell that Everson was reluctant to answer, but he finally said, "Yes. But listen, Roger, think about—"

Roger ended the call. Not only that, but he turned his phone off when it was over. He took a deep, steadying breath, closing his eyes to focus on it. He could feel his heart beating, he could hear the streets below, and even the gentle crashing of the ocean from two blocks away.

He took one last calming breath and looked at his watch again. Somehow, it was 7:53.

No more hesitations, no more putting off.

He thought of Maggie as he picked the rifle up. He thought of Thomas as he hefted it and brought it to his chest. And he thought of all of the lives overseas that could very well end if the President remained in power.

That thought pushed him forward. Roger pocketed his powered-down phone and with an eerie calm, he walked directly to the window and raised the rifle.

46

The window was just high enough to not allow Roger to kneel. Instead, he had to adopt an uncomfortable squat that caused his abdominal muscles to clench and start burning. He'd assumed a perfect shooter's stance amid his awkward crouch; the butt of the rifle was square against his shoulder and the barrel was just barely protruding out of the window frame.

With his eye pressed to the scope, Roger took in the scene down on Miller Pier. He looked to the area that had been set aside for the interview and saw the nationally recognized female host speaking animatedly to someone behind the camera. The co-host of the show, a rotund man wearing a purple suit, was laughing with a few other people just to the side of the area. Roger estimated that there were sixty or seventy other people all along the pier, stretching from the back of the building that served as its entrance to the interview area. The sea churned beautifully behind them.

But so far, there was no sign of Seibert. Roger allowed himself to come out of his uncomfortable position, knees back on the floor. He thought of how to get out of this once the act had been done, internally scolding himself for not wearing gloves. His prints would be all over the rifle. He looked around the room and saw a solution. The sheets of insulation lying on the floor would not only wipe away his prints, but also slightly scratch and diminish the polished surface of the rifle. He'd have to leave the weapon behind because in the moments following the assassination of the President he certainly didn't want to be seen out on the streets with a rifle. And he wasn't going to have time to take it apart and put the pieces back into the case.

He also knew how the Secret Service worked. There would be dozens with Seibert, some of them probably in separate vehicles. Roger figured it would take about two seconds for the reality of what had happened to sink in. After that, the immediate area would be a ring of chaos. But as soon as possible, the local PD along with Secret Service would lock the area down, including streets leading out of the city. He figured it might take them a grand total of five minutes to figure out the shooter had been a sniper, from a decent distance away. That would lead them to look for tall places within sight of the pier, which would then bring them to his building.

In other words, he was going to have to haul ass right after the shot.

He looked at his watch again. It was 7:57. With the same degree of eerie calm, Roger raised himself into that awkward position once again, propped the end of the barrel along the portion of exposed windowpane, and looked into the scope.

There was a slight buzz of activity near the center of the gathered crowd. Roger focused on this and was able to make sense of it right away. Seibert had arrived. He was being escorted through the crowd by local police officers and Secret Service agents. Other agents walked stoically behind him, like robots on high alert. Seibert was pausing here and there to shake hands with people in the crowd, but he was in a hurry to make it to the interview location several yards away. The host was already in her chair, getting some quick make-up touchups.

The closer Seibert got to the chairs and the lights, the clearer Roger's next few moments became. He was going to have a window of about five seconds when Seibert sat down to take the shot. He wanted to take it just before things settled down to silence on the pier. If he could take the shot before all the applause died down and before the interview started properly, it would buy him a few more seconds. And he was going to need all the time he could get in order to make a successful escape. It was truly going to be an instance of where every single moment would count.

Roger continued to watch as the President made his way toward the host and the chairs—the man who was choosing to turn a blind eye to news of a terrorist attack simply because he didn't want to strain relationships with foreign officials. The man who was playing political strategy games rather than looking out for the lives of thousands of people...most whom were members of the US military, volunteers who'd chosen to serve their country.

He was nearly there now, the spotlights to the sides of the chairs now brightening the right side of his face. He was smiling, chuckling, drinking it all in. Meanwhile, somewhere overseas, Nightwatch was putting the finishing touches on whatever plan they had put into motion.

The President had made it out of the crowd, heading to the host, who stood behind him clapping right along with the crowd. He made one last wave to the audience with his politician's smile plastered on his face. He then turned to the host, shared an informal half-hug with her, and walked to his seat.

Roger took a breath and held it in. The rifle was steady in his hands, the President's head lined up perfectly in the scope, his left ear in the dead-center of the crosshairs. Roger followed his movements as the President lowered himself in the chair and sat. Roger took one last moment to make sure no one else nearby would be hurt.

The President settled into the chair, still waving and smiling to the audience. He shifted a bit and then found a comfortable position. The lights shone on him, and the motion and applause of the gathered crowd died down.

Now... Roger thought.

He tightened his finger on the trigger, adding pressure, ready to take the shot.

Forgive me, Maggie...

He let his breath out, and the morning was torn apart by the cracking sound of a solitary gunshot.

47

Sometimes, Amber knew that the simplest solutions were best. That's why she listened to her police-band radio the entire way between DC to Virginia Beach. She knew the President was due to get some media attention there this morning. She knew the time and the name of the news anchor who would interview him. Because of the intricacy of her system, she'd even gotten a peek at notes from the President's valet and knew what he'd be wearing for the interview.

But the police band radio told her everything she needed to know about the scene on the ground. When she was still ten minutes outside of what would be considered Virginia Beach city limits, she already knew the route she would need to take in order to get around roadblocks set up for the Presidential cavalcade and any roads closer to the coast that were closed down because of the hurricane.

It was 7:13 when she pulled into a gas station parking lot and retrieved her trusty laptop from the backseat. Using her cellphone as a hotspot, she could get access to a civilian-restricted satellite mapping tool. Because of the lagging connection, it took a while, but she finally found a suitable lookout location. It was hard to tell by examining a computer screen, but she thought it might be perfect—so long as the images used by the mapping software were up to date.

Getting to the spot might be tricky, but she supposed there was only one way to find out. She got back out on the road and continued on toward

Virginia Beach. Traffic was already slightly congested, and she was sure the President's visit had a huge role to play in that bit of inconvenience.

Just as she began to worry that she hadn't properly planned things out and would miss the interview, she came to a police roadblock where she saw signs for beach parking. They were letting cars go through one by one, simply doing what they could to keep the flow of traffic at a manageable pace. Rather than trickling straight ahead with the vast majority of traffic, Amber turned right. She knew that at some point, she'd be able to turn back toward the coast and, according to her watch, she still had exactly twenty-four minutes before she had to be in position.

But those minutes ticked by quickly as she came to a series of red lights and then a detour from where the hurricane had apparently caused damage at an intersection. By 7:45, she worried that she truly wasn't going to make it in time. But after the detour was behind her, the stoplights were green the rest of the way. She eventually took a left, meandering closer to the coast. As she came to an intersection, she looked ahead and saw a tangled mess of traffic and the glittering blue green of the sea just beyond it.

She checked the satellite imagery once again and confirmed she was now only two blocks from where she needed to be. Looking to her left again, she realized that she'd just now passed the pier where the President would give his speech. She checked her watch again: eight minutes.

Damn, I couldn't have cut this any closer.

When she came to the last turn she'd need, she noticed that there was a small police presence in the parking lot she'd planned to use. This spooked her, but only a bit. Instead of going to the parking lot, she began searching for street parking instead. She didn't see one right away, but she saw a bank to her right, with a strip of parking beyond the ATM drive-thru lanes. She pulled into this little lot and killed the engine.

She stepped out of the car, pocketed her keys, and walked to the trunk. As she popped it open, she checked her watch again. It was 7:54. She could still make it, but she was going to have to really rush...and hope no one stopped her. She glanced ahead and slightly to the right, in the direction of her final destination. It was out of sight, though, blocked by a large office building.

She reached into the trunk and took out the two items that were essential to her success. First, there was, of course, the case with the rifle inside. She'd switched out the cases back at her apartment, placing it instead into a scuffed-up attaché used for carrying audio equipment. It was a tight fit, but it had worked; she'd had to remove the scope and tuck it into the side. The second item was a lanyard that she placed around her neck. There was a plastic sleeve at the end of the lanyard, showing an ID card with her face. The logo of a prestigious news organization was in the right corner—a genius rendering by one of her many less-than-reputable friends. A sticker reading PRESS was along the bottom of the plastic sleeve. It always felt juvenile to wear it, but she'd lost track of the number of times this little prop had gotten her through security in tight situations.

Amber closed the trunk and hurried to her left, toward the beach. When she came to the end of the street, she looked to the right again and this time, she could just barely see the uppermost edge of her destination. She hurried along the next block, doing her best to fit in, to make sure people who might be questioned later would only remember the rushing member of the press, in a hurry to get to the pier.

"Excuse me," she muttered to a man dressed in business attire, holding a coffee cup in one hand and a briefcase in the other. "Sorry...so sorry," she said to a young mother pushing her baby in a stroller.

And then, when she was nearly to the corner with just one more street separating her from the beach, she saw her destination in full. Half a block to her right—roughly two and a half blocks from where President Seibert would be interviewed on the pier—was a billboard. Currently, it was advertising a local beach shop. A mother and two children were digging for seashells while a cartoon dolphin leaped into the air behind them.

Amber crossed the street in a hurry, weaving her way through clogged traffic. Through it all, no one questioned the case. She knew how people operated—how they thought. The lanyard was bouncing on her chest and the case in her hands was roughed up and looked like it had seen some wear and tear over the years. No one would assume the worst. No one would see it as overly suspicious.

She came to the other side of the street and took a right, headed toward the billboard. It was behind a small building—a yoga studio of some kind from the looks of it. And when she turned into the small alleyway that led to a wide strip of pavement that separated the businesses from the beach, she didn't look back a single time.

Her eyes were on the large, black column that held the billboard up fifty feet in the air. Thin rails of the installed ladder ran up the back of the column. She dashed to it, making sure no one was in the area to see her. All she saw was a single delivery truck pulling in behind a store several spaces down, the back of the truck facing her.

She made it to the column, now standing in the shadow of the beach shop billboard. And as she reached out for the first rung on the ladder, she quickly glanced at her watch.

It was 7:58. She'd just barely made it.

Not sure how the next several minutes would play out, Amber took a deep breath and started to climb.

48

Most of the people on Miller Pier didn't hear the shot. The ocean and the softening applause, as well as the distance, drowned out most of it. But there were a few—those younger and with better hearing, as well as those closer to the street-end of the pier heard it. They turned back to see what was going on, thus missing the eruption of movement near the head of the pier, where the President had just taken his seat.

The interview had not even properly started when the President gave a sudden jolt. His head snapped back and for a moment, he went limp in his seat before he collapsed from the chair and fell to the pier. It happened so quickly that no one screamed or reacted until his body thudded against the old, salt-water infused boards.

It happened so quickly that only a few would later tell the police and the FBI that they'd actually even seen the blood. This was not the case for the estimated 3.58 million watching the broadcast. The morning news footage showed it all clearly, but it lasted only a split second, and it took a while for most people to understand what they had seen: a sudden red splash, almost cartoonishly bright in the lights, and then the President falling.

With his body crumpled on the pier, the morning host screamed and nearly tripped over her chair in an effort to step away. Cops and Secret Service agents rushed forward instantly, guns drawn. When it dawned on the onlookers that the President had been shot and that they were in the middle of an active-shooter situation, everyone in the crowd bolted for the entrance behind them. Cops who had not been close enough to the President to lend a hand did their best to keep some sort of control over the crowd, but it didn't last long. In a wave of running and screaming, several people were knocked down. One person was actually pushed so hard against the side of the pier that the railing broke loose, and they fell into the ocean twelve feet below.

It took another two minutes for the police and the handful of Secret Service agents to organize a proper search for the shooter. And even when they decided to do so, the flood of people rushing off the pier and out into the streets made their task much harder.

The closest thing to a medic on the scene was one of Seibert's Secret Service agents—a man with a basic understanding of medicine and trauma care. He was the second man to kneel by Seibert, and he knew without even checking for breath or a pulse that the President of the United States was dead. There had only been a single shot, and it had been a deadly one. It had entered the President's head just above his right ear and exited from the other side. The entry wound was a precise hole, but the exit was the exact opposite.

That was all he needed to see to understand the situation. He looked back at the few cops and his other fellow agents with a grim expression. "We've got a sniper."

49

Roger's stomach felt as if it had been turned inside out. As he stepped away from the window, he was sure he was going to throw up. But there was no time for that. He swallowed the urge down and when he turned back around to face the partially finished room, he instantly rushed to the pile of unused insulation sheets in the corner.

As he scrubbed the rifle down, his mind whirled, trying to make sense of what had just happened. He trapped the rifle between two foam-like sheets and scrubbed hard. When he was sure there would be no traces of his prints, he left the rifle there, hidden between the two sheets of yellow-tinged material.

He raced to the stairs, his knees wobbly and his head feeling like it was on a spring. The world was dizzy, and he still had to fight the urge to stop and throw up.

What the hell. What the HELL?

He nearly fell down the first flight of stairs to the second floor. He caught himself against the wall, aware the clock was ticking against him. If the authorities did their job correctly, a lot of avenues out of the city would be closed, and he already had the mostly congested streets by the shore to contend with.

As he rushed down the last set of stairs, there was a small and slightly detached part of him that could swear he was still holding the rifle. His knees trembled, and his fingers still felt as if they were cupping the fore stock, still pulling back the trigger. He felt something very much like madness trying to creep in as his brain refused to accept what had happened. It made no sense. Something wasn't right, something wasn't—

Those thoughts fell apart like sand in the wind when he came to the first floor and saw the back door. Through that door was the street and then his car and hopefully freedom.

Are you not prepared to pay for what you've done? Did you really think you were going to get away with it?

He didn't know. All he knew was that he had to get to his family. Whatever happened to him next, he had to make it to Maggie and Thomas to explain himself.

Only...explain what, exactly?

The world continued to totter and spin as he blasted through the back door. He nearly stumbled and fell out in the dirt lot but managed to stay on his feet. Roger forced himself to remain standing still for just a moment when he realized it was incredibly hard to breathe. He supposed this might be some sort of panic attack—something he didn't have time for.

He waited for the world to stop spinning and then ran to the sidewalk that would lead him to his car. He made it three steps, nearly placing a foot on the concrete of the sidewalk, before a voice shouted from behind him.

"Hey! Stop right there!"

He turned without stopping and saw a cop. He was a larger fellow, maybe middle aged, and he was already reaching for his gun. Roger turned back toward the car and his instincts told him to run. It was less than fifty yards away. But he also knew that given what had just happened down on the pier, this cop might very well shoot him.

Fighting every urge in his body, Roger stopped. He turned, putting his hands up. He'd explain what he could...though, the end of it made no sense. It made no sense to him, and it sure as hell would not make sense to this cop.

"I'm not—" Roger started, but the cop was already firing.

Only, in the last moment, Roger realized it wasn't a sidearm that had been holstered at the cop's side. Instead, it was a taser. He felt the prongs sink into his chest and then the jolt of electricity passing through him.

As he fell to the ground, the pain came swift and hard. He was vaguely aware of the cop saying something, maybe speaking into a radio or shoulder microphone. But beyond it all—the taser and the cop's faint voice—there was one more thing that loomed over it all. It was a giant thought that followed him deep down into the darkness that waited for him as he came to the verge of passing out.

He'd scoped the President perfectly and had his finger on the trigger, ready to take the shot.

But he hadn't done it.

Roger had momentarily frozen, unable to pull the trigger. But all the same, Seibert had been killed, taken by a bullet from somewhere else, as Roger peered through the scope and saw the left side of his head explode.

And that begged the questions: from where, and by whom?

They were questions that followed Roger into the uncomfortable darkness, taunting him the whole way down.

50

When Roger opened his eyes, the first thing he became aware of was the intense pain in his head. As his nerves tried to make sense of the pain, he began to process other information as well. First of all, he was lying on his back in a dull, bright room. He was in a strange bed and could see the shapes of his legs and feet under a thin, white blanket.

But it was the small sink across the room and the depressing fluorescent lights that really clued him in: he was in the hospital.

He looked to his arms and saw that there was a single line fed into his left wrist, connected to an IV containing clear fluid. Slightly groggy, he noticed that his watch had been removed. He wasn't handcuffed to the bed or restrained. He glanced around the room, hoping to find a clock, but there was none.

He recalled the cop and how he'd been tazed, but that was it. If he'd been apprehended for the assassination of the President, certainly he'd be in a much more secure room than this.

Confused and slightly scared, he reached to the right side of the bed where the small remote with the Call button was hanging. He pressed it and waited, again trying to take an inventory of his body. The ache in his head was the most notable thing, and there was a strange, itchy irritation all along the right side of his chest. His wrist was hurting again, a reminder of the violence from yesterday. Wait...*had* that been yesterday? He wasn't sure for a moment; it was all starting to blur together.

There was a soft knock at the door to his room, a door he couldn't quite see from where he was lying. Before he could respond, the door opened, and a doctor stepped inside. On the older side, his hair almost completely gray, he wore a stern expression, the sort of look that made Roger think the doctor really didn't want to be pulling this duty.

"Mr. Commer," he said. "Welcome to the waking world. How are you feeling?"

"My head hurts like hell, and I'm slightly confused."

"That would make sense. You've had a pretty eventful four hours."

"Four hours?"

"That's right," the doctor said. "You're currently at Hampton General Hospital, about forty minutes away from the beach. You—"

"How did I get here?"

The doctor's face tightened a bit as he seemed to understand what Roger was really asking. With a small sigh, the doctor leaned against the wall. "A police officer called for an ambulance after you'd been tased. And that's all I'm permitted to say. I'm only allowed to discuss your medical status. There are, however, two men waiting for you just down the hall who can probably answer everything else you're wanting to know."

This did nothing but send another jolt of worry through him, but he understood the reasoning behind it. "Okay," he said. "So what can you tell me about my medical state? For starters, what's in the IV?"

"That's just what we call a Myers Cocktail. A vitamin B complex and a dose of B12. When you arrived, you were showing signs of extreme exhaustion...which is why you passed out the moment the taser took you off your feet. Have you not slept much over the past few days?"

"That's putting it mildly."

"Other than exhaustion, you took a pretty good whack to the head when you fell down. You've got a mild concussion and a pretty good goose-egg on the right side of your head. We haven't done any X-rays yet, but I'm also betting your wrist is fractured...maybe broken. And there's one hell of a bruise on your left side, but that looks a day or two old."

"So, am I...I mean, am I okay?"

"Yes. I'd recommend getting that wrist checked out and to stay where you are for another few hours just because of the concussion."

"I can do that…I think." He thought back to that last moment in the room above Beachside Counseling and Support. He thought about seeing Seibert's head in the scope and how he'd started to pull the trigger.

But apparently, someone else had beaten him to it. Then again, he'd been tased…and if any cop or Secret Service agent worth their salt had thoroughly searched the scene, they would have found a lot of damning evidence against him: the broken door to the building, the torn piece of plywood across the window, the rifle, and the borrowed LR car from the Pentagon's private garage.

"You said your head is hurting," the doctor said. "Do you feel up to speaking with the men down the hall?"

"Yes, please."

With a nod, the doctor started for the door and said, "I'll send them in."

When he was alone again, Roger took a moment to appreciate the gravity of the situation. The conversation that was about to take place was likely going to determine the course of the rest of his life. There were many people who might come into his room. Depending on who they were, things could go badly or better than he could've hoped for. The tension made his head pound even worse.

Less than two minutes later, the door opened again. Two men stepped inside, both dressed in respectable suits. The first man was a total surprise—someone he hadn't seen in several weeks. His name was Albert Pinault, the Chairman of the Joint Chiefs of Staff. An immense African American man, he'd served twenty years in the military and was one of the President's primary military advisors.

This is going to be terrible, Roger thought.

But then the second man entered, and Roger was confused all over again. It was Frederickson. He looked tired, his eyes wild with the intensity of a man who was being pulled in about a million directions at once.

When Roger saw him, he couldn't help but blurt out the first thing that came to mind. "Henry, it wasn't me. I was there, and I was—"

"We know," Frederickson said.

"But someone took the shot, right? I saw it through the—"

"Roger, stop talking for a second," Frederickson said. He nodded toward Albert Pinault and said, "You and Mr. Pinault have worked together several times in the past, correct?"

"Yes," Roger said, uncertain of where this was going.

"Well, I can tell you right now, away from the White House and any official channels, that Mr. Pinault has been assisting Walter Everson over the past three weeks. He's been feeding Everson information about the President."

Roger looked at Pinault, baffled. Pinault nodded and stepped closer to the bed. He spoke softly, as if afraid there might be prying ears just outside the door.

"I'm the one who provided him with Seibert's schedule for today. And I've been putting together a list of names of people that were believed to be part of Nightwatch here on US soil. In fact, Homeland Security arrested five people in Pamplin, Virginia."

"So Devante Abdul wasn't BS-ing me?" Roger asked.

"He wasn't. When Dean Page was killed, it made me think Nightwatch must have someone on the inside. Perhaps someone that had the President's ear, and maybe Seibert didn't even realize who he was talking to—or didn't want to admit it to himself. We might never know who."

"Why not?"

"Seibert's gone now," Frederickson said. "He was pronounced dead on the scene, and personnel changes will occur wholesale, so the mole from Nightwatch might slip out with the others. Right now, Speaker of the House Pelingra and Vice President Warren are acting as a sort of Presidential tag-team while the Vice President wraps up things involving his hospital stay. He's being discharged later this afternoon."

"So he's the President now."

"Yes. Officially. But, as I said, Pelingra is assisting until he's on his feet. And about that..."

Though Frederickson stopped here, Pinault picked up. "I spoke with the Vice President on the phone on the way here. Despite what the hospital records say, Vice Pres...*President* Warren says that he recalls a strange, small pinch, followed by a tingling sensation in his hand after taking a pen from the former President to sign a document. He compared it to a pins-and-needles sensation. He also described a tightness in his throat and an accelerated heartbeat before he blacked out. I am only speculating here, but that sounds a lot like what I know of succinylcholine."

Amber, he thought. And the mere idea of her brought Roger back around to the original question.

"Do you know who did it?" he asked. "Who pulled the trigger?"

Frederickson traded a look with Pinault and said, "The Secret Service has found a location a quarter of a mile away from the pier, a billboard on top of an apartment complex. There are fresh prints and tracks in the ground along the backside of platform. It would have provided a clear shot."

A quarter of a mile, Roger thought. The shooter would've needed access to a top-of-the line rifle and be an expert shooter. He again thought of Amber. Had she changed her mind *again*, willing to do the job just because she believed it might bring the best results—not necessarily that it was the right thing to do, but the best option given the circumstances?

"What about me?" Roger asked. It came out bluntly, and he wished he hadn't asked.

"Probably nothing," Frederickson said. "This conversation will never leave this room, so I'll tell you this. Cops and Secret Service found a perfect little sniper's nest in the third level of a building two and a half blocks away from the pier. A sniper rifle had been embedded between layers on insulation on the floor, and plywood sheeting and been pulled from one of the windows. The building was just forty feet away from where the cop stopped you. But," he said, looking over to Pinault, "you were probably just in town to make sure the President was safe. After all, you *have* been paranoid about the Nightwatch movement. And after the events at Dean Page's house, you worried about the President's safety as well."

"Perhaps," Pinault said, "you feared pushing the issue with Secret Service or other security forces because you knew you'd already irritated the President with so much Nightwatch talk. So you took matters into your own hands and decided to privately come to Virginia Beach as an extra layer of security. Only, the sniper who took the President's life got around you somehow…one-upped you, if you will."

Frederickson nodded. "Does that sound about right?"

Roger was speechless, so he only nodded. He finally managed a "Yeah," and then rolled his head back on the pillow. He didn't quite understand the feeling of guilt that came with it, but the relief that swept through him made him feel much lighter—as if he might float right out the hospital bed.

51

Roger understood perfectly that both Frederickson and Pinault couldn't just hang around the hospital and wait for him to be discharged. They had a new president to advise. So, when his doctor finally cleared him and signed his release forms at 2:45 that afternoon, he wasn't surprised to see that they had already departed.

What *did* surprise him, though, was the suited man sitting in the waiting room. Roger headed for the elevators. He sprang to his feet and quickly approached him.

"Hello, Mr. Commer," he said. "I'm Special Agent Sheldon Parks, with the CIA Security Task Force." He showed his badge and ID.

"Okay," Roger said. "Nice to meet you. But I'm sort of on my way out. Did Frederickson send you?"

"Well, sir, Mr. Frederickson *left me.* I've been tasked with driving you back to DC, sir."

"What? That's unnecessary."

"You know the rules, sir. Concussion protocols. You've got a three-hour drive ahead of you. Or, rather, a three-hour *ride.* These are my orders, Mr. Commer."

Roger appreciated the gesture and knew better than to argue. Besides, even the doctor had seemed very unhappy about the idea of Roger driving and had come very close to denying his discharge.

"Well, thank you very much, Agent Parks. Let's get the hell out of here. What do you say?"

They didn't speak on the way out, giving Roger time to wonder what things were like in DC right now. He assumed it would be utter chaos for at least another week with not only the transition of Warren into the Presidency, but with all the solemn rites surrounding Seibert's funeral.

And, he hoped, a strategy would be implemented to stop the Nightwatch plans overseas.

When they got out to the parking lot, Roger saw that someone had brought his LR car over. It didn't surprise him, but he was a bit confused.

"How'd this get here?" he asked.

"From what I understand, Frederickson was directing a team of FBI agents on the scene. They investigated the spot where the cop tased you and saw the car just down the street. Frederickson ran a quick check on who checked it out, and I think the name you inserted into the records tipped him off."

Roger nodded as he slid into the passenger seat and secured his seatbelt. He also wondered how much Everson had to do with his quick discovery.

"How much have you been told, Parks?"

"Just that you were downed by a police officer over a severe misunderstanding about what happened to the President this morning. I was told you suffered a concussion and were exhibiting signs of exhaustion. Other than that, I was only told to bring you home safely. Which I intend to do."

In other words, Roger thought. *I won't be getting any real updates from you.*

He took his cellphone out of his pocket and saw that he had missed calls and messages from an abundance of people: Frederickson, Everson, Maggie, Moreno, and a few unlisted numbers. He opened up a text thread for Frederickson just as they came to the hospital parking exit, but Parks stopped him.

"Don't use your own phone," he said. "Mr. Frederickson instructed me to have you use the phone in the glove compartment. He placed it there specifically for you when the car was delivered to the hospital."

The move made sense, but it was a reminder to Roger that no matter how smoothly things might play out for him in the coming days, he was likely never *truly* going to escape the trouble and shadow of what he'd nearly done. He opened the glove box and found one of Everson's go-to burner phones waiting for him. It was already powered on and there was a long string of texts waiting for him. They'd all come from Frederickson and Everson.

He read Everson's first, as there weren't quite as many. Starting from the top, and beginning at 1:17 that afternoon, the texts read:

Make no phone calls today. Maybe not tomorrow, either. Let US reach out to YOU until the smoke clears.
- *FYI...before Warren even saw the Oval Office, he made calls concerning NW. There's already movement, a team being assembled outside of Bagram.*
- *I've removed Dean Page's name from LR car logs. No trace of that car being taken this morning.*

Roger wasn't sure how to feel about the idea that so many people were making so many moves to ensure he wasn't found out as a would-be assassin. Even thinking such a thing brought the memory of peering at Seibert through the scope, his finger applying weight to the trigger.

Before the image of it could take root, Roger shook it away and turned his full attention back to the phone and read the rather long thread that had come from Frederickson.

Lay low for a few days. Stay at home. No work calls. If needed, I'll call you.
- *Warren and Pelingra are already working on plans to stop Nightwatch. In secret, it's #1 priority. Will keep you updated.*
- *I've informed your wife that you are in the hospital but shared no details of why. Figured it wasn't my place. She knows you're fine but that's about it. Told her you weren't being allowed visitors.*
- *Questions of your involvement in this morning's actions are circulating around Washington, but we (myself, Moreno, Everson, even Warren*

himself) are denying it and pushing the story we gave you this morning.
- *Initial forensics and ballistics show the shot that did the job was not the caliber of your rifle. Once that is confirmed, whispers of your involvement should die out completely.*

There was a break in the thread here, a space of exactly fifty-six minutes. But when it picked up again, there was a lot to process. And as Parks drove Roger closer to home, each bit he read was a minor relief...and a confirmation that even though the end of it all had resulted in a nationally televised death, it had been the right move.

- *2 arrests made locally, both NW members. One cracked hard under investigation. Giving up names, locations, plans.*
- *1 arrest made in Parwan Province by military police. Second in command of current NW.*
- *Small task force of soldiers and military police to stake out 4 locations of suspected compounds in Afg within the hour.*
- *One NW nest found and exploited. 6 members dead, 1 wounded, 8 arrested.*

That was the last text to come through, arriving half an hour ago. Roger forced himself to place the phone back into the glove box because it was taking far too much restraint to not reach out to Frederickson to request more details.

However, before he closed it, he took the phone back out and manually typed in Maggie's cell number. There was so much he wanted to say but he knew that in his current situation, there was only thing he could tell her that would be safe. But really, it was all she'd need to know...the most important thing.

Coming home, he typed. *See you soon.*

And with that, he put the phone away and closed the glove compartment. He then settled back against the headrest and watched the highway unspool ahead of them.

***

Another of Parks's instructions had been to take Roger directly home—not to his office, not to the garage where he'd left his car. Roger didn't argue with this, either. Truth be told, he couldn't remember the last time he'd yearned to be home so badly.

As a testament to just how long the day had been, he was shocked that it was only dusk when Parks pulled the LR car into his driveway.

"Do you need anything else, Mr. Commer?"

Before Roger could say anything, the front door of his house opened, and Maggie came out. She didn't waste time lingering in the doorway, instead hurrying down the stairs and making her way across the yard. Behind her, Thomas waited at the door; Roger figured he wasn't sure how to handle the situation.

"No, Agent Parks," he said. "I think I'm good for now. I've got just about everything I need. Thank you."

He shook Agent Parks's hand and got out of the car. As he stepped forward to meet Maggie in the yard, he saw that though she was clearly concerned, there was also a bit of anger in her expression.

"I know," Roger said. "Maggie, I'm so sorry."

She met him and wrapped her arms around him. With her head buried in his shoulder, she let out a sigh of relief and said, "You had me worried sick, you jerk. The President was killed, and you were missing, and...."

"I know. I'm sorry."

"What the hell happened?" she asked as he broke the hug. "Where did you go when you left so early this morning?"

"Can we go inside? Let's all sit down, and I'll tell you everything—well, everything I can."

"Are we...Roger, are we okay? Are you *safe?*"

"Yeah, I think so. Come on. Let's go in."

They walked inside and when Roger passed through the door, he met Thomas with a hug too. Thomas asked no questions, though. The poor kid looked scared out of his mind. When they entered the kitchen, Roger saw that Maggie had written down the scant details of his hospital stay. From the bare bones information, he saw that Frederickson had told her next to nothing.

"There's a nasty knot on your head," Maggie said as she sat down to the table. "You know that, right?"

"Yes."

"So...tell us," she said. She nodded to the chair next to her, and Roger sat down. Thomas did as well, still looking a bit out of sorts.

Roger took a seat and looked at them. He felt a swell of love in his heart for both of them and he knew there was no way in hell he would be able to get through the entire story without breaking down. But he'd do his best...and he decided he'd tell them absolutely everything, secrecy of his job be damned. They were his family, and they deserved the truth.

So he started telling his story and, as he'd promised himself, he didn't leave out anything. He didn't break down completely but did start weeping at a couple points. Maggie reached out and took his hand both times and as he told them about the immediate response to Nightwatch once Warren had taken over, he again felt reassured that he'd done the right thing by pushing the matter.

But when he told them about that upper room over Beachside Counseling and Support and how he'd had the President perfectly aligned with his scope, that feeling of reassurance faded. He still had no idea if it had been the right decision or not...if he would have pulled the trigger after all.

But now, he supposed he'd never know. And if that was the only price he had to pay for it all, the price had all been worth it.

52

Five weeks later

The San Juan coast stretched out before Roger like a perfect streak of beautiful pastel. He sipped a beer and looked out to the ocean, taking in the scenery. It wasn't a bad way to spend the last days of what had turned out to be something of a forced vacation. And it was also a beautiful glimpse into what retirement could be like; a subject that he and Maggie had discussed quite a bit during their week in Puerto Rico.

Maggie's voice called out to him from inside their private bungalow. "Roger, is that *really* what you're wearing to dinner?"

He chuckled, looking down to his khakis and what he thought was a rather tasteful—and only slightly tacky—Hawaiian shirt.

"Yeah, it is. Do you not approve?"

"That shirt is God awful."

Smiling, Roger got up and walked inside, leaving the beach scenery behind.

He and Maggie had drawn closer than ever over the five weeks he'd spent away from work. He'd kept her abreast of all of the updates concerning Warren taking over in the Oval Office and of updates on the official disintegration of Nightwatch. He did maintain the rules of secrecy, telling her only what she would learn on her own in the news anyway, only he gave her the un-biased and factual story.

That story included President Warren stamping Nightwatch out completely. In one of the three raids to eradicate the group, laptops filled with plans of terrorist plots had been discovered…one of which included the plans for an attack on Bagram Air Force Base. The attack was to be carried out just three days after the day Seibert had been killed. Those plans had, of course, been thwarted when Warren started applying pressure the moment he became President.

The results of the raids had been worth celebrating, but Roger had a hard time with it. Two American soldiers killed and five injured. Fourteen Nightwatch insurgents killed, and more than thirty arrested. Countless lives saved as a result of the group coming to an end.

But all Roger took away from it was the image of former President Seibert's head in his rifle scope.

He was thinking of it even now as he changed shirts. It was an image that popped up seemingly out of nowhere, sometimes as a nightmare while he slept and sometimes as nothing more than a drifting thought in the middle of the day.

As he slipped into a shirt Maggie had approved days before, his phone rang from the hutch across the room. He went to it and saw FREDERICKSON on the caller display.

"Work!" he called out. She'd apparently slipped into the bathroom to finish getting dressed for their dinner date. After the stress and tears of revealing the entire story of what had happened five weeks ago, they'd both thought it would be a good idea to let Maggie know whenever he was about to take a work call.

"Now?" she asked, slightly exasperated but in good fun.

"I'll keep it quick."

"You better! It was *them* that wanted you to take this time off."

Smiling, Roger took the phone onto the patio. He answered it while looking back out to the flawless stretch of beach.

"You know I'm on vacation, right?" he said in lieu of an answer.

"I do. So I'll keep this short. I do come bearing some…well, some *interesting* news."

"Okay…"

"I got an encrypted email from Everson this morning. He said, and I quote, 'The lid is about to come off. I've tried keeping it on for as long as I could. In the coming days, headlines about a drone spotted not too far from where Seibert was shot are going to start popping up. Can you work on some sort of story as to what it was used for before it becomes a bigger news item than it needs to be?'"

Roger opened his mouth and nearly said *"I don't understand."* But just before he spoke, the significance of that flared like neon in his head.

Perhaps it wasn't Amber after all. Maybe the president's assassin was someone piloting a military drone.

"Did...did Everson have a hand in that?" Roger asked.

"He swears he had no involvement."

"Pinault?"

"Doubtful. But...I do have a few possible stories you can roll out to answer for it."

Which was convenient if Frederickson had taken matters into his own hands—or had one of his people do it. As Secretary of Defense, he would've had ample access to hardware and a loyal soldier he could trust. Roger remembered the look Frederickson had traded with Pinault in the hospital room. Maybe they were both in on it.

Even using their encrypted phones, he knew he'd never get Frederickson to confess. Instead, he said, "Send me what you've got. I'll attend to it when I return."

"A not-subtle reminder you're on vacation," Frederickson said with a chuckle. "I'll let you get back to it. I guess I'll see you in...what? Three days?"

"Yeah, three days."

"See you then, Roger."

They ended the call, leaving Roger to once again look out over the crystalline water, the perfect white crests of waves, and the almost peach-colored shore. He smiled at the sight of it all, taking it in as an image he hoped could help to combat the Seibert-in-the-scope image that had been haunting him.

"Is everything okay?" Maggie asked as she stepped out onto the patio.

He turned to her and did a slight double take. She was wearing a lovely sundress, and she'd put a slight bit of curl to her shoulder-length hair.

"Yes," he said, taking her hands and pulling her close to him. "Everything is fine."

He didn't truly believe this, as he still had a lot of things to work through. But for now, as things in Washington and here in San Juan seemed quiet, he took the bit of peace as a blessing. There would be hard times ahead as he went back to work and countless Secret Service, FBI, Homeland Security, and CIA hours would be wasted in the search for Seibert's killer. But for now…?

Yes, everything was fine.

About the Author

Alex Contorno is the pen name of an Atlanta-based consultant with national experience in a variety of industries. He has a master's degree in counselor education from Georgia State University. This is his first novel.

Note from Alex Contorno

Word-of-mouth is crucial for any author to succeed. If you enjoyed *The President's Assassin*, please leave a review online—anywhere you are able. Even if it's just a sentence or two. It would make all the difference and would be very much appreciated.

Thanks!
Alex Contorno

We hope you enjoyed reading this title from:

BLACK ROSE
writing™

www.blackrosewriting.com

Subscribe to our mailing list – *The Rosevine* – and receive **FREE** books, daily deals, and stay current with news about upcoming releases and our hottest authors.
Scan the QR code below to sign up.

Already a subscriber? Please accept a sincere thank you for being a fan of Black Rose Writing authors.

View other Black Rose Writing titles at www.blackrosewriting.com/books and use promo code **PRINT** to receive a **20% discount** when purchasing.